The
Blackhope
ENIGMA

The Blackhope ENIGMA

Teresa Flavin

CANDLEWICK PRESS

For P. R. and K. J. R., with love and appreciation

Copyright © 2011 by Teresa Flavin

The author acknowledges support from the
Scottish Arts Council toward the writing of this book.

First U.S. edition 2011

Library of Congress Cataloging-in-Publication Data

Flavin, Teresa.
The Blackhope enigma / Teresa Flavin. —1st U.S. ed.
p.   cm.
Summary: Fourteeen-year-old Sunni, her stepbrother Dean and an art-student friend trace the footsteps of a labyrinth built in Blackhope Tower by a mysterious and brilliant sixteenth-century artist, and suddenly find themselves trapped inside his enchanted painting, trying desperately to get out.
ISBN 978-0-7636-5694-2
[1. Painting—Fiction. 2. Space and time—Fiction.
3. Adventure and adventurers—Fiction. 4. Magic—Fiction.
5. Italy—History—1559–1789—Fiction.] I. Title.
PZ7.F59861Bl 2011
[Fic]—dc22   2010047654

11 12 13 14 15 16 BVG 10 9 8 7 6 5 4 3 2 1

Printed in Berryville, VA, U.S.A.

This book was typeset in Adobe Caslon.

TEMPLAR BOOKS

an imprint of
Candlewick Press
99 Dover Street
Somerville, Massachusetts 02144

www.candlewick.com

fausto Corvo

15 82

Prologue

Venice, 1582

"Soranzo is out for your blood, Fausto."

The candles in the astrologer's study flickered as he spoke, sending light dancing over a table covered with star charts and calculations.

"I know, Vito," said the man with the hooked nose and dark eyes. "You are the third friend to warn me."

"I fear for your safety, Fausto. Soranzo is not a man to be toyed with. He did not become one of the most powerful men in Venice without destroying the lives of those blocking his way."

"And he is also greedy." Fausto Corvo paced back and forth as he spoke. "I fulfilled my contract with him for four new paintings. I wanted that to be the end of my dealings with the snake, but he wants others—paintings he has heard rumors about."

"Enchanted paintings?"

Corvo came to an abrupt stop.

"Yes, enchanted paintings—those that by their very nature challenge all that we once understood. And I wonder," he added, turning to stare deep into the eyes of his old friend, "who might have started such rumors."

The astrologer looked at him steadily. "None of our friends would do such a thing. We are all sworn to protect the ancient knowledge—and the way you have used it to bring your artwork to life."

"I know that." The painter's eyes were like flint. "But there is a traitor among us who has whispered a tale to Soranzo about my work. I have my suspicions about who it is, but no proof. I am not sure I can trust anyone, Vito, not even my apprentices . . . and they are like sons to me."

"The enchanted paintings," asked Vito, "are they safe?"

"Yes, they are well hidden, but I dare not leave them for long."

"That is a relief," the astrologer said with a sigh. "Such enchantment is not meant for the likes of Soranzo, who would use it only to gain more power for himself at the expense of others. If he were to get hold of the paintings, who knows how he would twist your knowledge for evil means?"

"Rest easy, Vito. I will not allow the paintings to fall into the wrong hands, and neither will I allow that villain to learn how they were made. But his spies now watch my workshop at all times, day and night. I realize that the time has come for me to act. That is why I am here today." Corvo waved his hand over Vito's table of papers. "Have you examined the portents, as I asked?"

The astrologer stirred himself and held a magnifying glass over a complicated chart. "Yes, yes. The heavens will look favorably upon travel by water for the next three days. The moon is strong and will aid you. But after three days, there is major opposition from the planets. I fear the stars will then favor spies and traitors instead."

Corvo let out a long breath. "So be it. We must move quickly."

"Do you have all your arrangements in place?" Vito asked.

"Yes. My apprentices and I will scatter to the four winds, though I have not yet revealed their destinations to them. We will be transported beyond Soranzo's long reach. That is all I can tell you. Vito, say good-bye to our friends for me. I will miss our discussions. But they know as well as I that my work must be protected at all costs."

Vito embraced the painter. "Godspeed, Fausto."

Corvo pulled up the collar of his cloak and smiled.

"Thank you, Vito." Moving quietly and swiftly, he closed the door and descended the stairs into the darkening Venice night.

Chapter 1

That's where they found the skeletons. Right where you're standing."

Startled, Sunni Forrest whirled around and found a lanky dark-haired boy smiling at her from a bench by the wall.

"Blaise! You scared the life out of me!" Sunni hopped away from where she had stood, in the center of a large, rectangular labyrinth picked out in black tiles on the stone floor. "Try saying hello next time."

"I'll just start over." Blaise said, looking sheepish. "Hey, Sunni, how are you?"

"Fine. Just waiting for my heart to stop pounding."

"I'm really sorry. You walked past without seeing me."

"I'll live." Sunni let out a long breath. "I came in to look at the painting and didn't notice anything else."

She nodded at the picture on the wall behind her. A medieval city, crowded with twisting lanes and buildings, sprawled across the huge canvas under a sky of robin's-egg blue. From the sailing ships moored in the foreground to the craggy hills behind the city, every inch teemed with tiny, brightly dressed figures. The plaque on the elaborate gold frame read, "Fausto Corvo, *The Mariner's Return to Arcadia*, 1582."

"I know—it's like a magnet," said Blaise. "Gets me every time. It had you in a trance, too, didn't it?"

"A trance bordering on panic," said Sunni. "I was wondering how I'll manage to copy the whole thing into my sketchbook."

"You just have to draw everything really small. That's how I'm doing it, anyway," said Blaise.

"You're copying it, too?" A feeling of dismay crept over Sunni as she noticed the open sketchbook in his lap.

"Yep. I'm doing my project for art class on Fausto Corvo."

That was typical. Blaise Doran would have to choose *her* artist. Sunni's afternoon was going from bad to worse.

"But *I'm* doing Corvo for *my* project," Sunni said. "It's probably not allowed, two people doing the same topic."

"No, it is. Mr. Bell said it was OK for some of the others to do the same artist," said Blaise. "Anyway, so what if we both do Corvo? Our projects will still look totally different."

And yours will totally look better than mine, Sunni thought. She pictured Blaise leaning over his drawings in their art classes, his hair falling in front of his face. Drawing, always drawing, even during break times and in the dining hall. Last year her project would have been the best, but then he had to sweep in from America. Now Blaise was always in the spotlight while she was shunted off to the wings.

Sunni dragged her shoe along the edge of a black floor tile. "But I wanted Corvo as *my* artist. I've loved his paintings forever. There's no other artist I like as much."

"Then I guess we've got a problem." Blaise tapped his sketchbook with a stubby pencil. "I'm Corvo's biggest fan.

I couldn't believe it when we moved to a town that has one of his paintings in its castle. I've been here every afternoon working on my project, so I'm not changing artists now."

"Well, I'm not changing either," said Sunni, tossing her honey-brown ponytail over her shoulder. "I'll leave you and come back another time."

She was stalking toward the door when Blaise said, "Wait a minute, Sunni. Don't get all upset." He moved over on the bench to make room for her. "There's space for both of us."

"Lucky me."

"I can show you my sketches so far. They're not that great."

"Oh, yeah, right." Sunni pulled off her school backpack and sat down beside him, unable to resist a closer look at the competition.

She looked carefully at each drawing, her spirits sagging even further when she saw how much he had already done. There was one of Blackhope Tower, the sixteenth-century castle they were in, its silvery stone walls and turrets surrounded by skeletal trees. And another sketch of the two stone lions at the gate, dusted with snow.

"You stood outside and drew these?"

Blaise nodded.

"Are you crazy? It's freezing!"

The American boy just grinned. "Fingerless gloves," he said.

The next pages in Blaise's sketchbook were crammed with drawings of armor, statues, and portraits from around Blackhope Tower. The unfinished last sketch was of the Mariner's Chamber, the room they were in. Blaise was painstakingly copying the painting and the tiled labyrinth on the floor. He had even drawn a section of the ceiling's wooden beams, decorated with mermaids and sea monsters.

Sunni handed his sketchbook back. "You're right," she said. "You have done a lot already. More than me." She halfheartedly offered him her sketchbook in return.

She cringed inside as Blaise studied her pencil portrait of Sir Innes Blackhope, the rich sea captain who had built Blackhope Tower. It had taken her an hour to copy his stern face and the white ruff around his neck.

"It's terrible," Sunni murmured, snatching the book back.

"No, it's good," said Blaise. "As usual."

"Are you making fun of me?"

"No way. I don't get you, Sunni. You want me to say it's bad or something?"

They sat, silent and vaguely embarrassed, until Blaise began sketching again. Sunni made a tentative pencil mark on her blank page, but her eyes kept drifting over to watch him draw. She could sort of see why other girls thought he was cute. Several even went out of their way to be around him, but Sunni was most definitely not one of them. Blaise Doran already got more than enough attention from everyone else.

He caught her looking and grinned.

Don't think I was looking at you, Blaise! I am not one of those giggly girls who always try to sit next to you in Art. "So, what do you know about the skeletons you mentioned when I came in?" Sunni asked hastily. "Blackhope Tower's big claim to fame."

"Not much," said Blaise, sniffing the air. "Except it definitely smells like bones in here, all musty and moldy."

"Bones don't smell."

"They do when they have rotting flesh on them."

"That's disgusting!" Sunni's short laugh echoed. "The skeletons they found didn't have any flesh on them anyway. They were dressed up in clothes from centuries ago. They just appeared out of nowhere, right here in the middle of this room."

"Somebody must have dug them up from the cemetery and dumped them here," Blaise said. He scanned the windowless chamber. There was nothing else in it except the painting, the floor labyrinth, the bench they sat on, and the door. "Someone with a key to this room."

"No, it couldn't have happened that way. They appeared one by one over hundreds of years," Sunni replied. Her grandmother had once told her that the skeletons were always laid out as if they were asleep—like they'd slipped from a long, deep sleep into death and all that was left was bleached bones and saggy old clothes. No one had ever even found out their names.

At this thought, a pang squeezed her heart, but she kept her voice steady so Blaise wouldn't notice. "They found the last skeleton in the 1800s. It was a man dressed in clothes from a hundred years earlier. He was lying in the middle of the maze like the others."

"Labyrinth," said Blaise as he drew.

"What?" Sunni was trying to swallow the lump in her throat from thinking about Granny and lonely skeletons.

"That's a labyrinth, not a maze. A maze has a lot of dead ends and you have to hunt for the right path to the center. A labyrinth has one path that twists and turns through all four corners, but if you stay on it, it takes you to the center eventually."

"Oh, right. I stand corrected," said Sunni sarcastically.

"Sorry," said Blaise. "But I'm kind of interested, especially since Fausto Corvo designed this one. You knew that, right?"

"Yeah. Who doesn't?" answered Sunni.

Blaise pulled a leaflet from his back pocket and handed it to her. Its title was printed in bloodred letters: *The Blackhope Enigma.*

"I read about it in here." He rubbed his hands together. "The enigma of the skeletons—the mystery that can't be solved. Excellent."

"Horrible, more like." Sunni skimmed the leaflet. "I probably already know all this. '*The Mariner's Return to Arcadia* was Sir Innes's prized possession.' Yeah, I knew that. 'He wouldn't ever let anyone take the painting down' . . . blah, blah, blah . . . 'Sir Innes stated in his will that nothing in this room could be changed'." She stopped and looked up. "That's kind of weird. It's not like there is a lot you *could* change, unless you take out the bench and the painting and chisel the labyrinth out of the floor."

"Maybe he just wanted to keep everything the way it was . . . to protect it."

"Of course he wanted to protect it. It's worth a lot of money," said Sunni.

"Yeah, but maybe Sir Innes didn't want to disrespect Fausto Corvo and his work. I wouldn't want to. Corvo could do everything: paint, invent things, speak a bunch of different languages, fight with swords, ride fast horses, write poems. . . ."

"Poems?"

"Uh, yeah." Blaise cleared his throat. "They were all for this one lady. But her family made her marry someone else. Apparently he was pretty cut up about it."

I can't believe it. Blaise Doran is blushing. Sunni suppressed an amused smile. "Really? Corvo doesn't seem like the poetry type. She must have been something special."

"Guess so." He suddenly slid from the bench and went up to the canvas. "You know, whenever I think I've seen everything in the painting, I catch something I missed."

"Me too. It's going to take me at least two weeks to copy it all."

"See this guy?" Blaise pointed to a man on one of the ships in the harbor. "Do you think that's Sir Innes Blackhope?"

Sunni shrugged. "Well, he's much bigger and better dressed than everybody else around him. Sir Innes paid for the painting, so maybe it was part of the deal that Corvo put him at the front."

"Yeah, I think you're right." Blaise's voice trailed off as he examined the picture, his nose practically touching its surface. "But something's really been bugging me about this painting."

"What?"

"You know how its title is *The Mariner's Return to Arcadia*? Well, I looked up *Arcadia*, and it's supposed to be a paradise, with mythical creatures and stuff like that."

"So?"

"Look at this. And this." Blaise pointed to a group of ragged, shackled men being marched onto a ship and a thief stealing oranges from an old woman on crutches. "Doesn't look like paradise to me. More like the opposite."

Sunni crossed the chamber and peered at the place he was pointing to. "That is odd. And look there — a little girl alone, crying, and an old man lying in a gutter."

"The painting's title doesn't make any sense, but Corvo got away with it anyway, so Sir Innes must have liked what he did." Blaise's finger moved down to the painter's signature: the symbol of a flying raven and the date, 1582. "Corvo painted this and made the labyrinth in the same year. But pretty soon after that, he disappeared."

"I already knew he vanished, but that's about it."

"This book I read said he escaped from Venice, chased by some rich guy called Soranzo. He'd bought some of Corvo's paintings, but then something happened between them, and all of a sudden Soranzo was out to get him. Corvo was never seen again."

"I heard something else about him," said Sunni, another of Granny's stories about Blackhope Tower coming to mind. *I bet you don't know this, Blaise.* "They say that Corvo made magical paintings."

Blaise leaped on this idea. "You've heard about that, too?"

"Yeah, maybe that's another reason he had to disappear — to save his skin from people who thought he was a sorcerer."

Before Blaise could say anything, a figure in a padded jacket and red knitted hat clomped into the Mariner's

Chamber and planted himself between them.

Sunni grimaced. She had forgotten all about her stepbrother, Dean. "Take him with you after school. He's been spending far too much time in front of a screen, playing those games of his," her stepmother had said. "I'll pick you both up at quarter to five."

Sunni had been stuck with Dean more and more lately, as part of her stepmom's quest to hook him on fresh air and educational pursuits. Her last good deed had been to take him to the Science Museum, where he'd hogged the interactive exhibits and trash-talked them loudly when he didn't get the highest score. Later, in the café, he'd spilled his drink on her. At twelve years old, Dean was only two years younger than her, but to Sunni they seemed worlds apart.

She braced herself for something embarrassing to come out of his mouth now.

"You done, Sun?" Dean's voice was like a horn blast. Then he turned to Blaise. "Who are you?"

"This is Blaise, and no, I am not done. I've barely started," Sunni said.

"Huh? You've been up here for ages!" Dean sized Blaise up and said, "I'm Dean. She's my stepsister," in a man-to-man kind of way.

"Hey. Nice to meet you."

"So, what're you doing, supposedly?" asked Dean.

"Drawing that painting, supposedly," said Sunni. "Why don't you go and look around somewhere else?"

"I've seen it all twenty times before. Boring. I'm going to hang out here till Mom comes."

"You'd better be quiet."

"You won't even know I'm here," said Dean.

Blaise was back on the bench, scribbling in his sketchbook. Sunni sat down next to him and resumed sketching in hers.

Dean managed to be quiet for about two minutes, while he glanced over *The Mariner's Return to Arcadia*. Then, in a mocking voice, he started reading the information card aloud.

"Dean!" Sunni hissed. "Quit it!"

"I'm helping you," he replied, and kept reading. "'Fausto Corvo was a prominent sixteenth-century Venetian artist' . . . blah, blah . . . 'This painting is a fine example of . . .' Hey—how do you say this? C-H-I-A-R-O-S-C-U-R-O."

"It's 'kee-ar-oh-skoo-roh,'" said Blaise. "Mr. Bell says it means 'light and dark' in Italian. Like the way artists paint highlights and shadows. See how Corvo put highlights on the people and animals to make them pop out against the dark background?"

"Don't encourage him," said Sunni. "You don't care what chiaroscuro is, Dean. You're just trying to get attention."

"No, I'm not. I'm helping," said Dean, strolling over to the edge of the labyrinth. "'This painting is a fine example of kee-ar-oh-skoo-roh!' Kee-ar-oh-skoo-roh!"

He skipped along the winding path through the first quarter of the rectangle and into the second, chanting loudly as he went. "Chiaroscuro, chiaroscuro."

"Dean, stop it!" Sunni said. "I can't concentrate with you doing that."

Without pausing, Dean turned into the third corner and

then into the fourth, repeating "chiaroscuro," now under his breath, and looking slyly at Sunni.

She glanced up from her sketch and noticed her step-brother nearing the middle of the labyrinth, still muttering.

"You're blocking my view, Dean!" she said, furiously erasing a line on her page. "And you're incredibly irritating!"

There was no reply. She looked up, ready to tell him off again, but the labyrinth was empty. Dean had disappeared.

Something in the painting seemed to glow for a moment, near the center, as if a firework had exploded.

Sunni blinked and turned to Blaise. "Did you see where Dean went?"

"What do you mean? He's right there." Blaise looked up and stared at the place where Dean had been. "Oh."

"He's gone." Sunni scanned the four corners of the room.

"He would have had to pass by us to get to the door," Blaise said. "Maybe he snuck out."

"It's the sort of thing Dean would do to make me mad, but he didn't go out that way."

"Come on, Sunni. How the heck could he have left without going through the door?"

"Well, he was there. We both saw him. I only looked away for a split second," Sunni said, her voice taut. "And now he's gone. There's nowhere to hide in here except for under this bench, and he's not there." Just to make sure, she bent down and peered below the seat. Then she jumped up and darted out the door.

Blaise followed as Sunni hunted through the other rooms that opened off the long corridor. There was no sign of Dean or anyone else. Blackhope Tower was almost empty on this snowy Tuesday afternoon. At the spiral staircase that led down to the exit she called, "Dean!"

Her voice echoed in the dank air.

"This is pointless," she said. "He didn't leave the room. I just know it."

"There's no way he just disappeared."

"He did—I know he did. Come on." Sunni scurried back to the Mariner's Chamber with Blaise at her heels and stopped in front of the painting, searching for the place where she had seen the explosion of light. "Help me look."

"For what?"

"For Dean!"

"In the painting?" Blaise stared at her as if she had a screw loose. "You've totally lost me now."

"I saw something flash in the painting right after he disappeared."

"It was just an optical illusion or something. And anyway, what's it got to do with Dean?"

"I don't know—everything!" Sunni pulled her hair back from her face and yanked it into a tighter ponytail. "Look, are you going to help me or not, Blaise?"

"OK, whatever," Blaise muttered, and moved closer.

Sunni located the man they assumed was Sir Innes on his ship, the *Speranza Nera*. He was resplendent in crimson, a sword dangling from under the black cape draped over his shoulders. One hand was raised before him as if to show off his magnificent ship to viewers, while the other rested on his hip. All around him, sailors hauled bundles of goods and worked in the rigging. Ladies waved fans from the dockside as hawkers sold oranges from baskets.

Sunni followed one lane from the docks to a busy square with an ornate fountain. Each person wore a different-colored outfit, and she felt overwhelmed at the sheer number of them.

Then she thought she saw one of the splashes of color move. She was sure it had.

"Blaise, in there, around that crowd by the juggler," she said, pointing at a man in a jester costume tossing three golden balls in the air. "Right there!"

A figure in a padded jacket and red hat stepped from the crowd and stood underneath one of the balls, staring up at it.

Sunni squinted at the minuscule boy, her heart starting to hammer in her chest as the horror of it sunk in. "Dean."

"Whoa." Blaise rubbed his eyes and looked back at the canvas. "Oh, man. I can't believe this."

As they watched, amazed, Dean moved away from the juggler toward a dim alleyway. He was half walking, half running, looking wildly around him.

"He's so small," said Sunni, her voice breaking. "And terrified. Like a bug that's going to get squashed any minute. I have to get him out!"

"But how? I mean, what did—?"

"The labyrinth," Sunni said, turning to Blaise. "That's what took him there."

"What do you mean?"

"That's all Dean did. He walked around the labyrinth."

"Loads of people do that, but they don't vanish!" replied Blaise.

"I know," said Sunni. "It must have been what he said while he did it."

"Chiaroscuro."

"And that triggered something that pulled him into Corvo's painting."

Blaise crouched down and touched the labyrinth's black tiles. "They're just pieces of stone. That painting is just a bunch of colors on a piece of cloth. How . . . ?" His voice trailed off.

"Magic." The word flew from Sunni's mouth like a bullet.

"You think those rumors about Corvo are true."

"Seeing is believing." She packed her sketchbook and drawing materials into her backpack and hauled it over her shoulders. "I'm going in after Dean."

"That's insane, Sunni." Blaise threw his arms up in the air. "You might not get out again."

"There's a way in, so there must be a way out. Why would Corvo make a painting you can't leave?"

"How do we know? He might have."

"Then why make a rule that the labyrinth can never be dug out of this floor? Because it's the way in and *out* of the painting."

"Maybe. But you don't have to be the one to find out, Sunni." Blaise's face was bone-white.

"I'm not leaving Dean in there."

"And I'm not telling you to do that! Let's get help. Let's find the guards and tell them."

"They won't believe us. No one will. We'll just be in

loads of trouble for losing Dean and I'll end up having to go in to get him anyway. At least if I go now, I know roughly where he is."

"Then I'm coming with you," said Blaise.

"Like I'm going to drag you into it." Sunni stepped up to the labyrinth's entrance. "This is my problem. Dean's my stepbrother, and I'm supposed to be looking after him. My stepmom will have my head if she finds out what's happened."

"But I'm part of this, too," Blaise protested.

"You have to stay behind to explain if I don't come back."

"If you don't come back?" He nodded his head in disbelief. "Is that what I'm supposed to do? Tell your parents I stood by and watched you disappear?"

Sunni wound her lavender-striped scarf around her neck and buttoned up her coat. Her heart-shaped face was pale but composed. "Look, I might find Dean and be back in five minutes. Or it might take longer. But hopefully you won't have to tell anyone. And who's going to believe you, anyway? So keep it quiet for now, huh?" She started to follow the labyrinth, murmuring "chiaroscuro" as she went.

Blaise trailed her around the perimeter as she went. "Stop it, Sunni, this is crazy!"

Sunni held one arm out to ward him away. Her heartbeat calmed as she walked along the path. At first she was aware of Blaise just behind her, begging her to stop, but then he and the rest of the Mariner's Chamber fell away. There were only the black tiles snaking around and around at her feet. As she neared the last corner, she felt sleepy in the way she had when her mother had gently brushed her hair a long time ago.

There were distant footsteps somewhere. Sunni noted the sound and let it go. *It doesn't matter.* The weight of her body was draining away, as if she had thrown off a huge stone that was keeping her anchored. Only her feet were still grounded enough to stop her from floating away, to move her steadily and irrevocably into the labyrinth. When at last she stepped into its perfect center, her feet broke free of gravity and she was released like a leaf on a breeze.

Blaise stood frozen to the spot, staring at the dissolving girl in the center of the labyrinth. Sunni was as dreamy and still as a statue, her eyelashes fluttering slightly. She began to look vague around the edges, as if someone had thrown a gauze curtain in front of her.

Someone's footsteps in the corridor were coming closer, and Blaise looked away, momentarily distracted. In that split second, he knew he had missed his last glimpse of Sunni. He jerked his head back, but she was already gone.

A security guard looked into the Mariner's Chamber and saw a boy standing alone in the empty room.

"You OK, son? Seen a ghost?" he asked.

Blaise shook himself and answered, "No, I'm all right."

"Then make your way down to the exit please. It's closing time."

The guard left, whistling down the corridor.

Blaise moved close to the painting, his head reeling. He

had noticed the burst of twinkling lights there after Sunni vanished. *The way her body melted into nothing,* he thought, bewildered. *How could someone ever come back from that?*

The chamber walls seemed to be closing in on him, the idiot who let her go and stayed behind himself. If only he could run his hands over the painting's surface and somehow pluck her out, chisel her out if he had to. But she was embedded in there now. Blaise's eyes raced over the area where he had seen the lights. There were hundreds of little people and no time to search.

A distant voice called, "Son, come on. I have to close this floor."

Blaise wanted to pound the walls and shout for the guard to give him just fifteen more minutes. But he knew the man would say no and tell him to come back tomorrow.

Come back tomorrow. That's all I can do. He shoved his sketchbook and pencils into his bag and left the Mariner's Chamber, barely managing to mutter "Thanks" as he passed the guard and flew down the spiral staircase.

Another guard on the ground floor ushered Blaise outside and locked Blackhope Tower's main door. The wintry night air hit him like a hard slap.

He trudged along the winding driveway, snow crunching underfoot. The only other person in the parking lot was a woman sitting in a car, its engine thrumming, but Blaise was so preoccupied that he didn't even notice her.

The woman glanced at him as he went by, then continued to watch the main door for a sign of her son, Dean, and stepdaughter, Sunni.

Chapter 2

Sunni was aware of someone standing over her. Her eyes fluttered open to find she was lying on the ground. A palm holding a few coins was thrust under her nose. The woman whose hand it was stared at her from under an elaborate hairstyle, woven through with pearls. Sunni cried out and pushed the hand away, but the woman did not blink or flinch.

Sunni glanced down at a bundle of rags beside her and realized to her horror that it was a person's legs; one knee jutting out sharply, the other just a stump wrapped in filthy cloth strips. Her heart thumped double time, sending bolts of fear shooting along her spine. She rolled away and scrambled to her feet, ready to sprint.

The richly dressed woman was bending down to offer coins to a one-legged beggar. His face was grimy but smiling at the lady. Neither had moved.

Sunni hugged herself and felt the familiar density of flesh and muscle under her skin. *I've seen these people before — in the painting. And now I'm in it, too.* The weightless, dreamy feeling she had experienced on the labyrinth had gone. Her feet were firmly rooted to the ground, and there was no way to fly off.

The medieval buildings in the small square where she

stood were bathed in a slanting lemony light. The air smelled of nothing. Not sea, nor smoke, nor food.

There was no sound. Not a rustle or hum or breath except for her own.

"Dean!" Sunni screamed to crack open the deadness of the place. It was as if she were shouting into a cupboard. No echo, no response. "Dean, Dean! It's me!"

She shouted his name until she doubled over, coughing. Where was he? How far could he have gone? Had he even heard her?

Slowly Sunni walked back to the woman and the beggar. She touched the lady's stiff dress. Then she gingerly touched her hand. Not exactly waxy, not exactly cold. Just not alive.

Sunni moved through the square, around a pack of young men with fixed laughing mouths and some toothless old ladies soundlessly shouting at street urchins. She hunted for something, anything that looked like a way out. But there was nothing.

She shivered. Although there was no breeze, there was also no heat from a real sun. She spoke out loud just to hear something. "Dean! How are we ever going to get out?"

Get a grip, girl. She stopped and faced a church with a tall spire. *Did I draw that earlier?*

She pulled her sketchbook out and found her rough sketch of the painting. If she had had time to finish copying it, she would have had a sort of map of the painting to follow, but she had hardly drawn anything of importance. At least she had marked out the church spire. Its tip pointed her gaze in the direction of something even more interesting: the castle on a hill overlooking the city. That must be the highest place in "Arcadia." She flung her backpack over her shoulder and set off toward the hill.

Dean sat curled up in a dark corner of a deserted alley and looked at his watch. Three thirty a.m. He had been wandering around for hours and hours. But it was still bright sunshine here. The shadows hadn't moved. Nor had anything else.

He rubbed his swollen eyes, feeling slightly calmer inside now. Not like when he'd first woken up and found himself lying on a road in this place, whatever it was. He'd thought he must have been dreaming and had punched himself in the arm. It had hurt. This was no dream.

He'd ventured over to see the golden juggling balls suspended in the air. He didn't know why, but he could stand underneath them and they didn't fall on him. He had looked around the crowd of people staring at the juggler, some with mouths hanging open, some pointing. Only the ones at the front had complete faces.

Dean felt sick at the horrible memory. The people near the back had shadow eyes, no noses and their mouths were just a stroke of red.

He had run away, panicked. Everywhere figures were planted like statues.

He had yelled for his mom and been answered by silence. Hurling himself through the streets, he had fallen over a mangy dog and tripped into a wall. He had finally dragged himself into this empty alley and hidden himself in a corner.

His stomach rumbled. He had taken a bit of bread from a baker's basket, but it felt odd and he decided not to try it. The same thing had happened with an orange he'd picked up. He'd tried peeling it, but it was as solid as if it had been carved from wood. If everything here was like this, he was going to starve to death.

Dean wished he were back in Blackhope Tower with Sunni, before he'd walked around those tiles in the floor and begun to feel dizzy. The last thing he'd seen before his vision faded was that painting.

A feeling started to tug at Dean from deep inside. The strange clothes people wore in this place, the odd houses, even the animals seemed familiar. The more it made sense, the more dreadful it was.

His head slumped forward into his hands. How could he be inside a painting? Would anyone ever figure out where he was? And how could they get him back?

After a while he pulled his jacket hood up over his head, hugged his knees even more tightly, and fell over onto his side. Moments later, he drifted off into a fitful sleep.

Sunni turned into another twisting lane and looked at the scene around her. *More clone people,* she thought. Fausto Corvo hadn't given his figures much variety. She saw the same nose over and over, and the same eyes, which was almost as unsettling as the weird, unfinished faces in the shadows and behind the crowds.

A donkey and cart loaded with sacks of grain caught her eye. She pulled the hat off the driver's head and perched it between the donkey's ears. If she came back this way, she would recognize them.

She drew the lane into a sketch map of the streets she had walked already and labeled it "Donkey with Hat." So far she had lanes labeled "Oranges in Fountain," "Upside-Down Dog," and others, making up a trail she could follow back if she had to.

"Donkey with Hat" Lane curved up a hill into a park surrounding the castle. Its towers and turrets gleamed in the perpetual morning sun, while its red banners and pennants were apparently flying in the nonexistent breeze.

Sunni walked along the castle walls until she came to an ancient tree. She hauled herself up until she was on the highest of its limbs and sat down, her legs dangling.

The view was not as good as she had hoped. She could see some of the lanes she had followed, but others were hidden below. Where the houses ended, masts of ships poked above the rooftops. There was no sign of her stepbrother. On top of that, she felt as if she had been awake for days, with her stomach rumbling continuously.

"Dean!" Sunni shouted, but the sound was still muffled, as if she had a box over her head. She rummaged through her backpack and pulled out her phone and a half-eaten bar of chocolate.

Nibbling on one square of chocolate, she stared at the phone. All she wanted to do was to call home and hear her dad's voice telling her he was coming for them. But the signal was as dead as everything else here. Her eyes prickled as she pushed back frustrated tears.

Sunni stuffed the phone down to the bottom of her backpack and glanced at the landscape outside the city. A few cattle stood in pastures edged by woods. In the distance were craggy hills.

Suddenly she saw something small and dark scuttling along the road through the fields. It was wearing a red hat.

Chapter 3

For what seemed like the fortieth time, Blaise flipped over onto his left side and then onto his right. He was asleep, but only just. First he dreamed he was standing outside *The Mariner's Return to Arcadia*, looking in. Then he was inside it, hunting for Sunni and Dean.

His mouth was dry and sour when he finally dragged himself awake. He tiptoed to the kitchen and poured some juice for himself, then dropped the container with a thud.

His father poked his head around the door. "Blaise? What's up?"

"Nothing, Dad," replied Blaise, mopping the countertop. "Just can't sleep."

"That's not like you, buddy. You feeling sick or something?"

"Or something, yeah." He drained his juice and rinsed the glass.

"Anything going on at school?" Mr. Doran stood in the doorway.

"I'm fine."

His father gently caught his shoulder as Blaise pushed past him.

"You know you can tell me anything," he said.

"I know, Dad," said Blaise. *But not this time.* He padded down the hall and fell back into bed.

He couldn't get Sunni out of his head, her image translucent and fading, the sleepy look on her face. *Chiaroscuro, chiaroscuro.* Blaise's mind spun around and around till dawn, when at last he drifted into a deep, dreamless sleep.

The next day, Braeside High School's corridors hummed with discussions of Sunni's and Dean's disappearance. Boys shook their heads and girls hugged each other as teachers tried to herd them into classrooms.

Blaise darted in and out of his friends' conversations, agreeing with them that the disappearances were freaky and tough for their family. But when his friends asked each other when they had last seen Sunni, he kept quiet.

That afternoon, Blaise sat in Mr. Bell's art class, staring at the blank sheet of paper in front of him. This was the place he usually felt happiest, with its colorful jumble of artwork on the walls and relaxed atmosphere. But today he couldn't wait to get away. Gazing at Sunni's empty seat, he wondered where she was in the painting and whether she had found Dean. *Could they have escaped by now?*

Around him the other students whispered to each other, and as they worked, Blaise picked out the words "Sunni" and "Blackhope Tower" and "police investigation." Feeling out of it from lack of sleep, he could only manage to draw a few scratchy lines before erasing them in disgust.

At the end of the lesson Blaise dropped his scrunched-up drawing in the trash and waited by Mr. Bell's desk until the other students had gone.

"Is everything OK, Blaise?" said the art teacher. "You didn't seem your usual self today. Are you worried about Sunni?"

Blaise thrust his hands into his pockets. "Uh, yeah," he said. "And I'm having some problems finding information on my artist for the project."

"Oh? That doesn't sound too serious. Who are you researching?"

"Fausto Corvo."

"Corvo? You too?" Lorimer Bell's hand trembled as he ran it over his shaved head. "I do have a book about him, but I'm afraid I lent it to Sunni. Did you know she's also doing Corvo?"

"Yes, but we talked about it."

"I would tell you to share the book with her, but under the circumstances—well, you know that's not possible." Mr. Bell shook his head sadly. "There is a painting by Corvo at Blackhope Tower—"

"I know. I've been there," interrupted Blaise. "Do you know anything else about Corvo, Mr. Bell? Did you, like, ever hear anything unusual about him?"

The art teacher looked up at Blaise sharply. "Well, yes," he answered. "There have been lots of rumors and stories over the centuries. They are part of what makes Corvo so fascinating."

"So, you heard that he was chased by someone named Soranzo? What did Soranzo want?"

"I believe he was after some particular paintings of Corvo's," Mr. Bell said. "Soranzo was a very powerful man in Venice, and he didn't take it very well when Corvo disappeared. He was so angry that he even offered a reward for information on Corvo's whereabouts."

"Did you ever hear that Corvo was a sorcerer?" Blaise asked.

Mr. Bell stiffened. "There's no proof of that rumor, Blaise. I'm sure plenty of Renaissance artists were suspected of sorcery. Think about it. People were much more superstitious back then, and being able to draw and paint is kind of magical, isn't it? It's a skill most people don't develop, so many were in awe of those who had it. And maybe they felt a bit threatened by it sometimes, too."

Blaise thought about this.

"Does your question have anything to do with Sunni's disappearance at Blackhope Tower?" asked Mr. Bell, scratching his neck.

"Maybe."

The art teacher flinched. "In what way, Blaise?"

"The disappearances couldn't have anything to do with being in the Mariner's Chamber with Corvo's painting and the labyrinth, could it? I mean, that room's got a weird reputation already, with the skeletons and all."

"It certainly sounds as though you suspect there's a connection, Blaise." Mr. Bell scratched furiously at the back of his neck.

"Well, there's only one door and no windows in that room, Mr. B. From what everyone's saying, no one saw Sunni and Dean leave," Blaise said, "and there's nothing else in there except the painting and the labyrinth."

"And you think that poor old Corvo, even though he's long since dead, is responsible for their disappearances?" Mr. Bell forced a smile.

Blaise shrugged.

"I think your imagination could be getting the better of you, Blaise. My advice is that maybe you should choose a different artist to study—I can suggest some others you'd like."

"Corvo is my favorite artist. I want to finish the project."

Mr. Bell finally took his hand away from the raw red patch that had bloomed on his neck. "All right, then. But stay away from Blackhope Tower and let the police do their work. You've already seen the painting. You don't need to go back."

Blaise hurried out of the classroom, disappointed that he hadn't learned anything new. On his way down the corridor, he popped his head into the school office. "Mrs. Jamieson, have you heard any more news about Sunni and Dean?"

The secretary looked up from her computer. "No, Blaise," she answered. "The police are still searching. But I did just hear they're trying to trace a boy who was with them when they disappeared."

Blaise's heart skipped a beat, and in that second he realized that there was only one way forward now. After thanking her, he walked briskly through the school gates and in the direction of Blackhope Tower. On the way, he bought several bottles of water, some energy bars, bananas, and chocolate, jamming it all into his messenger bag as he ran for the bus.

When Blaise arrived at Blackhope Tower, the driveway was packed with news vans. He cursed under his breath.

Of course—Sunni's and Dean's disappearance was big news.

The hall was bursting with reporters talking to cameras under bright lights. Blaise edged along the side, hoping no one would notice him, and got as far as the spiral staircase before a security guard caught him.

"Sorry," the guard said. "The upper floors are closed for investigation."

"I know, sir. That's why I'm here. I want to talk to the police because I was the last person to see Sunni Forrest."

"That was you?" The guard jerked his thumb at a man being interviewed by several reporters. "That's the chief inspector. You'll have to wait till he's free."

"OK."

The guard was called away, and Blaise stepped back a few paces toward the staircase. He grew bolder and stepped onto the second stair, still facing the hall. The guard looked over for a moment and Blaise raised his hand in a half wave.

Carefully stepping backward, Blaise managed to move up one step at a time. When he was around the curve of the staircase and out of view, he turned and galloped up to the top floor.

Another guard stood at the top of the stairs. "No entry."

"They've sent me up here to talk to someone in the Mariner's Chamber," Blaise said. "I saw Sunni Forrest here before she disappeared."

The guard looked Blaise up and down, then nodded. "Yeah, they were talking about a boy who was with her. I'll take you to them."

Blaise peered into the Mariner's Chamber. A man in a dark suit sat frowning on the bench while a woman in a long overcoat strolled around, studying the labyrinth.

The guard called to them from the door, "Excuse me, but this young man has been sent up to speak to you," and then returned to his post.

Blaise put on what he hoped was a relaxed smile as he stepped into the Mariner's Chamber. "Uh, hello. I think I was the last person to see Sunni Forrest yesterday."

"Speak of the devil, Jim—the boy in the security recording. The guard on duty last night told us about you," the woman said, introducing herself as Detective Constable McNeill and her colleague as Detective Constable Nash. "Isn't the chief inspector with you?"

"He's busy getting interviewed," said Blaise.

"You're here on your own? Where are your parents?"

"My dad's at work. But you can call him." He fiddled with his phone and handed it to the policewoman. "I'm Blaise Doran."

"Blaise Doran." D.C. Nash scribbled this into his notebook as the woman phoned his father. "Address?"

"Twenty-one Braeside Road."

"You a friend of Sunni's?" asked D.C. Nash. "Boyfriend?"

"Uh, no," said Blaise, annoyed to feel a flush spreading up his neck. "We're in the same year at school."

"All right," said D.C. McNeill, handing Blaise's phone back to him. "Your dad's on his way over."

"I don't mind telling you now. I was drawing on the bench when Dean disappeared. Sunni and I are working on a school project, and we were copying the painting into our sketchbooks. The next thing I knew, she was telling me Dean was gone. We went and looked around the other rooms on this floor, but he wasn't there."

"Yes, the recordings from the camera in the corridor showed you doing that. But we haven't got full footage of this room. The camera is aimed at the painting—we can only see people walking past it and stopping to look. The corridor camera shows Dean entering the room, and we know he looked at the painting for a few minutes, but we can't see what happened next—all we know is he never left this room. Neither did Sunni," said D.C. Nash. "After you and Sunni searched the other rooms, why did you both come back and stare at the painting? That seemed odd."

"Well, Sunni kind of thought that Dean might have vanished *into* the painting." *There*, Blaise thought, *I said it.*

"Pardon? Did you just say she thought Dean was inside that painting?" Nash asked.

Blaise nodded. The two police officers stared at him and then at each other.

McNeill asked, "How did she think he'd done that?"

"By walking along the labyrinth and saying a special password."

"Like *abracadabra* or *open sesame*?" Nash was suppressing a smirk.

"Yes, sir."

"Well, come on, then. What did he say?"

"I'm not sure," said Blaise, crossing his fingers behind his back. "He whispered it."

The officers shook their heads in disbelief. "And I suppose Sunni did the same thing, did she? She walked around the labyrinth?" asked Nash.

Blaise nodded.

"What did you do then?" McNeill arched her eyebrows.

"I told her to stop, but she wouldn't listen to me," Blaise replied.

Nash said, "And then she was transported into the painting, because she said a magic word!"

"Yes, sir."

"Next you'll be telling us she's visiting Snow White and the Seven Dwarfs while she's there. This sounds ridiculous," said McNeill. "You're saying you just stood there as she went *poof!* Then you got your stuff, went and looked at the painting again, and left the room. Why?"

"I was confused. I didn't know what to do. The guard said it was time to leave, so I did. But first I went to the painting to see if she was there."

"And did you see her?" asked Nash.

"No."

"Why didn't you tell the guard or someone else what had happened?"

"Who'd believe me?" Blaise stared at the floor. After a moment, he said, "I can show you exactly what Sunni did."

Blaise hurried to the labyrinth and took a deep breath as he set off along the black tile path. Bowing his head low, he whispered, so no one could hear, "Chiaroscuro, chiaroscuro, chiaroscuro." He got through the first corner and then through the second. The detectives followed at his side, and he heard Nash say, "Blaise, speak louder."

Blaise ignored him and was almost through the third section when he heard the click of heels coming toward the Mariner's Chamber. He desperately hoped it was not his father.

Keep going, Blaise said to himself and whispered, "Chiaroscuro, chiaroscuro."

The steps came closer as he rounded the last turn. He stood in the middle of the labyrinth, eyes drooping, his body growing as light as vapor. The world went cotton-ball white around him, and he felt himself drift away.

Blaise disappeared.

"What the—?" The two detectives were sweeping their arms through the empty space just as the chief inspector stalked into the Mariner's Chamber.

"What's going on here? They told me you were questioning the boy," he said. "Where is he?"

McNeill's face was strained. "He was just here talking to us, sir. He was showing us what the kids did, and he just vanished into thin air!"

The chief inspector growled, "You mean he disappeared from under your nose?" His voice grew more irate. "Have this room closed off. I don't want anybody else in here until we've figured this out!"

He was so busy barking out orders, neither he nor the others noticed the tiny burst of light near the bottom of *The Mariner's Return to Arcadia.*

Chapter 4

Dean trudged along the road out of the city. The stillness of the cattle and the motionless trees here were not as eerie as the streets he had just left. He had no idea where he was going, but at least he had escaped the frozen people with half faces.

The road became a narrow path by a grove of trees. Dean gazed at the high hills in the distance. They were at the back of the painting, he remembered. But what was behind them? The way out?

Dean picked his way through the trees into a field of stone boulders at the bottom of the hills. The path petered out at a dark cleft between two tall boulders. He moved closer. The cleft was wide enough to squeeze through. He peered into the inky darkness, sniffing the air while trying to decide whether it was a good idea to go in.

Sunni was running through the fields after Dean. She had lost sight of him sometime earlier, but as there was only one road, she was certain she would catch him eventually. At the start of the grove, she pulled the lavender-striped scarf from her neck and tied it around a tree trunk as a marker.

Picking her way through the trees, she caught sight of a

familiar red blob. Dean was leaning against a boulder with his back to her.

"Dean!" she yelled, hurling herself toward him, her ponytail loose and flying in wavy tendrils.

Dean whooped with relief. He tackled Sunni and gave her a messy hug. "What took you so long?"

"Charming," said Sunni. "You're lucky I figured out where you were. I bet you don't even know how you got here."

"No. I must have blacked out or something. I woke up here with those frozen zombies and food you can't eat. I wish Mom had never made me go to Blackhope with you."

"So do I," Sunni said with a sigh. "If you walk around that labyrinth in the floor and say the word *chiaroscuro,* it transports you into the painting. But I don't know how to get us out."

"You don't?" Dean hung his head. "But you told my mom and Ian, right? They'll come and get us, won't they?"

"I didn't tell them anything. I came straight in after you."

"So, they don't know we're here?"

"No." Sunni saw his incredulous look, and her anger rose. "Well, they were never going to believe me, were they, so what was the point of telling them?"

"That's just brilliant. Nobody knows where we are," Dean spluttered. "We're doomed."

"You're right. Doom is the option I always go for." Sunni kicked at some loose stones. "Like you weren't doomed before I got here?"

"I can't believe you didn't tell anyone. Any grown-ups."

"Do you know any grown-ups who specialize in getting kids out of paintings?"

"No one else knows where we are," Dean bellowed. "Because of you!"

"For your information, Blaise knows. He was there."

"That guy you were with?"

"Yeah," said Sunni. She didn't add, *And I told him not to tell anyone.*

Dean let out a long breath. "Maybe he won't be as dumb as you and he'll get help. Maybe all we have to do is wait."

Sunni slumped back against the rock face, glaring at the sky. *Maybe. Maybe not.*

"I'm starving," said Dean. "You got any food?"

Sunni rooted around in her backpack and handed him her last piece of chocolate. "That's it."

He shoved it into his mouth and practically swallowed it whole.

"What're we going to eat now?"

"Forget about your stomach," answered Sunni. "Let's find the way out."

"We've got to stay here so they can rescue us."

"Who knows how long that will take?" *If it happens at all,* Sunni thought. "Let's try getting ourselves out." She gestured at the slit in the rock. "This must lead somewhere. There are no other roads."

"It's dark in there."

"Yeah, and . . . ?"

"I don't want to go in."

"Stay here, then," she said. "Though I would have thought you'd be used to creepy caves from all your monster and demon games."

"But this isn't a game," he said. "This is real."

"That's right: it is real. We can't just skip the scary bits." Sunni pushed through the opening, waving her arms in front of her. "Besides, what if the way home is just around the corner?"

They inched through dense, heart-stopping darkness. In the distance was what looked like a bright white door cut out of a black wall. Sunni tiptoed toward it, puzzled by its brilliance.

"Is it snow?" whispered Dean. "A blizzard?"

"I haven't a clue."

The door was just wide enough for Sunni to walk through. She and Dean emerged into the light like rabbits from a winter burrow.

There was nothing here except whiteness. No objects, no colors, only brilliant whiteness.

Sunni took a few steps and bumped into what appeared to be some sort of wall. There was no edge where it met the ground. She turned around. The door they had come through was now just a black slit.

"This is giving me a headache," Sunni said, feeling around the black shape. "There isn't a wall. But then there is a wall." She ran her hand up and down the whiteness. "It feels rough."

"It's got streaks in it," said Dean, sticking his nose up against it. "Like when your dad painted the kitchen table."

"Dried paint." She could make out great whorls and swirls, as if a huge paintbrush had sloshed white over everything. She edged sideways along the wall that wasn't a wall. "This is like an alleyway. Come on, let's just see where it goes."

Dean followed her, peering back at the black doorway in case it disappeared, until Sunni pointed and said, "There!"

A misty shadow loomed in the whiteness, shining through as though it was wrapped in lace curtains. For the first time in ages they felt a breeze.

"It looks like the trees in the fog on that day we went to Gran's last month. Remember? She called it a pea-souper," said Dean.

"Yeah. And you know what else it looks like? Like when I did a painting on a canvas and really messed it up, so Mr. Bell gave me some white paint to cover it and start again. It didn't quite hide everything until I'd done three coats."

"I don't get it."

"Maybe Corvo did the same thing. He painted something and then covered it over with white paint," said Sunni, heading toward the shadow.

"Because he made a mistake?"

"I don't know."

As they came closer, they could make out a deep gray tree trunk bleeding through the whiteness, its lower branches framing a patch of bare earth and scrubby bushes below.

"Come on," said Sunni. "This could be the way out. Maybe Corvo was trying to hide it."

"I dunno," answered Dean, pulling back.

"Do you want to go back to the frozen zombies instead? Look, we can find our way back there if we need to. The path only leads one way." Something struck her. "Just like the labyrinth."

"I wish I'd never walked on that thing," Dean muttered.

Together they stepped onto the patch of ground

beneath the tree. As they moved forward, the whiteness thinned out and Sunni and Dean found themselves in a green wood. It rang with bird songs, and the leaves rustled in a gentle breeze. The sky was the same blue as the one in the world they had just left, but this time clouds were moving across it. The sun was low, and the shadows gave them the feeling that it was afternoon.

"This place is alive," Sunni said in wonder. "Things are moving. *Inside* a painting."

"Maybe we're out of the painting now. There's wind and sounds." Dean looked around for anything he might recognize. "Maybe we're home, Sun."

"Not unless we skipped winter. It's warm here." Sunni picked a wildflower and stroked its petals. They felt silky, like real petals. Its fragrance was delicate, though not like any flower she had ever smelled before.

They moved along on a path lined with ferns, through groves of swaying trees. The sun sank a bit lower, sending even longer shadows across the glade they passed through. The birds grew quiet or fluttered away. Dean looked uneasy and pulled his jacket around him, even though the air was warm.

"What's up?" asked Sunni in a low voice. Dean had huddled against a tree.

"I've got a feeling we're being watched," he whispered. His eyes were riveted on dark shadows among the ferns.

Sunni was straining to see when they heard a new sound.

"One is one and all alone, and evermore shall be it so!" sang a deep voice.

The voice dropped for a moment and then burst out

again. "Five for the symbols at your door, six for the six proud walkers! Seven for the seven stars in the sky, eight for the April rainers!" Now they could see a man in the distance, heading toward them.

"Green grow the rushes, Oh!" the voice boomed as its owner thrashed into the glade. "Oh, I say, Inko, well spotted!"

Before them stood a man wearing slim trousers and a long blue coat, a top hat sitting jauntily on his blond head. He looked like someone from the TV programs Dean's mom loved, where snooty men rode around on horses and women sat in mansions waiting for one to propose.

The man tipped his hat, careful not to come too close. His eyes were bright with excitement. "Good day to you. Hugo Fox-Farratt at your service." He nodded toward the ferns behind them. "And Inko, of course."

A shorter, smiling figure stepped into the clearing and Dean recognized the face he thought he had seen among the ferns. It belonged to a barefoot boy of about his age. He had shaggy dark hair and wore a loose shirt covered by an embroidered vest. His baggy trousers were bound at the waist by a red cloth, like a pirate's.

"D-don't hurt us!" Dean stammered.

"Young sir, I have no intention of hurting you!" Hugo was horrified. "Heavens, that is the last thing we should wish to do. You have found Arcadia—and so few have of late. May I ask who you are?"

"I'm Sunniva Forrest," said Sunni as calmly as she could. "This is my stepbrother, Dean Rivers. We're here by mistake, and we're looking for the way out."

Hugo looked surprised. "Sunniva," he said thoughtfully. "That is an unusual name."

Sunni rolled her eyes ever so slightly. "My mother was Norwegian," she replied.

"Well," said Hugo, "I have not heard of anyone arriving here by mistake before. It is a difficult task to guess the password. Yet despite your youth, you have cracked it."

He paused for a moment. "Or perhaps you are the accomplices of some great personage, sent ahead to survey this place? You would not be the first." He nodded at Inko. "There is no sense in lingering here. Come, we will take you to the palace for a meal. We can speak freely once we are there."

Sunni remained where she was. She studied the man for signs of a shifty look or a fake smile. But his gaze was straightforward and his geniality seemed genuine.

"How do we know we can trust you?" she asked.

"I might ask the same of you," answered Hugo. "Let me put it this way. Of all those you are likely to meet here, we are the least threat to you. And if we leave you in this glade, your safety cannot be guaranteed."

"How is it not safe here? Who is—?"

"I will explain everything at the palace," interrupted Hugo. "I offer you my word as a gentleman that you will not be harmed."

Sunni and Dean exchanged a glance and a hesitant nod. "Don't let them split us up," she whispered as they moved away from the tree and followed Hugo.

"This way," said Hugo, leading them deeper into the

grove of trees, with Inko bringing up the rear. "It is not far." As they thrashed past overgrown greenery, he called out in a jolly voice, "By Jove, it has been some time since anyone found his way in. In fact, I believe I was the last one until now."

"But why are you still here?" Sunni asked. "Don't you know how to get out?"

"Ah." Hugo paused. "That is rather a good question. And one that I have not yet answered definitively."

"You're stuck in here, too?" asked Dean.

"Hmm . . . stuck. Not exactly the word I would use, but, yes, this is where I have ended up."

"Since when?" Sunni felt a growing sense of apprehension. She could hear the smile in Hugo's voice when he answered: "Since the 20th of September, 1859."

Chapter 5

L orimer Bell turned off the news and put his head in his hands. Now Blaise had disappeared, too, even after he had warned him to stay away from Blackhope Tower. Maybe he should have told his student everything he knew. Or thought he knew.

The computer on his desk beeped to say he had a new message. Lorimer frowned at the sender's name and opened the message.

It read: *I see some of your lambs have wandered into our pasture. See you soon. Angus.*

Beneath it was a scanned newspaper article with a photo of a well-built man in a cluttered artist's studio.

Paris, January 16
THE RETURN OF ANGUS BELL
International art forger Angus Bell is now using his original family name, Bellini, but can he change his infamous reputation as easily after five years in prison?

He thinks he can, and his accountant would probably agree. Bellini's first exhibition since he was released from prison has sold out within a week. The show, at Mimi St. Pierre's stylish gallery, is the talk of Paris.

But are the paintings any good?

"At least they're not forgeries this time," quipped Bellini.

"Angus is an undisputed talent," said Madame St. Pierre, "and having a colorful past has not hurt him one bit. In fact, it has made people want his paintings even more."

Fuming, Lorimer Bell studied the picture of his cousin, Angus, grinning cheekily at the camera as he aimed his paintbrush toward a canvas. Lorimer deleted the message in one swift move.

The doorbell buzzed insistently, and Lorimer squinted at his alarm clock: five in the morning. He stumbled downstairs to the front door. Through its glass pane, he could just make out a dark figure outlined by the streetlight. The bell buzzed again, and Lorimer jumped. He flicked on the outside light to reveal the smirking face of Angus Bellini.

"Stop gaping and let me in, Lor," ordered his cousin. Lorimer hesitated and then unlocked the door. Angus barged through, bringing a blast of icy air and French aftershave with him. He looked his cousin up and down.

"No hair left, I see. Due to the stress of your teaching career, by any chance?" Angus pulled off his dark fedora and triumphantly shook loose his own jaw-length hair. Then he crushed Lorimer in a bear hug.

"What are you doing here?" Lorimer asked stiffly, pulling away.

"Thanks, I'd love a cup of coffee. A couple of eggs on toast would be grand, too." He shrugged off his black overcoat and handed it to Lorimer. "I traveled all night to see you, Lor."

The art teacher snorted. "You're not here to see me, Angus. You're here because of the painting."

"Grumpy in the morning, aren't you? Of course I'm here to see you," said Angus.

"You've been out of the slammer for over six months and you haven't bothered till now. Not that I wanted to hear from you."

"I was busy making paintings for my comeback exhibition. You know what it's like. Art takes up all your time." Angus stroked his chin and said, "Actually, no, you don't know what that's like anymore, do you? You had your chance to be an artist, and you chose to babysit teenage brats instead."

"At least what I do is legal!"

"Oh, yes, you're the good one." Angus sat down at the kitchen table. "Coffee, Lor. Come on, then—we've a lot to discuss. Haven't you been reading the papers?"

While Lorimer grimly boiled water for coffee and cracked eggs into a frying pan, Angus said, "Those missing kids have done what we spent ages trying to do. They've found a way into *The Mariner's Return to Arcadia*."

"And they may never get out! Two of the three are my

students, Angus, and they have left frantic families behind. They also happen to be the most promising students I've taught in years."

"Very touching," said Angus, filling a cup with black coffee and settling back into his chair. "But it was the youngest and apparently least artistic of them who went into the painting first. So, how did he work it out?"

"I have no idea," muttered Lorimer, shoveling eggs and toast onto a plate and throwing it down in front of Angus. "But you have to stay out of this. Go back to Paris and live the good life that art forgers seem to have these days." He waved his hand dismissively at his cousin. "When you and I tried to get into the painting, we were only kids ourselves. It was a stupid idea, anyway. I've left all that in the past."

"Hmm." Angus munched his breakfast, ignoring Lorimer. "From what the police are saying, the kids all walked the labyrinth before they disappeared, muttering some sort of password. Something must have inspired them—something in that room. And we know that no one is allowed to change anything in the Mariner's Chamber. It's stayed exactly the same since 1582. Right, Lor?"

Lorimer said nothing.

"Actually, that's not strictly true, is it?" Angus continued as he wiped egg yolk from his plate with a piece of toast. "They added an information card about the painting, did they not?"

"How do you know that?"

"A news snippet I found. You were asked to help write

all the information cards about the paintings in Blackhope Tower, weren't you?"

"So?" Lorimer shot back.

"Tell me what you wrote for *The Mariner's Return*." Angus looked slyly at his cousin.

"I can't remember. It was three years ago." The art teacher stood up. "Leave this alone, Angus. It has nothing to do with you."

"On the contrary, it has everything to do with me. And with you." Angus rose, eye to eye with his cousin. "Fausto Corvo *did* make magical paintings. You and I wanted to believe it. We spent all that time trawling through dusty old books on magic and astrology but found nothing. Now your little darlings have come along and proved us right. Just think of the possibilities, Lor. For a start, a certain customer of mine would pay the earth for a painting he could disappear into whenever necessary."

"You haven't changed a bit, have you? Even after cooling off in prison," said Lorimer in a flat voice.

"Why should I change? I'm pretty marvelous as I am. Always was more marvelous than you, anyway. Better at drawing, more popular with girls."

"I'm not interested in helping you. Never again," Lorimer said.

"Even if there's a chance that Corvo's lost paintings are hidden inside *The Mariner's Return to Arcadia*?" Angus smiled.

"That's a bit of a leap, isn't it?"

"No one's ever found those paintings, so why shouldn't they be hidden in there? Just think what they'd be worth!"

"You're just as greedy as ever, Angus," Lorimer said. "I've heard enough. You can leave when you've finished eating."

"With pleasure. After you tell me what you wrote for *The Mariner's Return* information card. It's a shame, though. I was hoping we could work together again. We were a good team."

"In your dreams. And if you want to know what I wrote about the painting, you can go over there and read the card yourself," Lorimer said. "Oh, but I forgot: that's not possible now because the police have closed the Mariner's Chamber off. You're too late."

Angus's face twisted in anger. He grabbed Lorimer by the front of his bathrobe. "You're not going to stand in my way."

The art teacher grappled with his cousin, but Angus managed to flip him around and pin his arms behind his back. He pulled Lorimer into the dark front room and flicked on the light with his elbow. In front of them was a makeshift studio with shelves of art supplies and a few paintings propped against the wall. On the desk sat a computer.

"Turn it on." Angus pushed Lorimer into the chair at the desk and held him firmly by the shoulders. "And find what you wrote for Blackhope Tower. I know you. You'll have kept it all."

Teeth gritted, Lorimer searched through his computer folders, hoping he might have deleted the one Angus wanted. But there it was, efficiently marked "Blackhope Tower Visitor Information." He slowly found the right file and opened it, scrolling to the text for *The Mariner's Return to Arcadia.*

Angus read the paragraph hungrily. "This must contain a password that the kids found by chance. It was the only piece of information they could have seen in that room. And it would be a word in Italian since that was Corvo's language. The only thing it could be is *chiaroscuro*. Yes, that must be it!" Angus started laughing. "Right under your nose, Lor, all this time."

"I wasn't looking for it anymore!" Lorimer shouted. "It was exciting at the time, trying to see if we could get into the painting. But that was twenty years ago."

Angus released his grip and swiveled his cousin's chair around so they were face-to-face. "I'd given up on finding the secret, too. But now it's been served up on a silver platter."

Lorimer cut him off. "Well, I'm finished with the dark side of art, Angus. No more forging, no more scheming. I make my own art now—plain old paintings with no magic involved."

Angus leaned over and flicked through the paintings stacked against the wall.

"If this is the best you can do, I suggest you go back to forgery." He shoved the paintings upright again. "These are garbage."

"Forgery is your game, not mine."

Angus shrugged. "Enough of this. I've given you a chance, but you haven't got the guts to come with me," he said. "But once I get into the painting, you're to keep your mouth shut, OK? You never saw me here or knew where I was going. Got it?"

"How are you going to stop me from inside the painting?" Lorimer sniggered.

Angus smirked back. "I've put together a little package of information about you. An associate has been instructed to send it the minute you start causing trouble and it will go straight to your headmaster and the media. Then your teaching career will be finished. Nobody will hire a forger like you, however much you say you've sworn off it."

"I quit forgery almost as soon as you'd dragged me into it, and I destroyed all the paintings I did. You know that."

"*Almost* every painting, Lor. There were a couple that found their way out into the world. I forgot to tell you at the time."

"What!"

"Yes, two paintings," said Angus. "One is out there somewhere hanging on a nice museum wall. I was accused of forging the other, along with the rest I had done. But I protected you. I went to jail and never told anyone you had played a part. So you owe me."

The art teacher's face sagged.

"You understand your predicament?" said Angus.

"I understand." Lorimer flexed his hands in his lap. "If you manage to get into that painting—and I hope you don't—the least you can do is look out for the kids and help them."

"If I run into them," Angus replied. He sauntered into the hallway and pulled on his coat and hat. As he headed for the door he called triumphantly, "Thanks for breakfast."

Later that afternoon, a weary Lorimer Bell trudged into the corner shop on his way home from school. As he paid for his milk, the headline of the *Braeside Evening Sentinel* caught his eye. He bought a copy and read the article before he left the store:

ANOTHER ENIGMA GRIPS BLACKHOPE TOWER

In a startling development at Blackhope Tower, police have confirmed that an unidentified man vanished from the Mariner's Chamber this morning. Three local children have already disappeared from the same room since Tuesday.

The intruder was dressed in a dark overcoat, gloves, fedora-style hat, and a mask when he broke in through a ground-floor window and overpowered a guard at the door to the Mariner's Chamber. He was last seen entering the windowless room. Police are analyzing security recordings to determine how the man was able to get past guards and vanish in the same way as the children had.

Despite the huge public interest in Blackhope Tower since the children's disappearances, Archie MacQueeg, director of this historic castle, has decided to close its doors until further notice. He says he hopes that the public will understand that chances cannot be taken with visitors' safety.

He got in—blast him! Lorimer hurried home in the wintry dusk.

Snow swirled outside the art teacher's window. But Lorimer, crouching on his studio floor, surrounded by papers he had taken from an old box, did not notice the weather.

He chuckled at some of the scraps and frowned at others, especially one faded leaflet, which read:

> During the 1580s, Sir Innes Blackhope swash-buckled his way across the high seas. Always relishing a challenge, he battled pirates and privateers and sparred with the Spaniards.
>
> He spent as little time as possible on land, and though he loved Blackhope Tower, he grew restless there. When he was bored, he often disappeared for days or weeks at a time, though he was never seen leaving the castle. Some wondered whether Sir Innes had built secret passageways in Blackhope Tower, but none were ever found.
>
> Whenever he reappeared, it was said he looked as though he had been through a battle. He was once found on the floor of the Mariner's Chamber, barely able to move as a result of a leg injury, but deliriously happy. Servants reported that Sir Innes kept repeating, "He does challenge me well, the enchanter! His manoeuvres test my wits, but I prevail again and again over his beasts and villains!"

At first his servants worried that the sea captain was afflicted with an imbalance in the brain. But he always recovered quickly, stronger than ever. He never explained where he had been or how he had been injured.

The old wives in the village of Braeside gossiped that "the enchanter" was surely the devil and that Sir Innes was called away to fight him from time to time. Every time Sir Innes returned, the old wives said, "He's broken Lucifer's back once more!"

Sir Innes died at sea in 1590, taking his secrets with him. The identity of "the enchanter" was never discovered, nor did anyone find out whether the "beasts and villains" lived only in his imagination.

Lorimer stared for a long time at a scribble in the margin. It was a question he had written when he was a teenager: "Was Corvo the enchanter?"

That had been the start of Lorimer's obsession with the mystery of Fausto Corvo. And Angus had become just as involved as he was, if not more so.

Lorimer should have left the mystery alone, but he could not. Even now, twenty years later, when he thought he had finally let go, it had come back to haunt him.

With a curse, he crumpled up the leaflet and flung it into a corner of the room.

Chapter 6

A pink light flickered in the distance as Sunni felt her way through the dim forest with Dean at her elbow, following the swish of Hugo's coattails. The silent boy, Inko, was behind Dean, moving easily in the gloom.

When at last they arrived at a clearing, Sunni saw that the pink glow came from a shimmering lake laced with tiny bubbles. Mesmerized by the tumbling water, she watched in amazement as a translucent hand materialized and swept through the water. She saw arms and lithe bodies all flowing and turning beneath the surface. As they passed, the figures glided along, making tiny waves lap the shore. Occasionally a streaming face surfaced then vanished.

"Look," hissed Dean.

"I know. I can see them."

"The naiads have come to greet us," announced Hugo with a bow toward the lake. "Good evening, ladies."

"Who are the naiads?" asked Sunni.

"Why, they are the lovely water nymphs of ancient poems and tales. Corvo painted many subjects from Greek and Roman mythology. He brought some of them to life in Arcadia."

"Do they come out of the water?" asked Dean. "Do they talk?"

"If they do, it must be when I am not about. I have never seen them on land nor heard their voices, if they have them. Unlike the dryads — tree spirits who can walk on the land if they desire."

"Where are they?"

"In the woods, of course."

Hugo hurried ahead, guiding them away from the water. Sunni glanced over her shoulder to make sure no watery creatures had followed. She noticed that Inko scanned the ground behind him as he walked, as if he, too, were worried that something was trailing them.

Up ahead, Sunni glimpsed a luminous building that looked like an ancient Greek temple. Thick columns at the front held up an angled roof. And once again, a dancing pink-violet light poured out from tiny high windows, highlighting veils of mist caught in tree branches and drifting over the lake.

They reached a pair of monumental doors, which Hugo unlocked with a large key he took from his waistcoat pocket. He pushed one door open and ushered them in.

"Welcome," he said. Inko pushed the doors shut after them and bolted them with a heavy iron bar.

A chill ran down Sunni's back. "I hope we did the right thing coming here," she whispered to Dean.

Before them was a long marble corridor lined with carved stone heads of lions and boars and eagles, each breathing jets of pink-violet flame. On either side of the corridor were three huge doorways, revealing eerily lit chambers. Sunni strained to see in as they passed, noting that each room had a large mural on its far wall.

"Come, come," urged Hugo, leading them into a covered courtyard. "You shall see it all tomorrow morning. This is the Sun Chamber."

In the center of the courtyard was a massive table laden with food and drink. Hugo pulled up two stools and sat himself in a high-backed chair. The wall behind him was decorated with a mural of a yellow-bearded man standing in the center of a golden circle with a lion crouched at his feet. Over the man's head were the letters *SOL*, and a fiery sun was painted on his chest. Hovering above either shoulder were a phoenix and an eagle in flight.

Rows and rows of tiny pictures, with captions, radiated out above the golden circle. When Sunni squinted, she could make out a horseman with a falcon, a man with a python, a rooster, a lion, and a man in a chariot in the clouds.

"Please take whatever you wish. You must be ravenous." Hugo pushed a platter of roasted meat and a bowl of glistening fruits toward Sunni. Her mouth watered at the sight of the feast in front of her, but she hesitated to try any of it.

"It's good, Sun—go on!" Dean was already gnawing on a chicken leg and grabbing purple grapes with his other hand.

"Dean!" Sunni hissed. "It could be poisoned!"

"I've already eaten half a chicken and I'm not dead yet."

"You are understandably wary, Miss Forrest." Hugo put a slice of meat into his mouth, then washed it down with something from a goblet. "There, you see? I am also still alive."

Yeah, you are still alive, she thought. She tried to figure out how old Hugo might be. He looked younger than her dad. Maybe thirty, she guessed, but getting closer to two hundred if he had truly been here as long as he claimed.

Hugo passed Sunni a goblet of golden liquid, but she shook her head. "I understand. Eat and drink when you are confident you can trust us. I recommend the figs. Inko fetched them this morning." The boy in the embroidered vest bowed from his position just inside the doorway.

"Where does all this food come from?" she asked while Dean jammed something else into his mouth.

"We are well provided for here," said Hugo. "Il Corvo designed Arcadia to perfection: an abundance of food and drink that replenishes itself, gentle companions such as Inko and the naiads, and a lovely climate. Just like the paradise described in mythology."

"I thought Arcadia was the city with Sir Innes's ship and the castle, that we've just come from," Sunni said, peering into the goblet at the golden drink. It smelled like honeysuckle.

"No, no!" Hugo said. "That is the outer painting, just the entrance. This is the true Arcadia, the living world il Corvo made for Sir Innes Blackhope to enjoy when he was home from his travels."

Dean chewed noisily. "You mean, like a private theme park for the rich guy? He could come here to relax and then go home when he'd had enough?"

"Theme park?" Hugo pursed his lips. "A park to be sure — but 'theme'?"

"Oh," said Dean, "it's like an amusement park where you

can go on awesome rides and have adventures."

Hugo raised an eyebrow. "Then, in that case, Master Dean, Arcadia does resemble a theme park."

Dean rubbed his greasy hands together and said, "Ten out of ten to me."

"And why do you call him 'il Corvo'?" asked Sunni.

"That is his name, to most people. Il Corvo means 'the Raven' in Italian," said Hugo. "You must have seen his signature on the painting—the raven in flight."

Sunni nodded, trying to take everything in. "But how did il Corvo make Arcadia?"

"Surely you must know this," scoffed their host gently. "Why else would you be here, if you did not know about il Corvo's ability to harness the power of the planets and stars to bring pictures to life?"

"Yeah, right. Planets and stars made this?" said Dean, rolling his eyes at Sunni.

"It's quite true, young man." Hugo was indignant. Dean shrugged and pulled his red hat farther down over his forehead.

"Mr. Fox-Farratt," said Sunni, kicking Dean under the table, "we're telling the truth. We're here by mistake. Dean just happened to be with me when he stumbled on the entrance to the painting. I was sketching the painting, but all I know about Fausto Corvo is that he was an amazing artist who was suspected of being a sorcerer and vanished."

"And you have never heard about the ancient knowledge that was passed down in secret books that Corvo and his friends studied?"

"No," said Sunni.

Hugo's eyes lit up. He sat back in his chair and addressed them with a flourish of his hand.

"Then let me tell you about him. In 1575 il Corvo was about forty-five years old, a successful painter with a workshop in a respectable part of Venice. He made paintings for rich merchants and members of royalty who admired the way he painted the stories of Greek and Roman mythology. He had a very comfortable life." Hugo pressed the tips of his fingers together. "But our friend il Corvo had a secret life, too. He was interested in astral magic. He had heard of ancient texts that explain how to gain extraordinary control over the hidden powers of the universe."

The torches on the walls sputtered for a moment and flickered across Sunni's rapt face. Dean held a half-eaten fig in midair as he listened.

"Il Corvo had many wise friends: geographers, mathematicians, astrologers. They met regularly to share knowledge, and one day Corvo was given a copy of a twelfth-century book called *Picatrix*. It was a guide to the making of magical talismans, to the harnessing of power from the stars. Corvo became hungry for more of this knowledge and secretly read every magical text he could find. He imagined channeling these powers into his paintings to create a wondrous living world of treasures and beauty. By 1582, when he was forced to flee Venice, he had already succeeded in making several enchanted paintings." Hugo's voice rose excitedly. "Corvo had brought to life the paintings beneath his paintings. We are now beneath *The Mariner's Return to Arcadia*."

"Is that why everything was white before we came into

Arcadia—because Corvo painted over all this to hide it underneath the top painting?" asked Sunni.

Hugo nodded, his eyes dancing.

Dean pulled his hat even farther down over his eyes, shaking his head and saying, "First we're in a painting. Now we're in a painting under a painting. How do you know that's where we are?"

"Because I saw this place before I even came here, while I was in Venice," Hugo said. "When I arrived, I recognized the lake, the palace, the statues. Except when I first saw them in Venice, they were just a sketch by Corvo on a tiny piece of paper in a museum."

Sunni looked around her. There was no sign of a brush mark or a paint smudge to let anyone know this was a painting. Everything was as solid as she and Dean were.

"How?" she whispered. "How does someone control the stars to make *this*?"

Hugo sat forward. "During the Renaissance, most people believed the earth was a ball sitting in space at the center of everything, surrounded by the elements of water, air, and fire. The cosmos was believed to surround the earth in rings, or spheres, that circled the earth and its elements: first is the moon, then Mercury, Venus, then we have the sun, then Mars, Jupiter, and Saturn. Outside these was the sphere of the zodiac—the stars of the heavens, and above these, the realm of the angels." He drew great circles in the air.

"Il Corvo's labyrinth was created as a model of the cosmos. The outermost path is the longest to walk because it stands for Saturn, the farthest planet from the earth. Each inner path symbolizes the other six planets in order, and each is shorter than the previous one. The innermost path is the moon, its orbit shortest and closest to the labyrinth's center, which is Earth." He paused, looking at the children.

"By walking the labyrinth, il Corvo believed he could experience each planet's journey round the earth and become open to its influence. And then he would be ready to start his work. The magical textbooks he studied told him which days and times were best for connecting with, for example, the authority of the planet Jupiter. He learned how to prepare special enchanted chalks, paints, and canvases. The secret books taught him how to make his workshop a place that would attract the planetary powers to Earth and infuse his paintings with life. The chalk marks and paint strokes that made Arcadia are like the bones or blood in our bodies—we can't see them, but they are there. Because this world is a huge, living magical talisman."

Hugo folded his arms across his chest, waiting to see how his guests would take this information.

Sunni frowned. "I still don't understand. The earth *isn't* at the center of the universe, is it? So how come the magic works?"

Hugo sighed. "To be frank with you, nobody has ever really understood it, apart from il Corvo and perhaps a few alchemists who spent their lives searching for the answers to ancient mysteries."

Sunni looked across the courtyard, picturing Corvo at his easel watching his painted people wriggling to life on the canvas.

"So, if he used labyrinths to get himself ready to do the magic," she said carefully, "and we came in on a labyrinth, do you think the way out is on a labyrinth, too?"

"Possibly," said Hugo. "One must walk to the center to come in, so perhaps one must walk back to get out. But I have not seen a labyrinth in my time here."

Sunni shrugged. "It was worth a try."

Dean finally put the rest of the fig into his mouth and asked Hugo between chews, "How do you know all this?"

"I am passionate about il Corvo's work. I made it my business to learn all I could about the man and his mysterious disappearance," replied Hugo. "It so happened that I was forced to disappear myself for a time and left London for Italy. That is how I came to be in Venice. I visited the small museum that held some of il Corvo's sketches and paintings and studied the diaries of his friends in the old library there. I wanted to know whether the rumors were true—that he had learned how to concentrate the power of the universe in order to bring drawings to life and hide dazzling cities inside flat paintings. My search eventually brought me to Blackhope Tower, and then here, to Arcadia."

"How did you work out the password?" Dean rubbed his sticky mouth.

"Trial and error. And you?" asked Hugo.

Dean answered smugly, "I can't really remember, but I got it on my first try."

"You were goofing around, Dean, and got in by pure rotten luck," Sunni said. Remembering the labyrinth jolted her back to their problem, and she said to Hugo,

"Everything you've told us is amazing and I'm glad we are getting to see it for ourselves, but we don't belong here. There must be a way out of Arcadia if Sir Innes was able to come and go. Please, Mr. Fox-Farratt, do you know where the exit is?"

"I'm afraid I have never looked for it. I have never been particularly interested in leaving Arcadia." Hugo looked a bit sheepish.

"Why not?" asked Sunni and Dean together.

He sighed. "My inheritance has dwindled, and I have almost nothing left. There are certain debt collectors who wished to find me. Disappearing seemed the perfect solution. And I could hardly ask for a better refuge than this." Hugo glanced at Dean's jacket draped over a chair and at Sunni's winter coat. "I do not know how long I have been here, because time moves strangely in Arcadia. But I deduce from your clothing that you are not from 1859. What was the date when you walked the labyrinth?"

When Sunni told him, Hugo murmured, "It means the debt collectors who hunted me are long dead by now." He was still for a moment. "As well as everyone else I knew."

Dean began yawning, and Hugo stood up.

"I am a poor host," he said. "You surely wish to rest, and I am boring you with my own troubles. There is a bedchamber for you." He picked up a brass bell from the table and shook it once.

Inko appeared and beckoned to Sunni and Dean.

"I hope you will be comfortable for the night," Hugo said, clasping his hands together. "Most delightful to have your company, my young friends! It has been so long since . . ." He stopped, his eyes misting over. "Since I had anyone amiable with whom to converse."

Dean's whisper cut through the darkness of the bedchamber they shared. "What do you make of Foxy Farratt?"

"He's OK, I think," Sunni mumbled, half asleep on a bed of the softest feathers. "He knows a lot."

"Yeah, though he's nice one minute and strange the next. Maybe he's been cooped up here too long."

"Oh, only by a hundred years or so!" Sunni said. "Just try to be a bit less mouthy, huh?"

Dean's hoarse whisper rose. "I was just trying to show him I'm not a stupid little kid!"

"You don't have to prove yourself. He seems to want to help us," said Sunni. "Let's not make him change his mind."

Dean was silent at this and then asked, "What do you think of Inko?"

"Dunno. Didn't speak while we were there. Did he say anything to you?"

"No," answered Dean. "I don't think he talks."

Sunni didn't respond.

"Sun?"

"What now?" she groaned.

Dean whispered earnestly, "Sorry I got us stuck in here."

Sunni let out a long breath. "It's all right."

At the bottom of the naiads' lake, a commotion began. There had always been a patch on the lake bed that glowed white under the silt, but it had never erupted before. Now suddenly a tangle of arms and legs thrashed up through it, propelling clouds of bubbles and sending the naiads darting away. A young man emerged, kicking at something below him, forcing it back down. Struggling to hold his breath, the young man finally let go. Satisfied that the mud had settled and his pursuer had gone, he pushed himself up to the surface, bursting from the water with a low cry of relief. He swam toward the lights of the palace and staggered out of the water, shaking pink droplets from his black hair.

The naiads recognized him and shrank back into the water to let him pass. He hardly noticed them—his eyes were trained on the palace ahead. He stole along the palace wall and heard voices through one of the high windows; voices that were unknown to him.

The young man made his way into the woods and whistled. A collective breath greeted him from the trees, like the wind rising through the leaves.

"Newcomers," it whispered. "Newcomers are here."

The dust of melancholy had settled over Hugo Fox-Farratt, sitting alone in his chair. He looked up as Inko scurried into the room with a tray.

"Bit of a shock, Inko," he said. "Outside it is the twenty-first century already." He picked up his goblet. "I ask myself whether my enterprise was worthwhile. I have evaded my enemies, the debt collectors, but I have also evaded my friends. I shall never see them again." His head dropped to his chest.

Inko stood nearby, his face furrowed with concern. Hugo half smiled when he looked up and saw the servant's serious expression.

"Still, it is good to have company, eh, Inko? I would have preferred visitors from my own time and closer to my own age, but it will be most interesting hearing about the twenty-first century from our guests."

Inko nodded more cheerfully as he picked up plates and cups.

"I remember when I first arrived in Arcadia," Hugo continued, "and was astonished to meet Lady Ishbel. I did not expect to find anyone here, let alone Sir Innes's niece. And then to find out that Lady Ishbel was not the only one here, that others had also found their way in—"

Inko paused in his tasks, the serious look back on his face.

"Why, Inko, what makes you look so worried? Are you wondering about Lady Ishbel and the others? I think we are quite safe here. We have been for some time now."

The servant boy nodded.

"We will continue to have as little to do with them as possible," Hugo said resolutely. "And we shall hope they keep to themselves. After all, we don't want to scare away our new friends."

Inko picked his way through the forest to his hut without need of a torch. He knew every twig and branch, every lump in the ground. Meeting the two young strangers from the other world had made him think of Sir Innes, who had gone back there long ago and never returned. He had died, Lady Ishbel had told him when she arrived. *He was my uncle,* she said, *and he left me the secret of how to come into Arcadia. Now I am your mistress.* And she had been, until she had vanished below, like the others.

Inko, too, had once had a life in the other world, though he couldn't remember it. Sir Innes had told him he had been a cabin boy on his ship, the *Speranza Nera.* Inko had never been able to talk, but the captain had said that he was the best cabin boy he had known.

Inko tensed as his mind snapped back to the dark wood he was crossing. There was a light breeze, and he sniffed the air. Something was nearby, something he had not sensed in a long time. Suddenly he was caught around the chest by a long, curling arm. A woody fragrance breathed into his ear. He recognized the scent of a dryad, a tree spirit from the woods.

A blue lantern light burst out of the blackness, and a dozen tree spirits surrounded Inko. In this form, they were willowy maidens with polished gray-brown faces and sinewy arms. The somber dryads made him uneasy enough, but a deeper shiver ran down his back when he recognized the person holding the lantern. *He* was back, after all this time.

Inko cringed as the young man stepped forward from

the gloom, his hair tangled around his face and his clothes shining damp.

"Inko," he said, thrusting the lantern into the servant's face, "strangers have entered Arcadia and are with Fox-Farratt in the palace. Bring them to me tomorrow."

Inko shook his head mournfully. He had not seen his master so happy in ages, and he knew it was because of the two visitors from the other world. Hugo would not want them to go to the faraway woods with the young man.

Eyes flashed in the blue lantern light. "You know you have no choice. I will be waiting by the brambles at this time tomorrow." The young man turned abruptly and melted away into the trees, followed by the dryads, rustling along the ground behind him.

Chapter 1

I'm in *the painting*, Blaise thought, awestruck. He had no idea how long he'd been sleeping when he woke up on a wooden dock, sprawled at the chained feet of men waiting to board a galley ship. Through their legs, he recognized the oversized Sir Innes Blackhope standing at the top of his ship's gangplank, one arm raised to greet the crowds on the dock. The name of the ship, *Speranza Nera,* was painted in curly gold letters on its hull.

Excitement charged through Blaise as he got to his feet and took in the life-size buildings, people, and animals. It was like being on a film set of Fausto Corvo's imagination, stuffed full of his backdrops and characters.

Blaise couldn't see back to the bench he had sat on in the Mariner's Chamber or the labyrinth in the floor tiles. People there might see him in the painting, but he could not see out of it. He wondered whether the two detectives were watching him at that moment. His dad might have arrived by now, too.

"Sunni! Dean!" he yelled, puzzled by the muffled sound of his own voice. The place was dead silent.

Instinctively Blaise pulled out his sketchbook and pencil. Flipping to his sketch of *The Mariner's Return to Arcadia,* he drew a star on his location at the docks and then chose a route up into the city where, if luck were with him, he would find Sunni and Dean.

Blaise hunted the streets, stopping to examine Corvo's painted people. A smear for an eye, a dash for a mouth, he noted, peering closely at the petrified figures.

"Sunni! Dean!" he shouted again. There was no reply, so Blaise moved on, occasionally stopping to make a quick note of his location on the sketch.

After he had wandered through many lanes, tiredness overcame him. Hoping to find somewhere to rest, Blaise came upon a slightly opened door to a house. In an upstairs window, a lady looked out from behind her fan. *She looks nice,* he thought dreamily, and went through the door. There was nothing there, just an empty space.

Blaise spread his coat out and sat down. He ate a banana and half a granola bar and drank a little water.

He was plotting what route to take when he heard a deep voice from somewhere outside.

"You beauty!"

Blaise jerked around, his heart pumping, and scrambled to his feet. Limping toward the door, one leg half asleep, he peered out, trying to keep himself hidden.

"You flaming beauty! Lorimer, you donkey brain, look what you've missed! Every brushstroke, every shadow, every hair the Raven painted!"

The voice was moving closer. A man in a hat and dark overcoat appeared, sometimes pausing to study the belongings and clothing of the people in the street.

"Bellissima," the man murmured, staring nose to nose into the blank eyes of a woman in his path. "Were you his

lady love? He took more time painting your face than all the others in this street." He stroked the woman's cheek. "Did you know his secrets? Eh, not talking either?"

Blaise held his breath and kept watching. The guy seemed drunk or something.

Just then the man wheeled around and fixed his eyes on the doorway where Blaise was frozen in place.

"You're Blaise, aren't you?" the man asked, pushing open the door. "You looked younger in the newspaper photo."

Bewildered, Blaise sized up this big man. If it came to a fight, he wouldn't stand a chance, even though he was pretty tall for his age.

"I'm Angus Bellini. Your art teacher is my cousin. He sent me in after you and . . . Sunni. And whatzisname, of course, her brother."

"Dean," said Blaise, stunned. So Mr. Bell had known more than he'd let on. "Mr. Bell sent you? How did he know the way into the painting?"

"Lucky guesswork," said Angus. "We put our heads together and worked it out."

"Why didn't he come himself? Or call the police?"

"Call the police? I could ask the same of you, my lad. Thought they wouldn't believe your story? Well, you were right. They wouldn't have believed us either. Just be grateful I've come to help you out."

"Who else knows how to get in?"

"Nobody else. We wouldn't want the hordes streaming in, getting in our way and mucking up the place," Angus said.

"You know the way out?"

"Not exactly. But the four of us will figure it out."

"It's just me. I haven't found the others yet," said Blaise. "You've looked everywhere?"

"Not yet. This is as far as I've gotten." Blaise scanned Angus's face, still sizing him up.

Angus grinned and tapped the top of his head. "Look, Blaise, no devil horns. No forked tail either."

With a shrug, Blaise pulled out his sketchbook and flipped to the sketch he had made of *The Mariner's Return to Arcadia.* "I started down here at the docks and came along these streets. We're here."

Angus's face lit up. He grabbed the sketchbook and thumbed through it, chuckling to himself. Then he looked Blaise straight in the eyes. "Nothing else matters like the *capture,* does it? Catching a face or a tree or an animal with your pencil. You capture it and it's yours."

"I just like to draw," said Blaise, pulling his sketchbook out of Angus's hand and thinking, *Weirdo alert.*

"Of course. So do I." Angus took a small sketchbook from his overcoat pocket. "Go on, have a look."

Angus's drawings took Blaise's breath away. Faces twisted in agony. Figures fought each other. One figure huddled on the ground, maybe not even alive.

"Who are they?" Blaise asked.

"It's a long story. And we've got people to find." Angus snapped the sketchbook shut and put it back in his pocket. "Shall we move on?"

D.C. Nash stood in front of *The Mariner's Return to Arcadia*. He had been staring at the painting for what seemed like hours but had not seen the missing kids or the man who had caused his colleague a hospital visit. Nash looked at his watch. Only ten more minutes and then he could go home.

The painting was an anthill of people in endless streets, so how could anybody find four particular figures, even if they were somehow there? All right, no one could explain how Blaise Doran had vanished in front of them, but he couldn't accept the boy's explanation of where the kids had gone either. Nothing had moved in the painting while he had been looking at it. That's what he was going to tell the chief inspector. With any luck, he would never have to look at the painting again.

At the stroke of five o'clock, Nash turned his back on *The Mariner's Return to Arcadia*, nodded briskly to the guard at the door, and strode out into the corridor. The lights were extinguished, and the heavy door was locked behind him.

The painting was plunged into darkness. But inside the sunny world of its medieval lanes and squares, two figures set off, the big man striding like a general and the boy keeping himself slightly to one side, the better to watch his new companion from the corner of his eye.

Chapter 8

Sunni sat up in the feather bed and rubbed her gritty eyes. Her body felt sluggish, and her head ached. She had woken up several times during the night, unnerved by the silence. The thoughts spinning around her brain had been as dark as the bedchamber and almost as suffocating. *We might never get home. We might die here.*

Now the darkness had gone but not the trapped feeling, even though a buttery light beamed onto one of the chamber's walls. She touched the wall and felt the familiar sensation of cool marble. *Made by the power of the stars.* On a table nearby was a brass tray filled with real bread, fruit, and a jug of milk. *An endless supply of food, thanks to the power of the stars. No wonder Hugo hadn't wanted to leave,* she thought.

Inko peered into the room and smiled, gesturing at Sunni to eat. He ventured in, carrying their jackets, and draped them over a chair. He was wiry and alert, like a young deer.

"Can you talk?" Sunni asked softly.

Inko shook his head. He smiled at Dean, who was snoring away, his bare feet dangling out of the bed. Sunni tugged one of his ankles, making him groan.

"Get a move on, Dean," Sunni said. She stuffed some

bread into her mouth and washed it down with milk. She was ravenous, not having dared to eat the night before. She grabbed a peach and let Inko lead her down a corridor lined with animal heads.

In the courtyard, Hugo lounged on a couch reading a small book. "Ah, Miss Forrest! I was just enjoying some Tennyson. I hope you slept well."

Hugo wore a cherry-red coat and tweed trousers. His shoes shone, and one foot was crossed nonchalantly over the other. Sunni was suddenly aware that her hair was probably sticking up and that her school uniform looked like it had never met an iron. She smoothed her hair as much as she could and nodded.

Sitting down on a stool near him, she rolled the peach from hand to hand. "Mr. Fox-Farratt, don't you have any idea at all how to leave Arcadia?"

"An idea, yes." Hugo hesitated. "I believe the exit is — I believe it could be some way from here."

"Would Inko know?"

Hugo smiled. "Inko is a simple soul. He is not interested in hunting for exits. He belongs here."

"So you're not sure how Sir Innes got out?"

"No. By the time I arrived here, he was long dead," said Hugo.

Sunni bit her lip. "Could you show us where you think the way out could be?"

A look of alarm passed over Hugo's face. He turned the poetry book over and over in his hands. "There are things you don't understand, Miss Forrest. Last night I told you how il Corvo created Arcadia for Sir Innes. But . . ." His voice trailed off. "I am afraid things have changed here since Sir Innes's death."

Just tell me where the exit is, Sunni wanted to shout, but she waited for him to go on.

"It is not safe to go off searching for things." Hugo frowned.

"Not safe?" Sunni repeated. "What do you mean?"

But Hugo ignored her question. "As well as this magical work, il Corvo is reputed to have created three other paintings even more spectacular than *Arcadia*—paintings of vast, rich cities where all the knowledge of the ancients was stored in huge palaces." Her host had his dreamy look again. "The grandest of the paintings was meant to be a gift for Rudolf, the Holy Roman Emperor. It was called *The Chalice Seekers,* and it was said to show a procession of noblemen on horseback, traveling across a mountainous landscape. Below them a dead stag was sprawled at the bottom of a cliff with scavenger birds poised to feed on it. A city lay in the distance, a glowing silver chalice hovering in the sky above it." Hugo paused and looked intently at Sunni. "It is my belief that these paintings, like il Corvo himself, are here—here in Arcadia."

Sunni raised her eyebrows. "Why would they be here? Surely they could be anywhere."

"I very much doubt il Corvo would let them out of his sight," said Hugo.

"So you think Corvo is here, too? Why?"

"Well, although he was never found, Soranzo's spies reported several sightings of him."

"The Soranzo who chased Corvo out of Venice?"

"The same. His spies crawled all over Europe like a creeping plague, and some of them even went to the lands of the Aztecs and Incas," Hugo said. "One spy said il Corvo went about disguised as a monk in Munich. Others said he became an amber trader in Saint Petersburg. But someone claimed to see him leaving a ship in London and making his way north — to Blackhope Tower, it was deduced. This caused huge excitement. What better place for il Corvo to hide than with his patron Sir Innes?"

"But you've never seen him here," said Sunni. "Have you?"

"There was a moment once when I thought I did, in another — er — part of Arcadia." Hugo gazed down at the little poetry book in his hand. "But no. Hundreds of years have passed like a fleeting dream, with no sign of Corvo or any of the other magical paintings."

"Hundreds of years." Sunni was struck by a terrible thought. "How long do you think Dean and I have been here? A day? A month? Or longer?"

She jumped up and paced around. "What if my dad is already old and I never get to see him again before — before he dies? And my friends, what if they're not my age anymore?"

"I doubt that. You have only been here since yesterday."

"But one day here might be a whole month at home." She sank back onto her stool, dejected. "We have to get home before any more time passes. You've got to help us. Please."

"I suppose I could escort you part of the way," replied Hugo, looking none too pleased at the thought. "But there is no point in hurling yourselves into the wilds, not knowing who or what may await you. I suggest you stay a day or two in the palace to familiarize yourselves with Arcadia before we set out."

"Even that feels too long. We need to go now."

"It would be reckless of me to let you go before tomorrow," said their host. He pulled a gold watch from his waistcoat pocket. "It is already four o'clock in the afternoon and will be dark by six."

"I slept till four?" she asked, astonished.

Just then, Dean half ran, half slid into the chamber.

"Ah, good afternoon, Master Rivers. I was just saying to your stepsister that I would be delighted if you would both stay here for a while," Hugo said.

"What do you mean, 'a while'?" Dean exploded.

Sunni held up one hand. "It's OK. I'll explain in a minute." She asked Hugo, "Could you show us around then? After we've tidied ourselves up, that is."

Hugo leaped up from the couch. "Inko, fresh water and soap for our guests. And then I will show you the splendors of our surroundings."

When Sunni and Dean returned to the bedchamber, he threw his jacket to the floor. "We're supposed to be getting away, not hanging around with Foxy Farratt! I want to go now."

"So do I!" Sunni hissed. "But it's just for tonight. He'll help us search for the way out tomorrow."

"He doesn't even know where it is."

"I'm not sure what Hugo knows and what he doesn't," said Sunni in a low voice. "But he's not telling us everything. And I want to know why."

Chapter 9

When they finally reached the castle on the hill, Angus shielded his eyes and scanned the city below them.

Blaise pulled a water bottle out of his bag and offered it to Angus. "That sure took a while."

"Haste makes waste, they say. We owe it to your friends to look everywhere for them." Angus took a noisy slug and dragged his sleeve across his mouth, sending out a faint whiff of aftershave.

"We've seen every street there is," said Blaise. "Sunni and Dean are nowhere."

"But they did go through the city and have a bit of fun with the Raven's masterpiece along the way."

"You mean the hat on that donkey? And the upside-down dog?" Blaise rubbed water over his face. "I still think they left those as markers to show which way they went."

"Well, I've put them back as they should have been, whether they were markers or not. Can't have kids messing about with genius," said Angus, staring at something in the distance. "I spy a cow with a rooster on its back in that pasture. Let's see if it's another one of your markers, because I doubt the Raven painted it that way."

They trudged down the hill toward the outskirts of the city.

"So you and Mr. Bell are both artists?" said Blaise.

"More or less," Angus said with a smirk. "I'm more of an artist, and he is less of one." He slapped Blaise on the shoulder. "Only joking. Yes, Lorimer and I went to art school together, to become painters."

"How come he's Bell and you're Bellini?"

"Our great-great-something grandparents came from Italy and settled over here. They shortened their name to Bell, so that's the name we were both born with. But I changed mine back to its rightful spelling."

"Mr. Bell's never mentioned you before," Blaise said, "or shown us your paintings in class. Sometimes he shows us his paintings."

A sour expression passed over Angus's face. "He's never been too keen on my work. Always was a bit envious of me, but don't ever tell him I said so." He shrugged. "We don't see each other too often these days. I live in Paris."

Blaise had a mental picture of Angus cruising past the Eiffel Tower in a fast car with a glamorous woman at his side. "So you happened to be visiting when we disappeared?"

"Yes," said Angus. "Naturally I offered to help find you."

Naturally. You decided to rescue some kids you don't even know, thought Blaise. "Lucky for us that you were around."

Angus smiled. "And how could I refuse the chance to be in a painting made by my idol?"

Blaise smiled back. "Your idol, huh?"

"Since I was eighteen, Corvo's the man I always wanted to be like. Not only an artist with the paintbrush, but also with the rapier and the sonnet. Women swooned over him, men envied him, and royalty craved his company, as well as his paintings," Angus said, gleeful. "The Raven did exactly as he pleased. He was a true star. No one could touch him."

The words set light to a feeling inside Blaise. How great would it be if he could be like Corvo, a little bit at least?

"Eh, my friend?" Angus glanced at him, eyes gleaming. "You want to be as great an artist as the Raven, too. I'm right, aren't I?"

Blaise shrugged and gave a slight nod.

"I can always detect a kindred spirit," said Angus. "So what's your story, Blaise? How came you to our bonny land?"

"My dad's a professor at the university. We came over from Boston last summer."

"Your mom?"

Blaise stiffened. "She still lives there. They're divorced."

"And you're great pals with Sunni and Dean?"

"I wouldn't say that. I only just met Dean, and I don't know Sunni very well." *I've tried to be friendly, but she always steers clear of me for some reason,* he thought, *even though we seem to like the same things.*

"Quite brave of you to come after people you hardly know." Angus gave him a sidelong glance. "The knight in shining armor rescuing the fair damsel, perhaps?"

"Yep, another day, another damsel." Blaise flushed with annoyance. Why did adults always have to drag romance into everything? They seemed to get a kick out of embarrassing kids with it. Besides, Sunni was hardly a girl who expected to be rescued. That was one of the things Blaise liked about her.

Angus laughed. "Or perhaps you're like me?"

"What do you mean?"

"You came into the painting because you want to be part of the Raven's world, damsel or no damsel." There was slyness in the painter's voice. "To be privy to all its secrets."

"The only secret I'm interested in is how to find the others and get out."

"Good," said Angus, as if Blaise had just given the correct answer on a test. "Ah, the enigmatic Raven! Ever since my cousin and I were students, we've been gripped by Corvo's mysteries. We found every scrap of information we could and became convinced that Corvo made magical paintings you could enter. But we never worked out how until you and your friends came along to show us the way."

"All you knew was that we had disappeared—not how we got in."

"Well, let's just say we looked at it from a new angle and got a result."

"But I asked Mr. Bell about Corvo and the painting after Sunni and Dean had disappeared, and he didn't tell me anything. Why would he do that?"

"Knowing Lorimer, it was so you wouldn't get too curious and follow the others into the painting," Angus said. "He was trying to protect you."

"From what?" asked Blaise.

"From never getting out again."

Chapter 10

Here is the last chamber." Hugo led Sunni and Dean into a torch-lit room. "And this one is devoted to Mars, the god of war."

They had already seen the other six chambers and their murals, named after the sun, the moon, Jupiter, Mercury, Venus, and Saturn. The paintings shimmered with life, as if the gods and their creatures could leap off the wall at any moment.

The mural dominating this chamber showed a muscle-bound man down on one knee, his face contorted in a terrible grin and his black eyes blazing. By his shoulder was a hawk in flight. In his left hand he held an enormous bronze sword with a dragon engraved on the blade. Above this scene, as in the other chambers, were rows of tiny paintings with minuscule labels.

"More weird little pictures," said Sunni. "There's a man with no head up there. And two snakes fighting next to a man riding a dragon." A thrill ran through her, knowing she was seeing Corvo paintings that only a handful of people even knew about.

"I'm afraid I don't know what each drawing means precisely," Hugo admitted. "Though il Corvo certainly did."

"So this is the last of his memory chambers. Isn't that what you called them?" she asked.

"Yes. This mural contains all the information about the planet Mars's powers over animals and plants. Each new row of tiny pictures is higher and higher on the wall, closer to the heavens, closer to the angelic powers in their celestial realm. If you were able to remember all the pictures in each room, you would know everything about the seven planets and how to connect with them."

"I could never remember all this," said Dean. "I couldn't be bothered anyway."

"Good thing no one's relying on you to do any magic," said Sunni.

Hugo smiled. "You might be surprised at how much you could recall, Master Dean. It is often easier to remember a picture than words."

"At least you can't lose stuff if it's painted on a wall," said Dean. "I lose my notebooks all the time."

"Precisely!" Hugo beamed. "Il Corvo's knowledge was safer here than anywhere else. A notebook could easily be stolen or misplaced."

"Do you think Corvo actually came here and painted all this on these walls?" Sunni asked.

"I do not know," said Hugo. "Perhaps he drew them into this layer of the painting before he conjured Arcadia into being."

"So Corvo could remember all these pictures and he used the information to bring his paintings to life," Sunni said, wondering what Blaise would make of all this if she ever got to tell him about it.

Hugo ran his hand over the wall. "Il Corvo could probably even picture himself walking through these seven chambers, remembering each of his murals in detail. He would instantly know which planet to call upon to work his magic."

"It must have taken him ages to learn all this," Sunni murmured. "But he probably wished he hadn't when he ended up hiding out while half of Venice was trying to catch him."

As they followed Hugo out of the palace toward the lake, Dean whispered to Sunni, "Those murals give me a weird feeling."

"Everything's been giving me a weird feeling since I got here."

"Yeah, but listen," insisted Dean. "If I drew a beard on that Venus mural, or glasses on Mars, would it screw up the magic? Would this place start falling apart?"

"Don't even joke about it!" said Sunni. "But I don't think it works like that. Those murals were just to help Corvo remember all the information he needed to do his spells. Remember, Hugo said he also had to paint with special brushes at the right time of day and everything."

"Yeah, I guess."

As the trio wandered, the sun tilted lower in the sky, sending a dappled light through the leaves and across the tinkling streams. Fantastic multicolored birds flew above them and nestled in the branches.

Hugo had been happy throughout the walk, telling stories and asking them about twenty-first-century life. But he stopped abruptly when they reached the end of a garden, and announced it was time to turn back.

"That is enough for today," he said. "From here on is just the background of the underpainting. Hills and woods as far as the eye can see."

"What's that?" asked Dean, pointing at a grove of trees, where a curved stone arch was visible.

"A ruin. No doubt Corvo put it there to add a bit of detail. I can assure you, it looks more fascinating from afar than close up."

"I'd like to see it," said Sunni.

"Me too," said Dean.

"You will be disappointed." Hugo crossed his arms over his chest. "That arch is of no importance whatsoever."

Sunni gave Dean a fleeting glance. "You don't want us to see it?"

"No, I—" Hugo began.

"Why not?" Dean interrupted. "Just for two minutes."

Hugo could barely hide his irritation. "Very well. If you insist."

As they entered the dense trees of the grove, the sun vanished, leaving them shivering. There was no breeze and no sound at all. Hugo walked ahead of them, a stony expression on his usually cheerful face. Sunni remembered the dryads and suddenly felt as though a hundred eyes were watching them.

The arch stood in a clearing, a lonely entrance to nowhere. At its top, two faces were carved in profile, looking in opposite directions.

"Janus." Hugo nodded up at the double-faced head. "God of gates and doorways."

Dean stepped toward the arch, but Hugo suddenly grabbed his shoulder and steered him away. "It's time we left."

Dean twisted out of his grip and said, "OK, OK!"

"What's wrong?" Sunni whispered.

Hugo stood dead still, as if he heard something the others had not. "We must go," he urged. "It's getting dark, and we are not at all safe here."

He quickly herded them out of the gloomy grove and didn't slow down until sunlight once again warmed their skin. Everyone was quiet on the walk back to the palace, as if they carried some of that eerie place with them.

"I think we should talk to Inko after Foxy Farratt's gone to bed. Maybe he can show us the way out," Dean said when they were back in their bedchamber before supper. "I don't trust that Foxy one bit."

"Hugo told me Inko doesn't know where it is," answered Sunni. Her mind was still at the archway. She shuddered at the thought of the pitch-dark grove at night.

"He might be lying," Dean said.

"I know. I suppose it wouldn't hurt to ask Inko, if we can get him alone. But he can't talk, so we'll have to ask yes or no questions and maybe get him to draw a map or something."

Sunni and Dean ate supper politely while Hugo tried to lighten the atmosphere by telling them about his life before he came to Arcadia.

He finished a story and realized he was the only person

chuckling at it. "You are both very quiet this evening."

"Well," said Dean, "I have a question, but I know you won't answer it."

"I have tried to answer all your questions, Master Dean," said Hugo, "but if you have more, please, go ahead and ask."

"Why did you stop me from going under the arch?"

"It was becoming dark, and we had no lamp. I told you it was not safe to remain there."

"No," said Dean, "it wasn't just that. There was something about that arch. You almost pulled my arm off to keep me away from it."

Hugo stood up suddenly, clearly annoyed. "Despite my hospitality, I fear I do not have your confidence. Perhaps in your century it is customary for children to question their elders' wisdom, but it was not so in mine."

A smirk played on Dean's lips. Sunni had seen that infuriating look on his face so often at home, she nearly lost her own temper.

Hugo continued: "You do not realize how lucky you are that I did pull you away from the arch. I wonder now whether I should have allowed you to go through it and left you to fend for yourselves!"

Dean's smirk evaporated.

Hugo was now pink in the face. "I have said I will help you find the exit. And I will. But you must heed my warnings."

"Mr. Fox-Farratt," said Sunni, "we don't mean to annoy you. It's just that you haven't told us what the dangers are."

Hugo deflated slightly and collapsed back into his chair.

"The dangers are mainly in the layers il Corvo painted below this one. Yes—there are more underpaintings. Sir Innes Blackhope claimed to have met many brutes and monsters in his sea travels. He described them to il Corvo, who drew them and brought them to life in the underpaintings."

"You've seen them?" Dean asked.

Hugo nodded. "Heaven help me, yes. They were put there for Sir Innes's entertainment. He loved to fight and outwit adversaries. The arch is the way into their domain."

Dean hung his head. "I'm lucky you did stop me, then."

"Perhaps I should have explained my actions more fully, but I did not want to frighten you."

"But if the monsters are down there, then what are the dangers in this layer?" Sunni shivered.

Hugo fidgeted with his goblet. "We are not the only humans in Arcadia. When I entered the painting, I found that others were here already."

"Who?"

"Scoundrels who hunt down fugitives in return for money. Bounty hunters from Spain, Holland, and Italy seeking il Corvo for Soranzo. And, of course, those who had come in search of the lost paintings."

"And they're still here?" asked Dean.

"Some have gone, possibly killed off by the creatures below, or perhaps just vanished. Others may still hunt the underpaintings, but I have not seen anyone for some time." Hugo began counting on his fingers. "One notably greedy and deceitful character is Bashir, a pirate captain from the Barbary Coast who found out about the paintings from one of Soranzo's spies. Then there is Lady Ishbel Blackhope, Sir Innes's niece, who came here in 1600, claiming she had inherited Arcadia. She is determined to become its mistress and be rid of all the outsiders."

"Is that why you stay here rather than hunting for Corvo and his paintings, to keep safe from those people?"

"Yes. I have nearly been killed by all of them."

Sunni's eyes widened.

"Luckily, while trying to escape them, I fell into a weak spot between the underpaintings that led me back to this one. The palace was empty, so I have remained here ever since, living as quietly as I can and hoping none of them turns up." Hugo drained his goblet. "Anyone who comes between them and il Corvo's lost paintings is fair game."

"You say that almost as if it's all right."

"I do not mean it to sound that way. I am merely telling you what you will face once you leave the palace."

"Do we have to go into the underpaintings?" Sunni twisted her hands in her lap.

"I have found no exit in this layer, so if you are determined to leave, you will have to search for it there." Their host wiped a linen handkerchief across his forehead.

"I hope I have satisfied your curiosity," he said. "I will show you the way back to the archway tomorrow. For all of our protection, I ask only one thing. Do not stray from here without me. You will be leaving the safety of the palace soon enough—and you may wish you never had."

The palace was still, except for the hooting of an owl outside. Hugo had long since gone to his chamber, but Sunni and Dean sat alert on their beds.

"I still think we should ask Inko if he knows how to get out," Dean said. "Now."

"What's the point? We're going with Hugo in the morning."

"What if Inko knows a way that doesn't have any monsters and bounty hunters?"

Sunni shook her head.

"We're only asking," said Dean. "If Inko doesn't know, we'll go with Hugo. Yeah?"

"If we can find Inko," Sunni said with a sigh, "then we might as well ask him, I suppose."

"Where does he sleep?"

"No idea. He just seems to turn up when he's needed."

"Well, we need him now." Dean pulled the hood up on his jacket.

Reluctantly Sunni put her backpack over her shoulder and followed him out of the bedchamber.

They tiptoed down the corridor. The Mars, Venus, and Jupiter Rooms were all still and dim, but when they passed the Saturn Chamber, the silent figure of Inko materialized in the doorway. He smiled at them, but his eyes were clouded with worry.

"We need to talk to you," whispered Dean, pulling Inko into the Saturn Chamber. "Do you know how to get out of Arcadia? We want to go home."

To their surprise, Inko nodded sadly.

"Now? Can we go there right now?"

The servant boy beckoned them to follow him. Dean almost whooped with glee and began hopping up and down until Sunni held him still by the sleeve of his jacket.

"But wait. Do we have to go down below?" Dean gulped. "Where the monsters are?"

Still somber, Inko shook his head and shuffled into the corridor with Sunni and Dean at his side, both grinning from ear to ear.

Inko stealthily unbarred the doors, and they scurried out of the palace into a dark avenue of trees. There was the slight hint of a crescent moon overhead, and the lake glimmered with only a faint rosiness.

"Is it far?" Sunni asked. But Inko put his finger to his lips and urged them on, deeper into the darkness.

She could barely make out any landmarks as they stumbled along, but she was quite sure they passed a chillingly familiar one in a grove to her left. The ruined arch. It seemed to glow under the shard of moonlight.

They came to a halt beside a huge wall of shrubs beneath a hill.

"Where is it, Inko—where's the way out?" Sunni couldn't contain her excitement. "How did Sir Innes do it?"

Inko shook his head from side to side. Sunni and Dean could barely make out his features. But then he sniffed, and they realized he was crying.

"What's wrong?" Sunni soothed him. "Please, Inko, we need your help. You know the way. Please—"

Inko put his hands over his face and swayed from side to side.

"Why are you crying?" Dean said, alarmed.

They did not notice the rushing sound in the grass. Dean kicked at something tickling his ankle and, without warning, they struck. Curling, winding tendrils lassoed Sunni and Dean's legs and wound around their torsos, lifting them both off the ground.

Dean was hung upside down, and with his stomach full, he soon began to retch. His red hat was yanked off, and he clawed at the sturdy vines that caged him.

"Dean?" Sunni's voice was faint and a bit choked.

Dean could manage only a groan as he tried to stop himself from being sick.

From the corner of her eye, Sunni could see a blue light coming toward them. Its radiance brightened as it drew nearer. She could just make out Inko, his head bowed and his shoulders hunched in fear.

Holding the lantern aloft was a young man of about eighteen. His eyes gleamed as he surveyed Sunni and Dean, trapped like flies in the web of vines and branches. The lantern played on black hair that reached down to a stiff white collar. His clothing was like Sir Innes's had been in his portraits: knee-length breeches, dark striped jacket, black stockings, and flat shoes.

An unnerving thrill ran through Sunni. Though the young man's face was hard, as if it had been carved from marble, it was the most exquisite she had ever seen. His almond-shaped eyes were the color of amber; his olive skin was luminous over high cheekbones and a proud, firm jaw.

Her breath caught as he turned to look at her. Sunni

was painfully aware of herself: a fourteen-year-old girl with messy hair, still wearing her school uniform, trussed up like a pig ready to be roasted over a fire.

The young man shifted his gaze to the miserable servant boy. His deep voice had a foreign accent. "Inko," he said, "I congratulate you on the discovery of these trespassers."

Sunni could hear Dean thrashing and cursing under his breath at the word *trespassers.*

The young man held the lantern up and addressed them. "Have you brought others with you?"

Sunni managed to squeak, "No, no, we came alone."

The young man then shone the lamp straight into Inko's face. "Do not let Fox-Farratt know where the trespassers are. If you do, you know what your fate will be. Now, go."

Inko darted away into the night.

The young man's eyes were on fire when he turned back to Sunni and Dean. "Take them up!" he shouted.

The tendrils and branches unraveled slightly, letting their captives roll forward, only to be caught by yet more vines and passed up to waiting branches that hooked under their armpits and knees. The pair were hauled up the hillside, over thickets and thorns that nicked their hands and faces.

For a moment Sunni faced backward and saw the blue lantern gliding behind them. The young man moved like a panther up a rough staircase of branches, his eyes focused on a point above them.

Farther up the hill, the branches propelled them toward a tangle of thorny bushes in the rock face. They shut their eyes tightly and waited for their skin to be shredded. But instead, they landed on soft earth, and when they opened their eyes, they saw that the thorny tangle had parted to let them through into the mouth of a large cavern. The young man climbed in, hooking the lantern to a root that protruded from the ceiling. The mass of brambles closed behind him, and he stood over Sunni and Dean, who were now curled up in terror on the floor.

"I am Marin," he announced. "And this is your prison."

Chapter 11

Angus slung his coat over his shoulder and tossed his hat into the air from time to time as he strode along. He surveyed the fields as if he were visiting a kingdom he had just inherited. It wouldn't have surprised Blaise if Angus had turned to him and said, "Mine . . . all mine!"

Suddenly Blaise saw something lavender and striped hanging from a tree in the distance. Relief and elation surged through him.

"That's Sunni's scarf!" he shouted, charging through the trees to the foot of some rocky hills.

Blaise was so busy untying the scarf, carefully folding it up, and stowing it in his bag that he jumped when Angus's voice rasped in his ear like an enraged hornet, "Don't you ever run off like that again. We hunt together—you got that?"

Blaise gaped at him, taken aback.

Angus dropped his hat and coat onto the ground and said mildly, "It looks like there's an opening up there between those rocks. I'm going to have a look. Come on." He ran his large hands over the rock surface as he walked along it toward the gap. Blaise followed at a distance, jolted by what had just happened.

Moments later, Angus waved a snippet of bright red wool. "I found this."

"That could be from Dean's hat."

"Snagged it as he went through, I bet." Angus shoved himself into the narrow opening in the rock face. "Bring my hat and coat, eh?"

What am I, your slave? Blaise snatched up Angus's dusty clothes and sprinted to the cave opening. He heard the painter breathing in the darkness but could not see him until his black silhouette obscured the white doorway ahead.

"Hmm," Angus purred, emerging into the white corridor Sunni and Dean had passed through. "What have we here?"

Blaise and Angus stepped carefully from the white corridor into the sunlit woods. For a few moments, they stood there, shocked into silence at the sight of this new, living world. Angus pounced on a butterfly darting past and cupped it in his hands. He let it fly off with a flourish and began laughing as if he had just gotten some big joke.

"What's so funny?" Blaise gingerly stroked the leaf of a tree brushed by the breeze. Everything around him shimmered and released bursts of grassy fragrance.

"Not funny—amazing!" Angus started whirling around. "Yes, yes, yes, this is what it's all about! The ancient Egyptians said it could be done with statues, but our friend the Raven took it one step further. Pure genius!"

"What are you talking about?"

"This." Angus broke off a leaf and held it up in Blaise's face. Milky sap dripped from its stem. "It's alive. I reckon we're inside a living underpainting. Celestial magic, natural magic, whatever you want to call it—the Raven worked out how to control it and create other worlds from his imagination."

Blaise caught a droplet of sap and rubbed it between his fingers. "It—it seems real."

"Ha! What do you make of it?"

"I'm blown away. How could anyone ever figure out how to do this?"

"Others tried, years and even centuries before Corvo. They left behind secret books that he got hold of and studied. He worked out his own formula—and it works!"

Angus jerked his thumb at the foggy edge of the woods, where they had entered the underpainting. "Those white walls back there, they must be a layer of gypsum and glue."

"Gypsum—what's that?"

"A kind of chalk. During the Renaissance, Venetian painters mixed it with glue made from animal skin, then used it to coat blank canvases before they started painting. It made a smooth, white surface to work on," said Angus. "Corvo must have painted this world, brought it to life, and then somehow covered it over with gypsum so nothing could show through. Then he painted *The Mariner's Return to Arcadia* on top. I wonder how he did it."

Blaise crouched down on a patch of grass, still thunderstruck. The grass was cool and soft, springing back from his touch. He just wanted to lie down and wonder at

Corvo's clouds, watch the light sparkling in the trees.

"We should move on." Angus rubbed his hands. "Who knows what else there is to see?"

"I just need a minute," Blaise said, taking out his sketchbook and starting a rough drawing of the woods before him.

He glanced at Angus and thought he saw a flash of vexation before the painter said sweetly, "Of course."

When Blaise stood up, his sketch finished, Angus asked, "Well, Christopher Columbus, which way do you think we should go?"

So now you're asking me, Blaise thought. *Half an hour ago you were telling me what to do.* He pointed to a gap nearby in the foliage. "That might be a path."

"Fair enough," Angus replied. "We have a real sun here, and I reckon it's about two o'clock. Hopefully we'll pick up the trail before dark, if they left one."

They bushwhacked through undergrowth, often losing the path only to join it again farther along. There was no sign of any humans, only birds and a few startled rabbits.

Blaise traipsed along, his eyes trained on the ground, until Angus stopped abruptly and pointed at a huge statue on a plinth. A stone archer, his teeth bared, aimed a gigantic bow and arrow directly at them.

"Zut alors!" Angus exclaimed. "Wouldn't fancy meeting him in the flesh."

Suddenly Angus hauled Blaise down with him to crouch behind some shrubs. They peered out through the leaves as a boy in an embroidered vest hurried around from the back of the plinth, carrying a basket of food.

"Let's go talk to him," whispered Blaise. Angus held up one hand for him to be silent.

As the boy disappeared from sight, Angus dragged Blaise to his feet, and they set off to follow the boy, edging past the plinth and into a sculpture garden.

The boy bustled past a winged woman and a sphinx, completely covered with ivy except for one eye. Beyond the trees and statues lay a shining expanse of water, tinted tangerine by the afternoon sun. The boy skirted the shore, making for the grand entrance to a palace, glinting gold at the far end of the lake.

By the time Blaise and Angus burst from the sculpture garden into the sunshine, the boy was inside the palace.

They stopped to catch their breath at the lakeside, and the naiads swam over to have a look at them, churning up the surface in lacy ripples.

"Unreal!" exclaimed Blaise, staring at the naiads in amazement.

"I like this place more and more," said Angus as he watched them.

Blaise rolled his eyes.

"We're getting warm now." Angus's eyes glittered as he shifted his gaze toward the palace. "I can feel it."

THE ARCH

THE BRAMBLES

STREAM

PALACE

THE LAKE

THE SCULPTURE GARDEN

THE WHITE WALL

Chapter 12

It was the sound of groaning that woke Sunni. As she looked around, her spirits sank. She was at the foot of an ancient tree trunk, one of several that grew into the cavern, with roots covering the walls like veins. She tried to stretch, but the vines that were still wound around her arms and ankles would not let her. Her skin was red and raw beneath them.

Across from her, similarly restrained, was Dean, his head lolling onto his chest. He groaned again in his sleep.

The previous night, after Marin had secured them, he had sat down upon an intricately shaped chair and watched them, without a word, until the blue lantern light died and he became a fading specter in the gloom.

Now enough daylight filtered in through the lattice of brambles and vines covering the entrance for Sunni to see their prison. Around the dirt walls, branches formed structures almost like benches. In one alcove, Sunni noticed a sort of desk supported by a thick wooden trunk. On it were a few sheets of paper and scattered charcoal sticks, a bottle of ink, and some quill pens. A number of drawings had been hung above the desk, speared on a blackthorn branch.

Sunni's eyes moved along the wall. The thronelike chair where Marin had been sitting was empty.

Next to it was a screen of twisted vines from which came a rustling sound. Someone was moving. Sunni quickly closed her eyes and feigned sleep. She heard a thump and then something that sounded like the opening and closing of a zipper. Opening her eyes to the tiniest slits, she could see Marin kneeling on the floor, moving the zipper on her backpack back and forth in wonder. At last he unzipped the bag and started pulling out her belongings, placing each one on the ground after he had examined it.

Sunni watched Marin empty her wallet, staring at her plastic library card and money, bill by bill, coin by coin. He turned her phone over and over, running his fingers across its shiny surface before putting it down. Part of her was outraged that he was touching her things. But an unfamiliar, shivery part deep inside her was entranced. *He's looking at my stuff, and it feels like he's looking at me.*

Marin studied everything, even her sparkly comb and a pot of pink lip gloss. He seemed to delight in her pencil case, laying out all the pencils and erasers, and turning the sharpener first one way and then the other in his hand.

He leafed through her sketchbook, pausing on one or two pages. But it was the second book in Sunni's bag that made him gasp. He scrambled to his feet and turned it over to look at the binding, feeling its shiny jacket. When he sat down on his chair and carefully opened the book, Sunni caught a glimpse of its cover. She had completely forgotten she had it with her: Mr. Bell's book, *The Mysterious World of Fausto Corvo.*

Marin spread the book open on his lap, transfixed by the photos of Corvo's paintings.

Suddenly Dean stirred and swore as he tried to stretch out his legs. Marin snapped the book shut.

"Water," croaked Dean.

"My questions first, then water," Marin answered, getting up and walking over to Sunni.

"Who are you?" Sunni recoiled as he neared her.

"I have already told you. I am Marin. Now it is for you to tell me who you are."

"I am Sunni Forrest, and he's my stepbrother, Dean."

Marin thrust Mr. Bell's book in her face. "And how did you conjure this book?"

"Conjure? You m-mean, how did I make it? I didn't make it. A printer did."

"How could a printer put these paintings in a book?" Marin yanked the book open.

"They are just printed photos—um, copies, of the artwork." Sunni racked her brain for the right way to explain it. "The caption on that one says the original painting is hanging in a house in Paris."

"Impossible. Lies, as I would expect from a spy."

"We are not spies," Sunni insisted. "We came here by mistake."

"If your presence was truly a mistake, you would not have a book of il Corvo's work with you."

"I only have that book because I wanted to learn more about his art. It's borrowed from my teacher."

"How can this painting be in the book and in Paris at the same time?"

"In my century special machines can make exact copies

of paintings. And then the copies are printed smaller into books like this one."

"So you say. But I suspect sorcery." Marin opened the book again and scratched his thumbnail along the surface of the paper, as if he might somehow slice a membrane holding the painting inside the page. "This painting cannot be in Paris. It was made for a duke in Rome."

"How do you know that?"

"It is none of your business."

"Maybe someone bought it from the duke and took it to Paris," Sunni said, beginning to realize there was no point trying to explain anything to him.

"Someone?" Marin burst out. "You mean your master, Soranzo, or some other dog?"

Soranzo. The name hit Sunni like a blast of icy air.

"We don't have any master!" Dean shouted. "We're just children and we're here by mistake. How many times do we have to tell you?"

Marin spun around. "Children can be excellent spies. You are not the first and you will not be the last enticed into stealing secrets."

Sunni's voice was shrill. "Well, we aren't, and we don't know anyone named Soranzo. We're from the twenty-first century, and we're not trying to steal anything. We're just trying to go home. If you hadn't captured us, we would have been on our way by now with Hugo Fox-Farratt."

"Fox-Farratt," sneered Marin. "He is another who pries into secrets that are none of his affair. Perhaps you came here to do his bidding, then."

"No way," said Dean. "We don't even want to be in this stupid painting!"

Sunni held her head high. "If you let us go, we'll find the way out and leave."

"Impossible. I cannot release you. I do not know what you are capable of." Marin laid Mr. Bell's book open on the ground at Sunni's feet. He walked over to the far wall and unhooked a pouch hanging from a branch. He gestured to Dean, then poured a stream of water into the boy's mouth. Then he went over to Sunni and placed the animal skin to her lips. As she swallowed, trying to gulp down as much as she could, Marin fixed her eyes with his, as if he were trying to see inside her head. Despite her fear, she felt a flutter inside.

"You came into the painting to steal knowledge," Marin said. "Or perhaps to take something else — for yourselves or for your master."

"Didn't you hear me?" Dean shouted. "I said I don't care how this stupid place got made and I want to go home."

"Very well," said Marin. He hung the skin back up and dragged his chair in front of Dean. From his worktable he selected a piece of charcoal and a creamy parchment. He picked up Sunni's sketchbook again, settled himself in the chair, and rested the parchment on top of the sketchbook in his lap. Cocking his head to one side, he gazed at the grumpy boy through half-closed eyelids and mumbled a few unintelligible words.

"What are you doing?" Dean asked, looking anxious.

Ignoring him, Marin drew an oval shape on the

parchment with the charcoal. Then he sketched in two eyes and the bridge of a nose with a horizontal line for a mouth.

Sunni watched over his shoulder, with an uneasy feeling in the pit of her stomach as her stepbrother's portrait took shape.

As Marin leaned on her precious sketchbook, Sunni squeezed her eyes against tears. Inside was her favorite sketch, the one she had drawn of her dad dozing on the couch. The beach and sailing boats from their last family holiday in Cornwall were on another page. Farther along, there were caricatures of her friends Vic and Mandy, with silly thought bubbles over their heads. Only two days earlier, she had been in school with them, giggling at the cartoons. Now she fought hard not to cry at the predicament they were in.

"What do you think you're doing?" Dean screwed his face up and stuck his tongue out at Marin. "I'm not posing unless you give us some food."

"Do not move!" Marin instructed, but Dean froze his face in a hideous expression. "This boy is extremely vexing, but he cannot keep his face like that for long. So I will show you something while I wait for him to tire."

He lay down the sketchbook, parchment, and charcoal, then took two drawings from the wall and held them in front of Sunni.

"Look closely."

The first was of a man with a droopy mustache and a pointy hat. He had a white ruffle around his neck like the one Sir Innes wore in the painting. Then something happened. The eyes in the drawing moved, widening and then closing slightly. The head turned a little to the side.

Dumbfounded, Sunni studied the other drawing. This man wore a flatter cap and had a scar on his cheek. As she watched in horror, the man's mouth opened into a scream. Marin paraded the sketches in front of Dean, who gasped when he saw the faces move.

"Both were spies," Marin said, skewering the sketches again on the thorns.

"H-how can they move?" Dean asked.

"They can still move once I have caught them inside the page," answered Marin. "Though it cannot be comfortable to live in such a small, flat space." He sat down on the chair once more and took up his sketch of Dean.

"Inside," Sunni repeated, appalled. "You mean those men are trapped *inside* your portraits?"

"Yes. It is most convenient to be able to imprison an enemy in a drawing." Marin drew a few strokes of hair on the sketch of Dean. "Quite portable. My bag is full of them." He nudged a leather satchel slung over the chair so it started to swing back and forth.

"Wait a minute!" blurted Dean. "Is that why you're drawing me? To trap me, too?"

"It is a good solution. There are too many spies here already."

"You can't do that!" White-faced, Dean struggled against his restraints. "We don't know anything, and we are *not* spies!"

"That remains to be seen. I have no doubt that you know very little, but I am not so sure about her." Marin blew charcoal dust off the paper. "So, I will make your portrait first in the hope that she will reveal what she knows before I finish. Otherwise you will vanish into this paper."

Marin smudged a line with his fingertip, and Dean shrank back, terrified.

"I don't know anything either!" Sunni shrieked. "But how can I prove it to you?"

"How to prove you are not a minion of Soranzo or Fox-Farratt? I will ponder that."

"You have to give us a chance. It's not fair to trap Dean in a drawing because *I* don't know the answer to your questions."

"Life is far from fair," said Marin. "This I know only too well. But I value justice nonetheless. If you will not save the boy by telling me what you know, I will do the fair thing and draw you into a paper trap as well."

Angus knocked on the palace doors and winked at Blaise.

After a moment a man's voice asked from behind the door, "Who is it?"

"Good day to you. We are searching for our friends. Sunni Forrest and . . ." He trailed off, appealing silently to Blaise for help.

"Dean," Blaise called. "I'm Blaise Doran and this is Angus Bellini."

The door slid open. A man and a boy stood behind it. The man's face showed exhaustion, as if he had not slept for days. "Good heavens," he said without enthusiasm. "More newcomers."

"More?" repeated Angus. "And you are?"

"Hugo Fox-Farratt," the man answered wearily. "This is Inko."

He gave Angus and Blaise a searching look before he finally stepped aside to let them in.

"We're looking for two children, a boy and a girl named Sunni and Dean," Angus repeated. "Have they been here?"

Inko looked uncomfortable, shifting his weight from side to side.

"They were here, but they left during the night."

"Where did they go?" Blaise was crestfallen.

"I do not know," said Hugo, his face grave. "I gave them hospitality and showed them around. I thought they would stay, but they must have been determined to leave." He ushered them into the Sun Chamber. "Do sit down. Inko, food and drink, please."

Blaise slid onto a stool and looked around the room. He caught sight of the sun mural and noticed that Angus was looking at it, too.

"Interesting mural," said Angus. "I believe that's Sol, the sun, with some of his animals. What are all the little paintings above him?"

"I have no idea," Hugo said brusquely.

Angus took a moment before speaking again. "So, we find ourselves caught up in the strangest of events. How did you come to be here, Fox-Farratt? I don't think Fausto Corvo drew you into the painting, judging by your clothes."

The man sighed deeply before answering. "I came through the Blackhope labyrinth. As you must have, I imagine, a century and a half after me."

"Yes, yes, but *why* did you come?" asked Angus, seemingly unfazed by the fact that Fox-Farratt had just admitted to being somewhere in the region of two hundred years old. Blaise was open-mouthed.

"I cannot see how my history has anything to do with *your* journey," said Hugo, thin-lipped. There was silence.

Blaise shifted awkwardly on the low stool. "Have you looked for Sunni and Dean at all?"

"Of course. We searched all morning with no luck. You say you are friends of Miss Forrest and Master Rivers?"

"I am," said Blaise. "I go to school with Sunni."

"And you, sir?"

"I don't know them personally." The corner of Angus's mouth twitched in irritation. "My cousin, their teacher, asked me to help find them."

"I see," was all Hugo said.

"You must know a lot about this place, Mr. Fox-Farratt," Blaise said. "About where to look."

"Yes. But there is no sign of the children anywhere."

Blaise's hopes sank even lower. "I really hoped we'd catch up with them. Then we could find the way home together."

"Home," said Hugo. "To the twenty-first century? We have had four visitors from your century in only three days. How many more will follow now? I wonder."

"None, hopefully," said Angus.

"I presume you are here only to find the two young people?"

"Of course." Angus smiled. "That is all that matters."

"Where did you last see Sunni and Dean, sir?" Blaise asked Hugo.

"Here, before we retired last night."

"And they were all right?"

"Oh, yes. Absolutely."

"You helped them out," Blaise said. "So why would they leave without saying good-bye?"

"I wish I knew." Hugo's face was forlorn. "Though we did have a bit of a disagreement at dinner. They thought I was withholding information from them."

"Oh?" Angus sat up.

"But I explained everything. I thought they had accepted what I told them as the truth."

Inko slipped into the room with a tray of food and a jug of the golden drink.

Angus helped himself to a handful of olives before the tray had touched the table. "What exactly did you tell them?"

Hugo frowned. "We came upon a certain place while walking yesterday. It is a dangerous spot, and I warned them not to go there again."

"If you had told me not to go there, that's precisely where I would have gone, just to satisfy my curiosity," said Angus.

"They would dare to go there alone, even after I had warned them?" Hugo was indignant.

"I reckon they would." Angus gobbled up several slices of pink meat and drained his cup.

"They would never have found it again in the dark," said Hugo.

Inko's hand shook as he refilled Angus's cup.

"Someone must have helped them." Angus looked intently at the boy, who spilled nectar on the table and sopped it up with his sleeve before scurrying to stand by the door.

"Did you see Sunni and Dean last night, Inko?" Blaise asked, to which the servant boy lowered his eyes and shook his head.

Hugo cleared his throat. "Sadly Inko cannot speak—"

"That's too bad," interrupted Angus. "Well, we have a bit of daylight left. I suggest you take us to this place, Fox-Farratt."

"That is most ill-advised! I will not, sir."

"Oh, I think you will."

"Sunni and Dean might be in danger," said Blaise.

"I have already looked there myself, to no avail," insisted Hugo. "I say again, it is a place best avoided."

"Is that true, or do you just want to keep us away from something?" Angus stood up.

"Not at all!"

Angus shrugged and walked nonchalantly toward the door. Suddenly he stepped behind Inko and grasped him firmly by the shoulders.

The color left Hugo's face. "Good heavens, sir! Whatever are you doing?"

Blaise jumped up, outraged. "Angus! Let him go!"

"Calm down. No one is going to get hurt," said Angus. "If you won't take us to this forbidden place, Inko will."

Angus glanced toward Blaise as if trying to transmit

some reassuring signal, but Blaise could only see his supposed rescuer strong-arming a boy.

"If I have no other choice," said Hugo icily, "I will show you. But if the children are not there, we must leave immediately."

"Fair enough. Go ahead of us, Hugo. Blaise, you go with him," ordered Angus, with a firm hand on Inko's shoulder.

Rigid with anger, Hugo led them out into the groves and paths behind the palace. Blaise hurried alongside him. "I'm sorry," he said under his breath.

"You should choose your companions more wisely," answered Hugo.

"I didn't choose him," muttered Blaise. "I just want to find Sunni and Dean. But not like this."

Hugo said nothing but veered onto another path as the top of the ruined arch came into view in the distance. He glanced at Angus, who was pulling Inko along some way behind them, and called, "Hurry—the light is fading! Come along, this way!"

Marin stopped drawing and dropped the charcoal and sketchbook to the ground. He raced to the opening of the cavern and mumbled a few words that made the thicket part.

Peering past the jumble of thorns toward the ground below, he clapped his hands and commanded, "Stand up and walk here!"

Dean and Sunni looked at each other and gingerly stretched their feet out one at a time. The creepers loosened and extended like elastic. The pair stood up and trudged over to Marin, trailing long vines behind them.

Marin pointed in fury at the ground below. "More trespassers."

Below them, Hugo hastened along a path with Blaise at his side. A few paces behind them was a man in dark clothing, his hand on Inko's shoulder. They were heading for the ruined arch.

"It's that guy Blaise!" Dean said.

"Shhh!" hissed Sunni, hope erupting inside her. Blaise had ignored her instructions and followed them in after all! For the first time ever, she was glad to see him. And who was that man he had with him? He wouldn't have brought just anyone. It must be someone who could help them.

"Who?" demanded Marin.

"N-no one."

"You lied when you said you came alone," said Marin. "You know these trespassers."

Sunni and Dean were silent.

Marin continued, "Whoever they are, they are going to the arch with Fox-Farratt, as you did yesterday. I saw you with him."

So you were the watcher in the woods, Sunni thought.

Marin herded them back into the cavern and pointed Sunni toward her backpack on the ground. "Pack your satchel. Quickly!"

He swept up Mr. Bell's book and carefully stowed it in his leather bag with the sketch of Dean and a pouch of charcoal sticks.

Sunni knelt awkwardly on the ground and repacked her bag, her hands still bound by the vines. "Where are we going?"

"You will see." He dropped her sketchbook to the ground and she put it in her backpack, relieved.

With a dagger, Marin sliced the children free from the long vines. But then he hacked off several short pieces and draped them onto their wrists and around their ankles. The short vines curled themselves around and around into secure but loosely binding cuffs.

"Can you walk?" asked their captor.

Dean staggered a few paces and glared at Marin.

"And you?" Marin looked at Sunni's feet. She shuffled backward and forward. "That is good enough."

"Good enough for what?"

Marin murmured something. The brambly hillside began to come alive, its tendrils and creepers rearing like cobras and slithering into the cavern toward them. Dean hugged himself and squeezed his eyes shut in revulsion.

"You are coming with me to the arch," said Marin. "We shall see if your fellow trespassers will barter for you."

"Barter!" Sunni cried out as thick creepers wrapped around her middle and hoisted her off the ground.

"Bargain, trade. Your lives in exchange for full disclosure as to who sent you all here. And if they refuse," Marin said, patting his leather satchel full of prison portraits, "I will put you all in here with the others."

Chapter 13

The four figures gathered at the arch under a fiery crimson sunset.

Blaise shuddered at the carved two-faced head of Janus. "I can't see Sunni and Dean coming here alone unless they had a good reason. It's really creepy."

"Quite." Hugo surveyed the surrounding woods. "They are not here. We must leave."

"Why so jumpy, Fox-Farratt?" asked Angus. "There's nothing here. Or is there? Maybe something you don't want us to find?" He began pushing Inko toward the arch.

"Halt!" Hugo put up one hand. "That is unwise. This is no ordinary archway—"

"Very interesting. Does this arch lead somewhere you would rather we didn't go?" Angus held Inko tighter. "It wouldn't happen to lead to Corvo's lost paintings, would it?"

Blaise's jaw dropped.

"Ah, I see," Hugo said sharply, regarding Angus with hostility. "That, I cannot say."

Suddenly Inko made a hoarse noise and pointed away to the right at something red, caught on a bush halfway up the hillside. He was so agitated that Angus could barely restrain him.

"Dean's hat!" exclaimed Blaise. "How did it get up there?"

Hugo scrutinized the servant boy. "That is close to *his* cave. Has he returned? Does he have the children, Inko?"

Inko's lip quivered and Angus tightened his grasp. "Who's *he*?"

"His name is Marin."

"Go on."

"He is the eldest of il Corvo's apprentices. It is said that he and the other apprentices disappeared at the same time as il Corvo, along with all of his paintings." Hugo paused. "Sir, could you not release Inko?"

Angus relaxed his grip but did not let go. "So, this apprentice disappeared at the same time as the Raven?"

"Yes. Then a few years after fleeing Venice, Marin came into Arcadia. How he got into Blackhope Tower and then the painting, I do not know, but he was here when I arrived, a lurking menace in the shadows. He accused me of spying and bounty-hunting, forcing me to defend myself by any means I could muster. Eventually our feud settled into a standoff and he disappeared. I hoped he was gone for good, but it seems we are not to be so lucky." Hugo sighed. "He is clever at concealment. It was no mean feat to hide from Sir Innes, who would not have wanted him anywhere near Blackhope Tower."

"Why not?" asked Blaise.

"It was suspected that Marin was secretly working for a rich client called Soranzo, who sought possession of il Corvo's secrets."

"I read about Soranzo!" said Blaise. "Corvo did some paintings Soranzo wanted, but he wouldn't sell them to him."

"Exactly. So il Corvo shut up his workshop and vanished.

Soranzo promised a reward to anyone with information on his whereabouts. But il Corvo was never found." Hugo looked uneasily around him. "The trees here have ears. I'll say no more."

"Take us to this Marin's place," Angus said.

"I do not know how to reach it." Hugo folded his arms over his chest in defiance.

Angus looked down at Inko. "Why do I think that you do? Maybe it's because you squirm every time Marin is mentioned."

"Let the kid go, Angus!" Blaise protested. "He's terrified."

Angus ignored him and said to Inko, "You are going to show us the way. But first—"

He suddenly hurled himself at Hugo, hauling the servant boy with him. Angus grabbed Hugo with his free arm, shoving him toward the archway, and, with a mighty push, threw him under the arch. Hugo staggered and fell as he passed through. And then he was gone.

"What've you done?" Blaise shouted.

"Now we know what the danger is," panted Angus. "He did say it was a special kind of arch."

Blaise was incredulous. "I can't believe you did that!"

"I didn't like doing it. But we're in an extreme situation here, pal. It calls for decisive action."

"Like throwing people through arches to who knows where?" Blaise spat back.

"Listen, do you want to see your friends again? Do you want to go home? Well, making small talk with Hugo won't do it. Someone had to go through the arch so we could see what would happen. Did you want to be the one?"

"He could have helped us," insisted Blaise. "The guy's been in here for over a hundred and fifty years! Now he could be dead for all you care." He turned his back on Angus in disgust.

"He already told us everything he was going to. And it wasn't enough. He lost your friends when they were right under his nose."

"And he couldn't, or wouldn't, tell you where Corvo's lost paintings are, so he was expendable. That's the real reason, isn't it?"

Angus flashed him a pitying glance. "I'm going to pretend I didn't hear you say that. I don't have to justify myself to you or anyone else. Just be grateful I'm here to help you."

Blaise jutted his chin and said nothing, though there was plenty on his mind. Was Angus just pretending to be their rescuer? How much time did he have before Angus got rid of him, too?

"I want to know what this apprentice has to say." Angus turned the distressed Inko to face him. "Now, take us to Marin's place. Understand?"

Inko gazed miserably at the empty archway, as if hoping his master would reappear. Then he pointed farther down the valley and started to walk.

Blaise walked behind them, his eyes riveted on his companion's back. He didn't trust Angus as far as he could throw him. But for now he might still be his best hope of finding Sunni and Dean.

Angus, Blaise, and Inko strained to see Marin's cave in the waning light.

"It's up there?" Angus asked Inko. "How do we get through all the brambles?"

Inko shrugged.

"You know a way, Inko," Angus said. "I know you do." The servant boy shook his head vehemently. "Let's take a look then, shall we?"

Angus pulled Inko along the bank of brambles. Darkness was falling fast, but it didn't take long before they found a narrow trail almost overgrown with thornbushes.

Inko shrank at the sight of the path.

"Did you think I wouldn't find the way?" said Angus. "Just for that, you go first." He pushed the boy forward.

Blaise struggled to keep his temper. "It's not a good idea to do this when we can't see where we're going."

"What, do it in the daylight when Marin can see us coming? Use your head, Blaise," Angus said. "Move, Inko! Blaise, you go next."

Avoiding the thorns as best he could, Inko tiptoed a few paces along the path. Blaise pulled his fingerless gloves out of his pocket and put them on. Angus snorted at this, but Blaise ignored him and followed Inko.

Suddenly, the brambles came alive. Branches twisted and vines sprang up, waving in the air, seeking to trap the two boys climbing the path.

Inko gasped and struggled against the thorny arms that caught him. Blaise could just make out dark coils crisscrossing the servant's white shirt and red sash, pulling him deeper into the thicket. The path was closing up around Inko and Blaise knew he would be trapped, too, if he didn't do something.

A thick vine began winding itself around Blaise's ankle.

As he stamped on the creeping thing at his feet and thrust the encroaching branches away, he heard Inko make a hoarse, screamlike sound. But it was too late to help him. Blaise hacked at the vine with his heel until he felt it break.

Angus was shouting at him, but he couldn't hear him. Blaise broke into a run, crashing through the undergrowth back to the relative safety of the clearing, desperate to be free of the snakelike vines. He came to the clearing and ran around the arch, looking for the path back to the palace. But it was too dark, and he could not remember how Hugo had led them there.

Angus puffed into the clearing behind him, speaking gently as though Blaise were a skittish colt. "You're fine, pal. It didn't get you. You are absolutely fine."

"You made that kid go in there, and now he's probably dead!"

"Calm down. It's over and you're OK," Angus soothed.

"Shut up. Just shut up. Who are you, anyway?"

"I'm your friend." Angus held his hands up as he got closer. "Come on, relax."

"Stay away from me!"

Angus went to tackle Blaise, who lurched away, but not fast enough to stop Angus from grabbing the strap of his bag.

"Slow down," Angus grunted.

"Get off!" Blaise gritted his teeth and found his footing. Then Angus pulled his bag strap, and Blaise fell back again. They pulled each other around the arch in a clumsy tug-of-war.

Somewhere in the background, Blaise could hear voices shouting but he didn't dare to look. Angus was wearing him down, and he did not have much struggle left in him.

At the precise moment that Angus was about to overpower him, Blaise went limp. He ducked his head and shoulders through the strap of his bag and let it go as Angus gave a tremendous tug. The big man reeled, clutching the bag, and tripped—backward through the arch.

Sunni and Dean, surrounded by Marin and his dryads, hobbled as fast as they could into the clearing. They arrived just in time to see Angus evaporate before their eyes as his body crossed the stone threshold.

Marin's blue lantern cast a strange, almost underwater glow on the ruined archway and the figure of Blaise, sitting slumped against the stone, gulping huge mouthfuls of air, his chest heaving.

"Get up! Get away from there, Blaise! Don't go under the arch!" yelled Sunni.

"Sunni? Is that you?" Blaise looked toward the light, dazed but smiling, and tried to get up. But his hand strayed a few inches beyond the line of the arch and his body was suddenly jerked backward by an unseen force.

"No!" Sunni screamed.

Marin leaped forward, one hand outstretched to pull him free, but Blaise's arm and head had already gone.

Within seconds, the invisible force dragged him under until only his other hand was left, clinging to the arch.

Sunni shrieked Blaise's name, but he could no longer hear anything. All Sunni could do was watch, helplessly, as his hand was sucked away and nothing of Blaise remained.

Chapter 14

A fragrance of crushed leaves floated all around as the dryads circled Marin's two prisoners. Sunni looked at the spot where Blaise had clung to the arch, eerie in the blue light. She hadn't even been able to talk to him, to tell him how glad she was he'd come looking for them. Her shoulders drooped. Dean huddled close to her, and she was grateful for his warmth.

"We are too late. Too slow!" Marin wrung his hands. "And you know those trespassers. Do not try to deny it!"

"We know the boy. That was Blaise," said Sunni. "But we don't know the man with him."

"That is a great pity. He is somehow familiar," Marin muttered but then stopped abruptly, as if he had said too much.

"What's happened to them?" Sunni asked, pulling Dean closer. "Are they—are they still alive?"

"For now, yes, but later, who can say?"

Sunni bowed her head.

"This upsets you," Marin said.

"Yes, it upsets me. They might die!" *And it's my fault for getting Blaise caught up in this,* Sunni thought miserably.

"They would not be the first. Nor the last."

"Meaning us, right? And you wouldn't care about us dying, either," she said.

"The monsters took them, didn't they?" asked Dean, his lip trembling.

"What do you know of monsters, boy?"

"Hugo said—"

"Ah, yes, your friend Fox-Farratt." Marin hung the lantern on a branch and drew back the deep violet cloak he had put on in the cavern, to reveal the dagger at his belt. "Listen well. Do you still refuse to tell me the name of the dog you spy for?"

"We. Are. Not. Spies." Sunni began quivering with outrage.

Marin let his cloak fall back. "Then I will learn it from your two cohorts while they are still alive. And you will come with me."

"Through the arch?" Dean could hardly say it.

"Yes. You obey me and you stay alive. Disobey me and you die or become lost forever." He touched the leather satchel slung across his chest. "If I see trickery from either of you, I will finish the first portrait. And you will be next, girl."

Sunni wanted to shake him by the shoulders and shout in his face that he was making a huge mistake. But a voice inside said, *You're alone. They've all gone—Blaise, Hugo, and the stranger. Your only chance is to find them, if they're still alive. And you can only do that if you're with Marin.*

She nodded once at their captor. "All right. Whatever you say."

Marin pointed at the bonds around their wrists and

ankles. "Just as those shackles loosen and stretch, they also tighten if you try to run away." The vines contracted slightly as he spoke, as if to make his point.

"We get it," said Sunni.

He swept his arm toward the sky, and the dryads shuffled away, melting into the black woods.

"We go through together, as one, and stay together on the other side." Marin linked arms with them, marching them toward the arch. Dean's legs almost crumpled beneath him, but Marin hauled him up and dragged him along.

As they disappeared under the arch, a great breeze swirled, stirring the leaves into rustling whirlwinds.

Blaise had been yanked from darkness into light. He lay flat on his back, staring up into a blue canopy of sky. The air was perfectly still. What new world had the arch led to?

The last thing he remembered was Sunni, right there with Dean. He had to get back. Maybe she was still there, waiting for him.

Head spinning slightly, he sat up. He was on what looked like a long, narrow lawn surrounded by tall hedges. And he was not alone.

"Didn't want to leave you behind in that state. You're lucky I managed to pull you through." Angus sat cross-legged nearby, with Blaise's bag on the ground next to him. "Have you calmed down? I thought I was going to have to slap some sense into you back there."

Blaise was so astonished, he could barely speak.

"They . . . they were there, in the clearing, Sunni—and Dean, I think. They'd found us. And now . . . now they've gone. What did you do?"

Angus grinned. "No hard feelings, eh? I wasn't trying to hurt you."

Tell that to Mr. Fox-Farratt and Inko, Blaise wanted to yell. But he had to be cautious. A few minutes before, Angus had been wrestling him and now he was all smiles, acting like he had just been horsing around. The guy switched moods like a light going on and off.

Blaise tried to look casual as he glanced over his shoulder. "Where's the arch?"

There was only a hedge behind him with no sign of the stone ruin.

"There's no arch here. We've passed into another underpainting. Corvo must have painted this place first and then painted the arch and woods on top of it. After I pulled you in, that bush behind you just grew across and the path was cut off."

"It just grew in front of your eyes?" Blaise didn't think his spirits could sink any lower. How could he get back to Sunni now?

"Another example of the Raven's skills."

Blaise stood up abruptly and took a running leap at the hedge, scrambling onto its flat top. For the few moments, he clung there. He could see an endless network of hedges—they were in a vast garden maze in the middle of nowhere. There was nothing else in the distance, no trees, no sign of the palace or the hillside. No sign of Fox-Farratt, either. Blaise dropped down.

"We're in a giant maze. There's nothing else but this."

"Drat," said Angus. "Those Renaissance people and their fashionable amusements. Guess a labyrinth in the floor wasn't enough for il Corvo—he had to put a maze somewhere, too."

This could be the way out of the painting, Blaise thought.

A large leaf fluttered to the ground by his foot. He picked it up and saw that it was etched with brown lines and squiggles.

"I found one of those too," said Angus, pulling a similar leaf from his pocket. "It didn't come from any of these bushes. And it looks like bugs have been at it."

Blaise studied the markings. No bug had made them—they were too organized and regular. He ran his finger over them and came to an upside-down U shape. *These lines look like the shape of a maze,* he thought, tracing his finger along them. *This could be the arch. And this may be the pathway I'm standing in.*

"What do you reckon it is?" asked Angus.

"Just another example of the Raven's skills," said Blaise sarcastically. He snatched up his bag and walked away briskly, turning right into a new path. The leaf told him that the path would soon turn left. It did, but as soon as Blaise rounded the corner, the hedge grew up behind him, cutting off his way back.

"Hey!" Angus shouted from the other side of the thick, leafy barrier. "It cut me off."

"Follow your own leaf," called Blaise. With any luck, he was through with Angus for good. He was going forward alone, whatever happened.

He heard the painter swearing as he stomped in another direction. "Don't think we won't meet again, my friend!" he yelled.

Blaise was almost lighthearted as he followed his leaf map. Then a distant rumbling began, as if a far-off thunderstorm were coming. He looked up at the cloudless sky, but there was no sign of rain. The noise grew more insistent, like a drumbeat, moving closer. He stepped in close to the hedge.

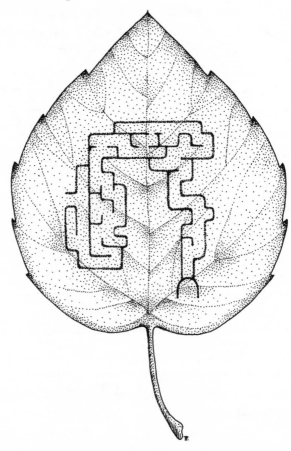

Suddenly a huge golden stag with a crown of antlers sailed over him, then vanished into the maze beyond. Behind it came eight hunters on horseback, their crossbows trained on the stag. The riders, clad in crimson and black, stopped to scan the maze from their lofty vantage point. Blaise shrank into the hedge, but one keen-eyed hunter spied him. He raised his crossbow, took careful aim, and fired.

Now that they were through the arch, Sunni had to squint hard against the bright daylight. There was no sign of Blaise or the other man in this odd garden of tall hedges.

Marin still gripped their arms and said, "Keep silent and do exactly as I say. Our lives depend upon it. We are in a maze made for Sir Innes Blackhope's amusement. There are many possible ways through it, but each one triggers a threat. The paths can close unexpectedly or open to reveal a predator."

"Predator?" Dean gulped.

"Yes, either human or beast."

A leaf tumbled from the sky and landed on the toe of Dean's sneaker. Marin snatched it up and, after studying the map on it, gave it to Dean. "It is yours. You came through the arch first."

"You're not getting one?" Dean asked.

"No, we came through as one. Do not let go of that leaf. It shows our route. We stay connected and go through together." Marin pulled them around the first turn. "If you become detached from us, the girl and I will not be able to follow the route and will have to make our own way."

Dean gripped the leaf in his shaking fist. He tripped over his own feet in his desperation to keep hold of Marin.

"Careful!" Sunni chided him.

"I'm trying!"

"Quiet," said Marin. "Listen."

In the distance a deep voice was shouting, "Get back or I'll banjax you in the snout!" and then, "Hah! That'll teach you!" The voice trailed away.

"Make haste." Marin pulled them even faster. "They are not far ahead."

But at the next turn, Dean came to a dead stop.

"Look!" he shrieked, his eyes focused on a place farther down the path. "It's coming to get us!"

"Dean, there's nothing there!"

"Yes, there is!"

Marin held their wrists tightly. "A predator — only the boy can see it. Quickly, we must get past it."

"No, I want to go back!" Dean shrank farther away. "Its heads, look at all of its heads!"

"There is no choice. Make him move," Marin said to Sunni. "Please."

He's telling the truth, Sunni thought, caught by something in the young man's eyes.

She whispered, "We have to trust him. Come on, Dean."

Marin and Sunni heaved Dean along, trying to shield him from the invisible predator. As they steered around a corner, he cowered, eyes wide in terror. Something rustled and rushed close by, knocking Dean's feet out from under him. Sunni and Marin struggled to keep hold of him.

Suddenly, Dean's body was yanked up by the foot into midair and something shredded his trouser leg. Deep punctures appeared in Dean's flesh, welling up with blood, as invisible teeth worked their way up his shin.

Marin unsheathed his dagger and slashed at the air around Dean's leg. The unseen predator brushed the hedge as it lurched away, and Dean fell over, pulling the others down with him.

Marin landed on top, his dagger still cutting the air above them in case the creature lurked nearby.

"Get off!" shouted Dean. "I can't breathe!"

Marin rolled off and knelt next to them. Blood was streaming down Dean's shin, and Sunni saw that he was swallowing hard, determined not to seem weak.

"Dean," she gasped. "I am so sorry I didn't believe you. Marin, you've got to let me help him."

Murmuring something, Marin sliced through the children's vine shackles and allowed Sunni to dab at Dean's wounds with a scrunched-up tissue she had found in her pocket.

"We have to keep moving." Marin started to help Dean up, but the boy stumbled and cried out in pain.

He pushed Sunni to Dean's other side so they could both support him while he limped along. "We must go," he said gruffly. "The predator will be back at any moment."

The hunter's bolt had narrowly missed skewering Blaise through the neck. The hunter himself had vanished over the hedge in a cloud of dust kicked up by his horse's hooves. In the near distance, Blaise could hear a man screaming in agony. *They got Angus,* he thought, panic rising in his chest. *But you're OK. Focus!*

He scurried to the next point on the map. There was supposed to be a path, but it was blocked by thick foliage.

The pounding of horses' hooves came nearer. Blaise huddled in front of the dense bush, the leaf shaking in his hand. When the hedge shifted sideways without warning, opening a new path ahead, it revealed the hunter coming straight at him, his crossbow trained on Blaise's chest.

He threw himself as far under the hedge as he could. As the horse flew past him, the hunter fired a bolt that just missed Blaise's ankle. Weak with terror and relief, he couldn't move.

Then, from nearby, he heard someone groaning.

"Who is it?" Blaise hissed into the hedge.

There was a gurgling and a sigh before a low voice, with a distinctive cut-glass accent, said, "I—I am here. By Jove, someone has come at last."

Taken aback, Blaise said, "Mr. Fox-Farratt? It's me, Blaise Doran."

"Ah, the boy with that r-ruffian. . . ." moaned Hugo. "N-no matter. Just help me, b-before it returns." There was a slight sob in Hugo's voice. "I have little s-strength left. The next time it comes, it will finish me. . . ."

"The hunter on the horse?" asked Blaise, scanning the path behind him and listening for hoofbeats.

"No!" Hugo's voice cracked. "B-body of a beast, wings of a-an eagle. Beak like pincers . . . tearing, tearing!" He suddenly screeched, and Blaise rolled backward from the hedge. There was the sound of thrashing on the other side, and Blaise craned his neck, looking for any sign of a winged beast above the hedge, but there was nothing. The sky was undisturbed and silent, but for Hugo's unbearable shrieks of pain.

Blaise dug his hands into the hedge to part it, but it was too dense. Instead he clambered to the top, expecting to see Hugo on the path below him. Astonished to find it empty, he was trying to decide whether to climb over when something caught his eye.

From farther down the path, the hunter was watching him, smiling devilishly as he lifted his crossbow and took aim. A bolt sped past Blaise's head, and he fell backward into the maze.

He heard Hugo moan again, but Blaise couldn't help him now. He ran blindly this way, then that, wherever the path was clear, until he came to a junction where there were three choices—which should he take? Blaise looked at the leaf and chose the middle one.

A horrible whinnying sound behind him made him run as he never had before. He nearly missed the next turn, which opened only as he reached it. *One more path. Left at the next junction,* thought Blaise. He ran straight for the hedge in front of him, ready to hurl himself to the left, but instead of finding the exit, he collided with the leafy barrier. Behind him, the horse was so close, he could almost feel its heat.

Crushed against the hedge, Blaise screamed, "Let me out!" He turned to see the hunter yet again lift his crossbow and fix it on his prey.

Blaise closed his eyes, waiting for the fatal shot, but suddenly the hedge shifted behind him and he tumbled backward through open space. The hunter lowered his crossbow and, with an imperious sneer, nodded his head once and disappeared over the hedge.

Blaise found himself rolling down a grassy incline. The blue sky was gone, covered by a thick mist. He came to a stop with his bag wedged uncomfortably beneath him and scrambled to his feet, looking around him in case the hunter sprang from the gloom.

He relaxed his curled fist and found the leaf map, crushed. As he smoothed it out with his finger, its jade color faded into gold and the soft surface dried up and crumbled away. All that was left was a burnished skeleton.

Marin hoisted Dean onto his back and grabbed Sunni's hand. His touch was warm and sent a current up her arm and straight into her chest, setting her heart racing.

Marin's dagger had just defended them against a second attack but not before Dean's shins were bloodied again.

"We are close," he panted, glancing at the leaf. "Just a little farther."

Ahead of them there was a gap in the hedge, on the other side of which swirled a pearly mist. Marin and Sunni summoned up all their stamina to reach it.

Dean suddenly whimpered, "It's there, waiting in the gap. We won't get past!"

"Pull out my dagger, girl," Marin croaked. "Hold it out straight in front of us as we run through."

Sunni reached under his cloak with her free hand and yanked the knife from its sheath. Marin pulled her close to his side and told Dean to hold on.

As they started through the gap, Dean let out an ear-splitting yell. Sunni gripped the knife, and it hit something in midair. She drove the weapon in, crying out as something invisible sliced its claws across her hand. After several moments of resistance, the adversary seemed to melt away.

When they staggered out of the maze, branches sprang up from the ground and filled in the gap.

Marin laid Dean on the ground and stumbled away to catch his breath. Sunni bent double, gagging at the thought of what she had just done. Then she put her arms around her stepbrother and examined his new wounds.

"Do they hurt a lot?" She spat on the soiled tissue and pressed it to the worst one.

"Naw. I'm all right." His face was white. "Do yours hurt?"

"Not yet. They're not too bad. You've been amazing. Really brave, Deano."

"You're the brave one," Dean said shakily. "You got it, Sun, right in its stomach. The guts spilled out and everything. Nice one."

Sunni almost gagged again. "Ugh! So glad I missed seeing that. What was it, anyway?"

"I don't know," he said, tossing the leaf map away. "It crawled like a giant crab with claws, but it could rear up and it had all these human heads growing out of its back. And it made this *sound*. . . ." He couldn't finish, and Sunni gave his arm a squeeze.

"It's over now." She nodded toward Marin. "It's a good thing he was here with his knife."

"Huh? We wouldn't even have been in the maze if it weren't for him! And don't forget he's got my portrait in his bag. One false move and he'll stick us both inside a sheet of paper."

"We're already stuck. And who knows where we are now?"

Marin watched the discarded leaf tumble to the ground and transform into a golden skeleton.

"Look there," he said. The mist that surrounded them had drifted apart, revealing a lone, dark-haired figure with a bag on his back, silhouetted in the distance.

"Blaise," breathed Sunni as the fog thickened again.

Blaise felt a surge of loneliness as he trudged down the hill. Sunni and Dean were still lost, Inko had been swallowed by the thorns, and something awful had happened to Hugo—the maze had either made him crazy or killed him.

Blaise shuddered. The mist around him formed strange shapes and added to his mood of despair. Then it grew still and thickened like porridge. The next thing Blaise knew, he had walked straight into a white wall. Gypsum and glue again. Another layer. What else had Corvo concealed beneath Arcadia? Blaise ran his hands over the wall. It was slightly rough, like sandpaper, with a strange but not unpleasant smell to it.

Stuck to the wall was a piece of parchment with drawings on it—it looked like a map. Blaise's fingers found a loose edge, like on a piece of wallpaper that hadn't been stuck down properly. Bit by bit, he pried it up.

A sound came from the direction of the maze. He tensed, ready to run, and saw Angus hurtling through the mist some distance away. He had nearly reached Blaise when he doubled over, heaving. Blaise hurriedly worked away at the map. When Angus finally straightened up, Blaise saw that three deep scratches had been raked down the older man's face from forehead to chin, and his overcoat was shredded, with one sleeve torn off. His fedora was gone, and his long hair was pasted to his face like strands of seaweed.

"You." Angus doubled over again.

Blaise gritted his teeth as he lifted more of the map off the wall—he wasn't leaving it behind for Angus.

The big man coughed and ran a hand over his bloody scratches.

"Did you see it?" he croaked, trying to draw something in the air with his finger. "Claws, tusks, fur—a bit like a wild boar and with a squeal that could turn you deaf. It seemed to be there at every turn!"

Blaise tugged harder on the map. More than half of it had come loose.

"What have you got there?" asked Angus, venturing forward.

With a final jerk, Blaise ripped the rest of the map free and took off.

He sprinted along the wall, praying for an opening. As he ran, he noticed a blue-green glow through the white. He changed direction, moving more slowly now, and ventured toward the color. A simple wooden walkway appeared under his feet.

The walkway became a sturdy pier, which Blaise followed until he stood poised at its edge. The world before him was a shining turquoise ocean with blue sky as far as he could see.

He pivoted around to look behind him. The other end of the pier faded into the white wall, and there stood Angus, a crooked smile on his bloody face.

Chapter 15

Blaise rolled up the map and shoved it into his bag. He looked down into the water, ready to jump, as Angus began limping along the pier.

Suddenly Blaise saw something gliding across the sea. Two triangular sails were moving swiftly toward him.

A galley ship drifted up to the pier, white sails shimmering and rows of oars protruding from its sides like a centipede's legs. The elevated poop deck at the rear was covered with a brightly decorated canopy, and a flag showing a panther fluttered overhead. The prow had a carved figurehead Blaise couldn't make out at first, but as it came closer, he saw it was a woman holding a lily in one hand and an apple in the other.

The main deck was bustling with sailors in loose shirts and breeches, bringing the craft safely alongside the pier. Muscular oarsmen were slumped with exhaustion on the benches that lined each side of the deck.

A sailor with an eye patch slung a rope around a post and gestured for Blaise to cross the gangplank that had been laid down for him.

As Angus's shouts grew closer behind him, Blaise jumped onto the ship. The air smelled of sweat and fish. He was greeted by several smiling sailors, ushered down the raised gangway between the oarsmen and up onto the poop deck, where the helmsman guided the rudder. A low rumble began as men grunted and pushed the oars out like the wings of a huge bird. Within seconds the vessel shifted away from the dock.

Heart still racing, Blaise watched Angus standing motionless at the end of the pier, his face twisted with rage.

Someone tugged at his sleeve, and he turned around, startled. The one-eyed sailor, whom Blaise immediately nicknamed "Patchy," bowed and looked expectantly at him. He seemed to be a first mate of sorts, dressed in neater breeches than the others and a tunic.

A boy peered down at Blaise from the crow's nest atop the mainmast. Everyone else on deck had stopped work to watch the newcomer.

Who were they? What did they all want, staring at him like that? The ship pitched and he clung to the side, his stomach lurching.

Some of the men had dark hair and some had light. The same went for their skin tones and clothes. But Blaise's stomach contracted again as he realized that their faces were all essentially the same.

They looked similar to the men in the frozen top layer of *The Mariner's Return to Arcadia*. But those men did not move, while these men climbed and rowed and stared at him without blinking.

A voice broke the standoff.

"Welcome, Captain. Where you want to go?" asked Patchy in a singsong voice, offering him a skin full of water. "You tell me. We take you where you wish."

"Captain? How could I be your captain? Don't you have one already?" Blaise guzzled water and poured some over his face.

"No. We been waiting for you, Captain. Now you're here, and this is your ship."

"But how did you know I was coming?"

"When Captain comes here to find his ship, we come to take him where he want to go."

Blaise noticed that many of the crew had gone back to their work. His stomach calmed a little. "But how do you know *I'm* the captain?"

"You were at shore," said the sailor. "So you're the captain."

"Is this the only ship here?"

Patchy laughed. "No, other ships are already here — other captains also. But *Venus* is your ship."

"Was Sir Innes Blackhope also a captain here?"

The sailor bowed. "Yes, yes, of many different ships, but not for long time now. Best captain, best fighter."

"That figures," said Blaise, and then he asked slyly, "What about Fausto Corvo? Was he here?"

This time Patchy's face was blank.

"OK, guess not." Blaise changed the subject. "Have you seen a boy and a girl about my age, maybe on another ship? She has brownish hair, dark pants, and her coat is green plaid. Her stepbrother is blond and has a dark jacket. They're my friends and they're lost."

Patchy screwed up his face as he pondered. "No, Captain."

"Well, I'm looking for them," said Blaise, knowing that they were probably very far behind him now. If he tried to go back, he would have to contend with Angus again, not to mention the maze. "If you see any girl or boy, tell me."

"I'll tell the crew." Patchy bowed and bellowed something across the deck in a language that could have been Italian. Heads nodded, and a few men grunted in acknowledgment.

"How do you know English?" Blaise finished the skin of water.

Patchy shrugged. "We all just know it, always."

"Corvo thought of everything, didn't he?" Blaise said.

"Corvo?" repeated the sailor.

"The man who made you and this ship and everything here," said Blaise, waiting to see how Patchy would take this.

"I don't understand, Captain."

"So you don't know how you got here?"

The sailor's eyes showed no spark of interest or curiosity. "Come now, Captain. I'll show you your cabin."

Blaise had to hunch over as Patchy led him below the poop deck to a small cabin containing a table, chair, and bunk. He folded himself down onto the narrow bunk and stretched out his legs.

A cabin boy scurried in, bringing dried cod and more water for Blaise. He ate with ferocity, ignoring the toughness of the salty fish, and drank the whole jug of water at once. It seemed a lifetime ago that he had sat in the comfort of the palace, being waited upon by the terrified Inko.

Patchy removed a yellowed nautical chart from a trunk and smoothed it out on the table, pulling a pair of dividers out of the drawer.

Mare Incantato was written in flowery lettering across the top, next to a painted compass rose, pointing north.

Below these the chart showed a sea full of islands, islets, and rocks.

"Where do you want to go, Captain?" Patchy asked again, sweeping his hand across the chart. "To find sea snakes or unicorn fish?"

Holding up the jug for more water, Blaise said, "If it's cool with you, I don't want to look for sea snakes right now. I really want to find my friends, but I don't know how."

He got up and scrutinized the chart with Patchy, hoping it would show him some way of getting back to the palace, or at least the way out of the painting, but it showed him nothing.

Blaise touched the ivory paper, and something tugged at his brain. He dived into his messenger bag, snatching out the map he had scraped off the white wall.

He flattened it on top of the chart and cursed himself. The map wasn't complete. In his haste he had left the top right-hand corner behind, still stuck to the wall.

The map showed islands and shoals, some with tropical vegetation and animals marked on them. The heads of fanged and spiked sea creatures popped out of the waters around the islands.

Blaise fingered the torn edge of the parchment. He had shorn off a piece of the northernmost island. Above the island were three drawings: a rectangle divided into four, with each quarter filled with smaller and smaller concentric squares; a woman holding a horn full of fruits and a wheel; and a woman with wings and a staff. Next to her was a fragment of another drawing that had been torn away.

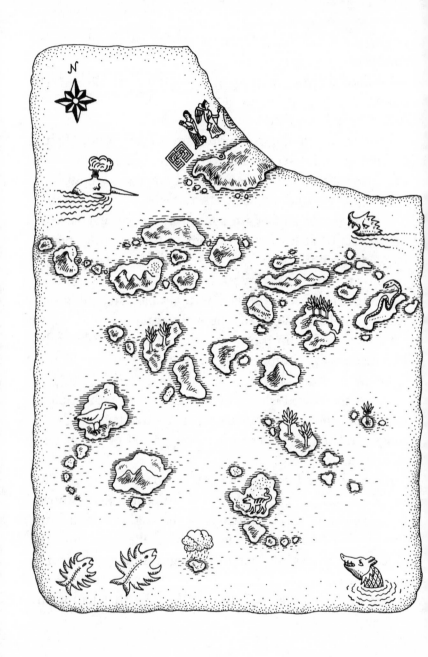

"Do you know what they are?" Blaise asked Patchy.

The sailor shrugged. But he pointed at the island and grinned. Lifting up the map, he jabbed his finger at the nautical chart below it.

"Same same," he announced.

Sure enough, the island was also on Patchy's chart. It, too, was the last island at the top, but there were no drawings next to it.

"Where are we right now?"

Patchy ran his hand down the chart and pointed to an empty expanse of sea.

"We're nowhere near that island," Blaise said, looking again at the tiny drawings on his map. He had no idea who the two women were, but he was pretty sure about the divided rectangle.

It was just like the labyrinth in the Mariner's Chamber.

"We go there, Captain?" The sailor measured the distance on his chart with the dividers.

Blaise furrowed his brow. Was it just a coincidence? Did he dare follow his hunch that the map had been left there for him, that his best way forward was to find the labyrinth—the way home?

"I guess so," he said. "It's somewhere to start, anyway."

"Aye, sir."

Blaise stashed the map back in his bag and followed Patchy out of his new quarters.

"Captain Doran," said Blaise to himself, and couldn't help but smile as he ducked his head through the low cabin doorway, emerging back on deck to survey the rows of straining oarsmen.

Angus's shouts became curses as Blaise's galley moved farther away.

"No one leaves me behind, least of all some idiotic boy!" he yelled. He stamped on the pier and dropped to his knees as it shifted suddenly beneath his feet, the wooden boards extending into an L shape.

When he got back on his feet, he saw a second galley ship coming across the water. Its wooden figurehead was Mercury, a young man with winged feet and a winged hat, holding a rod entwined with snakes.

Angus scrambled aboard as soon as it was tied up. A band of sailors greeted him as their captain, but he cut short their welcome.

"Captain—good," Angus said. "Is this my reward for fighting off the monster hog and making it through the maze? I get my own transport, too?"

"Yes, yes," said a gap-toothed sailor. "We take you where you want to go. We fight for you also!"

"Thank you, Raven, wherever you are," muttered Angus to himself. "Very useful."

He rushed to the stern of the ship and swung himself up onto the poop deck, from which he could see Blaise's ship heading out into open sea.

Two sailors followed. "You give us orders, Captain. You want to fight the giant octopus? We know where to find it. Or the giant eel?"

"Fight a giant eel?" Angus frowned. "I'm not interested

in sea monsters. I'm hunting a boy. He's taken a map that should have been mine."

The sailors nodded brightly at this.

"So here's my first order, lads," he bawled, pointing at the *Venus*. "Follow that ship!"

The crewmen scattered and took up their duties, shouting to the oarsmen. The ship turned and skimmed along the water's surface while Angus hung over the side, never letting the *Venus* out of his sight. The sailors watched their new captain with the torn clothes and scratched face as he laughed and muttered to himself.

But then Blaise's galley began to fade behind a ragged cloud of mist, and the *Mercury* slowed. Sailors called to each other in a rapid mix of tongues as they peered out to get a better view, while the ship's pilot studied his compass and compared it to a dog-eared chart.

Angus pounded the railing with his fist. "Faster! Get moving!"

He scanned the gray shroud surrounding them. Something dark had moved in the distance—he was sure it had. But when he looked back, it had gone.

"Change course," he commanded. "That way. They've gone that way!"

The helmsman glanced at the pilot, who returned a warning look.

"What's the problem?" demanded Angus, hands on hips.

"That way's no good, Captain," the pilot said, frowning. "Rocks."

Angus answered coldly, "You'll have to be careful, then, won't you?"

Sunni stumbled down the hill, her cries muffled by the thickening mist, calling for Blaise. He was nowhere to be seen. They reached the white wall, and Marin motioned for her to follow as he half carried Dean alongside it. When the whiteness gave way and opened to the sea, there was no sign of the pier Blaise and Angus had embarked from. Sunni collapsed onto her knees.

"Where did Blaise go? He must have come this way."

Marin sat Dean down by her side. He took a swig from his water skin, then passed it to them.

"A ship came for the boy, and he is gone. And he was followed," Marin said. "I saw the man for a moment only, running in the mist—the one you say you do not know."

"We're not liars. If we say we don't know him, we don't," Sunni said. "So, now what? Do we just sit here?"

"Patience," replied Marin. "Watch the sea."

"You know where we are?"

"Yes."

They sat in silence as the sunlight dazzled the water's surface. A patch of fog drifted far out to sea.

Then Marin pointed at a ripple in the water. A pier pushed up through the surface and came to a standstill, as if it had always been there.

Marin hoisted Dean up and walked him along it, with Sunni close behind. As they reached the end, a galley with a warrior carved into the prow moved alongside them. The figurehead's fearsome face and sword etched with dragons looked familiar.

"Mars again," said Dean as the ship pulled in.

Marin called out something to the sailors. Two of them hauled Dean over the gangplank and sat him up on the poop deck. One of them tried to clean his leg wounds with a wet rag, but he recoiled and said, "Get off!"

Sunni huddled next to him, watching Marin tell the sailor at the helm, "There are two ships out there somewhere, captained by a man and a boy. Find them."

The *Venus*, too, had been caught in the fog bank. When at last it drifted out, there was no sign of land in any direction, nor any birds. And there was no sign of Angus.

In his quarters, Blaise flicked his sketchbook open to a blank page and drew the hunter and his crossbow from memory, then Hugo and Angus. He spent more time on a sketch of Sunni standing on the labyrinth's center, her eyes closed. More drawings poured out of him, filling up page after page. In the white spaces, he wrote captions and made little diagrams.

When he finally stopped and leafed back through his work, a lump rose in his throat. If he didn't make it, at least someone might find his sketchbook and keep it. Maybe they would even find his dad and give it to him. That might help him understand what Blaise had seen and done before he died in this place.

Chapter 16

Angus drummed his hand against the railing of the *Mercury*, willing the oarsmen to catch up with Blaise's galley.

"Too slow!" He threw his ruined overcoat onto the deck, glaring down at the master of the oarsmen, and turned to the pilot. "Make them go faster."

"We must go slow in fog, Captain," the pilot answered. "Until it is safe."

"Well, when will that be?"

"I do not know." The pilot pointed at his chart. "Cannot see the rocks here, Captain."

Angus returned to the railing and swore at the mist. The echoing screeches of gulls drowned out the calls of the sailor in the crow's nest. The mist thickened and clung to everything, making the sailors look like phantoms as they darted around.

Waves grew from light swells to rolling juggernauts that crashed over the sides and sent the sailors skidding along the decks. Angus clung to the railing, drenched and spitting seawater.

A sailor tried to pull him away. "Come below, Captain, or you'll go overboard!"

"I give the orders," snarled Angus, "and I'm not going anywhere."

A towering wave drove over them and hit the ship with a thunderous slap. The sailor tumbled and was washed into the sea. Angus was spun across the deck and dashed against the opposite railing.

The *Mercury* righted itself long enough for the crew to get to their feet, then the stern suffered a massive blow. Horrendous screams came from above as the sailor in the crow's nest plummeted to the deck. The surge rammed the ship forward into rocks, tearing its underside apart with a sickening grinding sound.

The air was a cacophony of sailors' groans and splintering planks as the *Mercury*'s belly filled with water. The cloth canopy above the poop deck tumbled down, covering Angus, and the ship's lantern crashed on top of it in a shower of sparks. He battled to throw off the heavy fabric as waves buffeted the ship.

Angus glanced behind him and saw a red glow. Flames were eating up the canopy, igniting the deck's timbers. He clawed his way along on hands and knees until he found the edge of the cloth and flung it off.

He dived overboard and swam as far away from the broken ship as he could. Fog still hid everything, but he heard a sound nearby that he took to be waves smacking on stone. He paddled in its direction, his hands stretched before him, feeling for the shore.

The fog bank opened, revealing a pile of rocks. Angus floated forward and grabbed hold of the first rock he could. He hauled himself up, slipping over seaweed and barnacles to get to longer, flatter rocks. When he was high enough above the surf, he lay down on his back and closed his eyes, panting.

Suddenly he felt warmth on his face and his eyes snapped open. Sunlight was pushing the mists aside. But what he saw above him made him roll over and scramble away from where he had lain.

"Zut alors!"

Mercury's wooden face stared down at him. The wrecked galley was wedged between boulders only meters away from him.

As the fog retreated, he saw flames engulfing the ship. The empty deck burned orange against the blue sky and sea, and soon all traces of mist vanished. Fire ran up the ship's rigging, popping and cracking and sending ashes flying on the breeze. There was no sign of the crew.

Angus whirled around and scanned the empty horizon. "Shouldn't a new ship be turning up for me about now, Raven? Or is it just one per customer?"

As if in answer, a rogue wave crashed over the *Mercury* and dragged it backward. The charred deck disappeared, followed by the flaming masts, until at last the prow was pulled down into the sea, the figurehead's winged hat the last to be swallowed up.

"All right, you win this round." Angus shook his fist at the sea. "But I'm not finished yet."

Dean spat an olive pit onto the cabin floor and took a large mouthful of water offered by the ship's boy.

"Those are too salty," he said, grimacing. "Don't you have anything else?"

The boy held out a basket of salted dried fish. "Oh, man, what is that? It stinks and looks like it's a hundred years old."

Marin did not look up from the chart he was studying at the table. "You are fortunate to have anything."

"I don't see you eating it."

"If you do not eat, you will die and save me the trouble of keeping you alive."

Dean glared at his captor's back.

Marin called the ship's boy over and said something to him. A few minutes later, he brought in a basket of hard biscuits.

Dean gnawed on one and banged it against the bunk he sat on. "It's like a dog biscuit."

Marin ignored him. Dean eyed the leather satchel at their captor's feet. He would give anything to snatch his portrait from the bag and tear it up. But Marin kept it with him at all times.

"How come you know where everything is on this boat, Marin?" Sunni licked olive juice from her fingers. "You knew all about the predator maze and Hugo, too."

"I have been in the maze many times and on countless ships in this ocean," he answered without looking up. "I have met each sailor ten times before and eaten this food over and over again."

"While you were spy hunting," said Sunni.

"Yes."

"So you just go round and round, chasing people who are probably completely innocent and even putting them inside drawings. What gives you the right to do that? What are you looking for, anyway?"

Marin slapped the chart with his palm. "My master is missing and with him some very important paintings. I must find him or at least protect the paintings from thieves. It is my duty."

"Your master?"

"Yes," said Marin. "Signor Fausto Corvo, artist of Venice."

"Since when?" Sunni stopped chewing.

"Since I was ten."

"So you're his servant," Dean said, grinding his biscuit against the hull.

"I am no servant. I am il Corvo's apprentice! He was teaching me to be a painter." Marin rose from the table. "He could not trust many people with the secrets of his work, but he trusted me."

"Then why don't you know where he is? Why didn't he tell you?"

"I do not have to answer your questions." Marin stalked out of the cabin.

"Yes, you do. My stepbrother and I were just trying to find our way home, and you kidnapped us," Sunni said, scrambling to catch up with him. "Our parents must be out of their minds worrying about us, and we're stuck here with you for no reason."

"Yeah!" said Dean, limping behind them.

"Maybe you don't mind being trapped here for four

hundred years, but I do!" Sunni followed Marin onto the deck. "I want to go back to my time and carry on living my life."

"I want to see my mom," said Dean. "I want to see my stepdad. I want to see my friends. . . ."

"Me too." Sunni threw her arms up. "There are so many things I want to do."

"What can a girl do that matters?" The apprentice gazed out into the fog that surrounded the galley.

"Where do I even start?"

"For one thing, Sunni's going to be an artist," Dean piped up.

"Dean!" Sunni hissed as she felt him tugging the zipper on her backpack.

"Show him your sketchbook."

"He's already seen it. I saw you looking at it back in the cave," she said to Marin. "Leave it, Dean."

"Give me the sketchbook." Marin held out his hand. "I want to see it again."

"I'll hold it while you look at it, if you don't mind." She tossed her head.

Marin shrugged and watched Sunni leaf through her drawings. He laid his finger on one page. "You drew that one without help?"

She nodded, and he raised one eyebrow. "It is not bad—for a girl."

Sunni flushed and felt like snapping the sketchbook shut.

"Sunni's the best artist in her class," Dean said. Sunni was not sure whether she wanted to hug him or kick him.

"A girl who draws," Marin said. "Is there anything females cannot do in your century?"

"No."

"It would be amusing to see how you would fare in my master's workshop, preparing canvas for his paintings, mixing his pigments from dawn to dusk," Marin said with a superior air.

"Is that what you did?"

"Yes." He tapped another sketch. "Who are these people?"

"Friends from school. My father and stepmother," she answered.

"You are this boy's stepsister."

"My father married his mother, yes. My mother died five years ago."

"My mother is also dead," said Marin. "The plague took her and the rest of my family."

"Plague . . ." murmured Sunni. "How old were you?"

"Nine." The soft look of sadness that passed across Marin's face took her by surprise.

"So was I, when my mom died," Sunni said in a low voice.

"Captain!" the sailor in the crow's nest called. "The mist breaks. Another ship comes!"

The *Mars* emerged into clear skies and was confronted by another galley sailing in the opposite direction. Its carved figurehead was a melancholy lady holding a crescent moon, with an owl on her shoulder. *Luna*—the Moon.

As the ship passed, they caught a glimpse of a figure on its deck staring at them. It was a girl in a billowing golden dress shaped like an upside-down wine goblet. A moment later, she had gone, swallowed up in the thickening mist behind them.

A lone raven flew over the *Mare Incantato*, riding in and out of the fog and watching the sea below with its beady eyes.

One galley made its way north through the empty sea. Belowdecks a boy lay asleep, curled up in a too-small wooden bunk, hugging his bag to his chest. In Blaise's dreams, he and Sunni were in Mr. Bell's class, laughing and painting a mural together on the wall.

As the raven dipped lower, another galley cut through the mist, emerging like a butterfly from a chrysalis and following Blaise's ship. On the forecastle stood two boys and a girl, the wind in their hair. Sunni picked at a loose thread in her coat, staring at the speck on the horizon that was the *Venus*, carrying Blaise to an unknown destination.

Dean was nearby, daydreaming about sausages and mashed potatoes.

Marin stood with his back to them both, fuming at the sight of the girl on the other ship.

Chapter 17

The *Luna* emerged from the mist and headed straight toward a rocky shoal. The pilot bellowed commands and the galley heaved itself sharply to starboard as Lady Ishbel Blackhope appeared, squeezing her golden skirt up the narrow steps to the poop deck. The pilot, helmsman, and various other crewmen hung their heads in shame.

"Went off course, mistress," said the pilot, holding up a chart for her to see and dragging his finger to the place where they had found themselves.

"Who is responsible?" Lady Ishbel asked, her mouth set in a line. All eyes swiveled toward the wretched helmsman. "No food or water for you until eight bells tomorrow. You, take over."

Another sailor took charge of the tiller, and Ishbel turned back to the pilot. "Change course to catch Marin's ship."

"We lost it in the mists, mistress." The pilot looked worried.

Lady Ishbel flung her braid over her shoulder. "Find it again. Make the men row as hard as they can. Seven knots—nine, even!"

The lookout's voice came from the crow's nest. "Man on rocks!"

Lady Ishbel and the crew peered over the side.

A bedraggled man in a dirty vest and dark trousers was swinging a blue shirt over his head and shouting at them.

"Yet another one," she muttered, gesturing toward a small rowboat stored on the main deck. "Get in the skiff and bring him to me. And then we set off at once."

Lady Ishbel made her way down into her quarters, arranged herself on her chair, and waited to interrogate the stranger.

When Angus ducked into the cabin, now wearing his torn shirt and his most charming smile, he saw a young woman of about sixteen, with sharp green eyes and a frowning mouth. She saw a man with telltale claw marks across his face.

"Angus Bellini at your service," he said, bowing.

"You have been through my maze."

"Your maze, my lady?"

"Yes," she said archly. "Which of my beasts did this to you? The bear, by the looks of things, or perhaps the griffin?"

"Neither. It was a kind of boar."

The girl took this in. "And in order to cross this sea, you must have been on one of *my* ships. Where is it?"

"The fog drove us onto the rocks, my lady, and the ship was sunk. I am the only survivor."

Lady Ishbel waved his words away. "The sailors do not die. They merely disappear, only to reappear for the next voyage on a fresh ship. They belong to the painting."

"Most ingenious," said Angus. "A continuous supply of sailors and ships. Still, I am fortunate to be alive."

"That is true." Lady Ishbel nodded curtly. "I could have left you there, you know. You are a trespasser, and, as such,

I am not obliged to rescue you. There are too many of your kind here already."

"Why, my lady, that would have been tragic. I am merely seeking three children who came here by mistake. Two boys and a girl. I wish to take them home to our world."

"A girl?" Lady Ishbel sat up. "In boy's clothing?"

"That sounds like Sunni," said Angus, though he had caught only a fleeting look at her by the arch. "So you've seen them?"

"I have seen the girl, but she was with one boy, not two. His hair was fair."

"Ah, how marvelous; Sunni and Dean are safe. But I fear for the second boy—Blaise. He, too, is on one of your ships. He has something with him that may be very important. I must find him."

"What is so important?"

"He took something: a map that he peeled away from the white wall before he boarded his ship."

"That belongs to me!" Lady Ishbel burst out. "Everything here belongs to me. He has stolen it."

Angus cocked one eyebrow. "Well, now, I would have thought everything here belonged to Sir Innes Blackhope. The map must be his, too."

"But I am Lady Ishbel Blackhope. Sir Innes was my uncle. Fausto Corvo made this underworld, Arcadia, for him to enjoy adventure and amusements. When my uncle died, he left Arcadia to me, and I have been here since my sixteenth birthday. I repeat, everything here is *mine*."

"I see," said Angus. "Then it must be very frustrating for you to have so many trespassers here."

Lady Ishbel clasped her hands so tightly together that the knuckles grew white.

"So many thieves," she said, fuming, "who think they can steal what they like from Arcadia."

"What could anyone *possibly* want to steal?" Angus asked.

"Paintings. Magical ones that are apparently hidden here. They were created by Fausto Corvo as well. When I arrived, I found outsiders already here, behaving as if Arcadia was theirs. It is *not!*"

"Any lost paintings should be yours if they are found," said Angus.

"Yes," she agreed, showing a slight smile at this idea.

"They would be yours to do with as you like, and to give to whomever you wish."

"Yes," repeated Lady Ishbel.

"If only they could be found." Angus sighed dramatically.

"Indeed. Then the treasure hunters would have no reason to stay. I could evict them and live in peace."

"Why can't you evict them now?"

Lady Ishbel looked thunderous. "They do not believe I am the heiress of Arcadia." She fingered her pendant, an intricately worked golden ship studded with rubies and pearls. She flipped it over to reveal *Speranza Nera* engraved on the back, along with her name and the word *chiaroscuro*.

"This was bequeathed to me by Sir Innes and is proof of my right to Arcadia. But these rogues will not accept a mere girl as their mistress."

"I believe you, my lady," purred Angus. "And I'm sure they will listen to you if you secure the paintings. You will keep them well protected, I have no doubt."

Lady Ishbel frowned, looking flustered at this idea.

"What a lovely thought," he continued smoothly, "that after four hundred years you might find the lost paintings at last. If only—"

"Four hundred years?" Lady Ishbel was aghast. "It has been so long?"

"Yes, I have come from the twenty-first century. But just think—finding the paintings will be all the sweeter for the wait."

"I am no nearer to finding them than I was in 1600."

Angus seized his chance. "The map this boy has stolen—perhaps it reveals the secret of the paintings' location. But of course, he would never give it to you."

"I would compel him."

"He would destroy it before handing it over. One would have to approach him with great care," said Angus. "Now, my lady, where did you see the girl and fair-haired boy?"

A dark cloud passed over Lady Ishbel's face. "On a ship called the *Mars*. With Marin."

"Marin? A most dangerous character, I am told."

"You know him?" Lady Ishbel shot back.

"Only by reputation."

"We are in pursuit of his ship. I—I have unfinished business with him."

"This is most interesting, Lady Ishbel," said Angus.

She stared down at her hands, deep in thought.

"I wonder whether I may be of service," he ventured.

"How?"

"I want Sunni and Dean returned safely from Marin. They are friends of Blaise, the boy with the stolen map.

Perhaps they can help me retrieve it for you. In return for your assistance with the children, I can also help you finish your business with Marin."

Lady Ishbel's eyes narrowed. "I ask again, how?"

"In any way you require," he answered with a knowing smile.

"All you want in return is these three children? And then you will leave Arcadia?"

"That's all," Angus lied, holding his palms outspread before him. "The return of the children will be reward enough."

Blaise woke to the peal of a bell. He shifted stiffly on the wooden bunk, forgetting where he was at first, and groaned when he realized he was on the ship, far from home and his lost friends.

He climbed on deck and found Patchy.

"Captain, look." The sailor pointed at an island on the horizon, covered in lush vegetation and lit golden by the late afternoon sun. Just poking above the tree line on its southern shore were two masts and the tip of a furled sail.

"A ship's on the other side of this island." Patchy shook his head.

"Whose?" asked Blaise, suddenly alert.

Patchy pointed at the crow's nest. "The boy says it is Bashir—a pirate from Barbary Coast."

"Let's get out of here before they see us. Can we sail any faster?"

"Yes, Captain." Patchy gestured toward the back of the *Venus*. "Good idea, because another ship is following us."

Blaise cursed under his breath.

"Let's get out of here now. If that other ship is the one I think it is, the captain is a bad man and he's hunting for me," he said vehemently, and touched his messenger bag with the map inside.

Patchy saluted and left Blaise to watch the fleck on the horizon behind them, unaware that the ship in pursuit contained not Angus, but Sunni and Dean.

Chapter 18

Dean swung his jacket back and forth against the cabin wall, muttering. Sunni tried to ignore him as she doodled halfheartedly in her sketchbook.

Dean's jacket whacked her shoulder as she sketched.

"What are you doing, Dean?" she snapped.

Dean threw his jacket down on the chart table and burst out, "We're never going to get out of here."

"Don't say that!"

"Why not? It's true. All Marin has to do is finish drawing me, and I'm history. He can't wait to get rid of me."

"Just listen to yourself! Mr. Doom and Gloom. Marin's had plenty of chances to draw you, and he hasn't."

"Yeah, not *yet*," said Dean sourly.

"He could have let you die in the maze, and he didn't. He could have left us behind on the pier, too."

"It's only because he thinks he can trade us for information."

"We're together and we're OK, aren't we?"

Dean gave a weak shrug.

"We're not going to let Marin get rid of either of us, right? We'll stick together." Sunni gripped his wrist and made him look her in the eyes until he nodded.

"And even if he did put you inside a drawing," she said, trying to be cheerful, "I'd be next and we'd both be in there together!"

"Maybe, maybe not."

"Huh?"

"'My mummy died of plague, boo-hoo.'" Dean mimicked Marin's accent. "He might want you to kiss him better, Sun."

"What?" Sunni turned bright red. "You're asking for it."

She threw her sketchbook down and scrambled after Dean, who dangled his jacket like a matador. They ran around the cabin, knocking into the chart table and shrieking until she caught him.

"Stop it! Stop, please, Sun," Dean pleaded as she tickled him.

"Are you going to cheer up?"

"Yes!"

"Promise?"

"OK, I promise!"

"You'd better not say anything like that about Marin again," said Sunni, her face still hot. "Especially not in front of him."

Dean nodded, panting heavily.

"I can't stand it here, Sun. I want to go home," he said in a low voice.

"I know. But we have to keep going. There's no choice."

The floorboards in the passageway creaked, and Marin stepped in. "You are making a disturbance."

Sunni turned red all over again at the sight of him. *Had he heard what Dean had said?*

"We're just having fun," said Dean. "Laughing—do you know what that is?"

"I laugh when I find something amusing. How are your wounds?"

"They're scabbing over."

"Good." Marin looked around the cabin. "You will sleep in the bunk, and she will sleep on the floor. I will sleep on deck, with the other sailors."

The cabin boy entered, carrying an armful of hay and rough cloth, which he arranged in a corner. Another sailor brought more dried fish and water.

"Is this it?" Dean groaned.

"For now, yes. We will get fresh provisions as soon as we come to a suitable island." Marin turned to leave and said over his shoulder, "You must both remain in these quarters overnight, do you understand?"

Sunni and Dean nodded wearily.

Dean shook Sunni awake, his face close to hers. "Get up, Sun!"

"What?" She brushed straw from her face and hair as she got to her feet.

"Something's happening!"

Footsteps pounded up and down the steps to the poop deck above. The sounds of scraping and stamping mixed with shouts and oarsmen's grunts. A cry came from the crow's nest and sparked a hum of frantic voices all over the *Mars*.

Sunni and Dean went to the cabin door and peered out at the deck and the night sky.

"Everybody's running around," Dean hissed. "Come on!"

Sunni grabbed her bag, and they tiptoed out of the cabin. One or two sailors pushed past, paying them no attention. Others darted about or talked in clusters under lanterns dotted around the ship. Marin stood with the pilot on the forecastle, their eyes riveted on something to the port side.

Marin raised his hand to quiet the crewmen and then rattled away in Italian as he pointed at something in the sea.

"What is it?" whispered Dean, craning his neck.

"Something's out there, but I can't see. Come on." Sunni pulled him past the oarsmen's benches to a cooking area with a firebox stove and provisions stored in barrels and baskets, but they still could not see what Marin was pointing at.

"I'm going to climb up on that barrel. You get on the one next to it," said Sunni.

They hoisted themselves up and hunched close to the ship's rigging for support.

"That's what they're looking at." She gestured at the black outline of a ship in the distance. "It's a boat, but it looks abandoned."

"We're getting closer," said Dean. "He's taking us up to it."

Marin hung over the edge of the hull, staring at the silent hulk, as the oarsmen slowed their pace to maneuver the *Mars* nearer.

Suddenly a light flickered on the dark ship. Then another and another, till a web of lanterns lit up the other boat, revealing sailors brandishing swords, crossbows, and pikes. A bearded man in long robes and a turban stood on the forecastle, laughing as his galley's oars shot out from the side and propelled it toward the *Mars*.

"Bashir!" bellowed the lookout, and Marin's crew roared as one.

Marin, face taut with fury, shouted orders, and the master of the oarsmen stamped a rapid beat. With an awesome collective gasp, the men moved their ship away from Bashir's galley.

"Bashir—isn't that the pirate Hugo told us about?" Sunni shrank against the rigging.

"Yeah." There was a quaver in her stepbrother's voice.

"Maybe we should get back to the cabin." Sunni squinted at the far-off doorway, clogged with sailors running backward and forward, picking up cutlasses and daggers. "Only I don't think we can right now."

"We'll be cut to ribbons here!"

"Only if Bashir catches up," said Sunni. "We've got a head start."

The *Mars* powered away, with the pirate ship in its wake. A few sailors hung in the rigging, knives clenched in their teeth, while others lined the deck, taunting Bashir's men.

The pirates had caught up to within half a length when a bolt from one of their crossbows whizzed across the water and caught a sailor in the arm. He fell and was swiftly dragged away, his dagger clattering to the floor.

The oarsmen's master swore and banged a faster beat for his men. The *Mars* managed to pull a length ahead before the pursuing ship moved in directly behind it.

Dean held tight to the rigging and peered back to see where the pirate ship was. He couldn't see much, so he inched himself beyond the ropes.

Sunni heard an odd zinging noise and then a strangled cry, followed by a splash. When she turned to look, Dean had gone and a bolt was impaled in the hull.

Sunni strained to find Dean in the blackness of the water. His wet head was barely visible as he thrashed behind the *Mars*.

"Dean!" she screamed.

A sailor pushed his way over and shone a lantern over the side.

"Boy overboard!" he shouted.

Sunni pushed her way to the poop deck, pausing only to scoop up the injured sailor's dagger from the floor and shove it in her backpack. Before anyone could stop her, she hoisted herself up one of the canopy's poles and dived into the water behind the *Mars*.

She bobbed up to the surface and rubbed her eyes free of the salty water. The pirate ship was bearing down on the *Mars*, just meters away from her.

But where was Dean? She shrieked his name, and a thin cry came from the darkness.

Suddenly a large object was flung off the port side of the *Mars*. It landed with a deep splash and righted itself. In the light from the lanterns she could see it was the skiff.

Marin's ship shunted forward and slid away, with the pirate galley just behind. Within a few moments, they were just dark shapes dotted with constellations of twinkling lights.

"Dean!" Sunni called out.

"I'm here," came his faint voice. "Over here."

"Tread water and keep talking."

She swam toward his voice until she bumped into him.

"Come on! Swim!" she sputtered. "We have to get to that rowboat."

He made a choked sound and hung on to her, kicking as hard as he could as she guided him along. The skiff drifted toward them, pushed by waves from the wake of the *Mars*.

With all the strength she had, Sunni grasped its side and yanked herself up. She tumbled in and hauled Dean behind her, before collapsing onto the floor.

"You OK?" Sunni tugged on Dean's arm. "Did you get hit?"

"No, it j-just missed. But when I dodged it, I lost my balance."

"At least you're OK and we're still together." She patted the timber floor. "They threw this overboard for us."

"For us?"

"It must have been. They couldn't get us themselves with Bashir on their backs."

"Marin knew?"

"He must have known," said Sunni.

"And he let us have a boat?"

"Uh-huh."

They lay there, shivering and dripping. By the time they sat up and looked around, the lights that illuminated the two galleys were just pinpricks on the horizon. The darkness around them was so dense they could not even see each other, so they curled up together and were eventually rocked to sleep by the sea.

When the horizon grew light in the east and awakened them, Sunni rubbed her salty face and smiled at her stepbrother.

She fiddled with an oar. "I suppose we'd better start rowing."

"Uh, Sun?" Dean's eyes were riveted on something behind her. "We'd better row fast."

Sunni turned around to see. A ship was approaching and making straight for them.

"Is that the pirate?" Dean said with a gulp.

"Maybe. It's not Marin, that's for sure. His ship had a dragon on its flag," said Sunni, hurriedly pulling out another oar. "Wait, it's the ship that passed us yesterday in the fog. That girl is on the deck again. And the man from the arch is with her!"

With her mouth set firmly, she positioned the oars and tried to row. At first the boat went around in circles and she almost lost her grip, but slowly she managed to move it forward. The palms of her hands grew red and sore as she struggled to go faster.

"They're almost on top of us, Sun!"

"You have a go if you're so much stronger!" She yanked on the oars, but she knew they had no chance against a sailing ship.

The galley with the moon flag glided across their path. Its oars were drawn up, and it drifted slowly to a stop.

Lady Ishbel stood regally on the poop deck, framed by

its blue canopy. Next to her was Angus, a broad smile on his face.

"Ahoy!" he called, hanging over the railing. "Sunni and Dean, just stay where you are and some sailors will come out and help you."

A short time later, the pair was hoisted up onto the deck, where Angus and Lady Ishbel waited.

"Welcome to the *Luna*," said Lady Ishbel sweetly. "I am Lady Ishbel Blackhope."

"A lady," Dean muttered, and made an awkward bow. Sunni half curtsied and their hostess gave her a cool look.

"Sunni, Dean." Angus shook each of their hands. "I'm Angus Bellini, your art teacher's cousin. He sent me after you to help you get home. Am I delighted to see you!"

A memory flitted through Sunni's head. She was back at the Janus arch, watching this man tussle with Blaise. Suspicion began tickling at her mind.

"How did Mr. Bell know——?" Sunni started.

Angus held up his hand. "That's not important right now. Let's get you dried off. There's some water and food in the cabin."

"Not dried fish," moaned Dean.

"Yesterday was a fish day. Today is a flesh day. You will have meat," Lady Ishbel said, looking at Sunni's disheveled clothes with distaste.

Dean clapped his hands and started to make his way below.

"Where is Blaise?" Sunni asked Angus. "We saw you with him before."

"Did you? Where was that?"

"Near the arch that took us into the maze." Sunni looked down at her wrists, which still had faint red marks from the vine handcuffs.

"Oh, yes. Blaise and I got separated after that. He's on a ship up ahead somewhere. That's where we're headed, to find him."

The painter grinned down at her. The scratches running down his face and his tangled hair gave him the look of a jungle warrior. But although his mouth was smiling, his eyes were not.

Sunni felt a chill as she looked around the cabin. It was just like the *Mars* and made her wonder what had befallen Marin.

Lady Ishbel watched Sunni eat and drink, her eyes darting occasionally toward Angus.

"We're lucky to be with Lady Ishbel," Angus announced. He had been explaining to the children what he had learned from Lady Ishbel about the layout of Corvo's creation. "Everyone else here is a threat. They've been going round and round chasing and ambushing each other for ages with no idea how fast time was flying in the outside world."

"That's what worries me," said Sunni, "that we'll get home and find out years have passed."

"No, I think we'll be fine, with Lady Ishbel's help." He smiled knowingly at Sir Innes's niece. "And Blaise's."

"Blaise? How's he going to help?"

Lady Ishbel said haughtily, "He has a map—*my* map—which he found before he boarded his ship. The boy must return it to me."

"Right," said Sunni. "So that's how Blaise is going to help *you*. But Angus says you'll help us, too."

Lady Ishbel's lip curled. "You are very bold."

Angus jumped in. "Sunni, Lady Ishbel was kind enough to rescue us. Now she's taking us to rendezvous with Blaise. She'll get her map, and we'll get Blaise. Then we can go home."

Sunni lowered her eyes to the floor. "Any clue how to *get* home?"

"Yeah!" Dean chimed in.

"It could very well be marked on the map," Angus said. "That's why we all need to cooperate."

"What if it's not?" Sunni looked sideways at Lady Ishbel, whose pretty face was sour.

"Then we keep searching together."

"You must know your way around Arcadia very well," Sunni said to Lady Ishbel.

"You've probably seen all the monsters and beasts, too," added Dean.

Lady Ishbel nodded.

"Why did your uncle want Arcadia to be so dangerous?" he asked.

"He loved adventure and vanquishing opponents. He came here to test himself whenever he wished. Arcadia was made in such a way that he could have a new adventure on a new ship every time he visited."

"But he didn't tell you how to get out," Sunni said.

"No. He believed I would grow up to be clever enough to find the way myself."

"But you haven't," Sunni guessed. The two girls eyed each other.

"I have not wanted to leave," said Lady Ishbel. "If I had gone back, my father would have married me to the elderly suitor he had chosen."

"How old was he?" Dean piped up.

"Thirty-eight," said Lady Ishbel in a horrified tone. Then she rose from her chair and stalked toward the cabin door. "The air down here is stale. I will see you up on deck."

Angus frowned at Sunni. "Don't you think you might be a little friendlier? She could just have left us all in the brine, but she didn't."

"All right. I'll go up and apologize."

She found Lady Ishbel on the poop deck. "I'm sorry if I seem rude to you. The truth is that I'm tired and grumpy and I want to go home."

"I accept your apology."

"And thank you for saving Dean and me."

Lady Ishbel gave a dismissive shrug. "I saw you on Marin's ship. Where was he going?"

"We were following Blaise, too. Marin thinks he's a spy. He isn't, though, and neither are we."

"So, Marin is attempting to capture Blaise," said Lady Ishbel. "Then he may obtain my map before I do."

"Maybe," said Sunni, "except that after we went

overboard, Marin was chased off by a pirate called Bashir."

"Ah! They have skirmished many times. Bashir will not keep Marin from his aims."

"He may have delayed him, though. Have you skirmished with Bashir, too?"

"Yes. One day I will take my rightful place as heiress of Arcadia and force him and all other outsiders to leave. Except those whom I invite to stay with me, of course."

"I would be fed up with them all by now if I were you," said Sunni. "Who would you allow to stay?"

"There is one perhaps. But it is not for you to know who that might be."

"So you survived that maze, eh?" Angus winked at Dean. "And escaped from Corvo's apprentice."

"Yeah. That guy thinks Sunni and I are spies," said Dean. "He wants to trap me in a drawing."

"What do you mean?"

"He can draw you and then you disappear inside the drawing." Dean was happy to tell the story now that he was far from the *Mars*. "He showed us drawings he'd done of two other guys he said were spies. They were still moving, trapped in the paper."

Lady Ishbel appeared at the door. "Marin was never meant to know such secrets. They are il Corvo's."

"How do you know that?" asked Dean.

"Zorzi, the youngest apprentice, told me himself. He

rescued me from this very sea a long time ago. Corvo sent him from Venice to hide from Soranzo and his spies. My uncle Innes looked after him in Arcadia. Then Marin crept in, hunting for their master." Lady Ishbel flushed. "Zorzi ran, keeping one step ahead of Marin and searching for il Corvo."

"So, even the youngest apprentice believed Corvo was here." Angus licked his lips. "I find it hard to believe that none of you has found him yet if he is."

"No one has, though not for want of trying. I have myself traipsed over hills and crept under bushes searching for signs. I know the others have done the same."

"What happened to Zorzi?"

"I do not know," answered Lady Ishbel. "I have not seen him for years."

Chapter 19

W e've gotten that far already? That's excellent." Blaise and Patchy were looking at the nautical chart. "But I'm not even sure I'm on the right track. And if it turns out that I am, Sunni and Dean won't know about it."

Patchy listened but said nothing.

Suddenly voices rose on deck. Blaise and Patchy hastened upstairs as two men were pulled on board. They jabbered away, using sweeping gestures as they told a long story.

"Men from Bashir's ship," Patchy explained to Blaise. "The ship's sunk, Bashir's gone." He added, "Bad man, Bashir."

"Phew, these guys were lucky to survive."

"What you want to do with them, Captain?"

"Well, let them get cleaned up and give them some food and water."

The sailors were escorted below, and Blaise smiled at Patchy. "I guess we can keep going now, huh?"

"No, Captain. Big problem. The ship that sunk Bashir is ahead. It came through the big reef and is waiting for us," Patchy announced mournfully. "Marin is captain."

"Corvo's apprentice. We were trying to find him. He might be the one that has my friends! That's good news, isn't it?"

Patchy could only shake his head.

At sunrise Sunni and Dean stood near the prow of the *Luna*, watching two distant ships grow larger and larger.

"This could be it, Sun. If Blaise has the right map, we might be home soon." Dean hopped up and down against the railing.

"I hope so." Sunni stepped back to make room for Angus, who was sauntering up, hands in pockets.

"Good morning," he said brightly. "I see two ships over yonder. Any idea whose?"

Sunni squinted. "One's got a panther on its flag, but I can't make out the other. It's too far away."

"A panther—that's our boy!" Angus yanked his hands out of his pockets, and something dropped to the floor.

"That's Blaise?" Dean punched the air.

Behind their backs Sunni picked up the scrap of paper. It was a torn-off corner with nine little figures of people and animals drawn above what looked like a group of islands. She studied the figures carefully but couldn't work out what they were.

Angus wheeled around suddenly.

"Did you drop this?" Sunni asked, holding the paper out.

"Yes." He smiled as he stuffed the scrap back into his pocket. "Thanks."

Sunni excused herself and went to find a quiet place to dry out the damp pages of her sketchbook.

A raven hovered above the three ships, which now formed a triangle in the sea. Farthest north sat Marin's ship, the *Mars*, blocking a narrow strait between two islands—the only safe route to the northernmost islands, where Blaise was heading.

Southwest of the *Mars* was the *Venus*, moving cautiously. Patchy had convinced Blaise to go carefully, though he was all for overtaking Marin's ship and demanding Sunni and Dean back.

Sailing after him was the *Luna*, carrying Sunni, Dean, Angus, and Lady Ishbel, who were all hoping that their galley would overtake Blaise's ship immediately—but for different reasons.

"Fetch Angus," said Lady Ishbel to Sunni. "He should be on deck with us."

Sunni found the painter in the cabin, lounging on the bunk.

"Lady Ishbel wants you on deck. We're getting closer to the other ships. The first one is Blaise's, and the second is Marin's. We recognized the dragon flag."

"Actually, I'm glad you're here, because I need to tell you something." Angus sat up.

Sunni waited, curious.

"I don't think Ishbel intends to help us at all once she has the map," said Angus. "So I'm going to take charge of it."

"Excuse me?"

"The new plan is for you to get the map and bring it back to me, secretly."

"Me? Why me?"

"Blaise knows and trusts you."

"You want *me* to board Blaise's ship and bring him and the map back?" asked Sunni skeptically.

"That's right. Though whether Blaise comes with you or not, I don't care," said Angus. "But you'll give me the map for safekeeping either way. And you'll tell Lady Ishbel that Blaise lost it."

"I still don't see why—"

"I suppose I will have to spell it out." Angus stood up and flexed his hands. "This is how it works: you get the map for me and nothing bad happens to Dean."

"What kind of rescuer are you? You'd hurt Dean if I don't get the map for you?" Sunni backed away, wondering where Dean was and how quickly she could find him.

"It would be *nicer* for everyone if you just did as I asked."

"But Lady Ishbel—" Sunni started, her skin crawling with nervous sweat. "I'll tell her you're going to take the map—"

"Not if you want to see Dean again, you won't. And anyway, why would she believe you?"

"There's no way you can keep that map for yourself if she orders the crew to take it off you." She took another step toward the doorway.

Angus darted forward and caught her wrist hard in his grip. "If you want to go home, just do it."

Sunni could hardly breathe. Angus's fingers dug deeper into her skin.

"What will it be, Sunni?"

She glared at the floor because she couldn't bear his hard eyes. "All right, I'll do it."

As the ship's boy rang eight bells, Sunni stood with Dean on the main deck of the *Luna*. She had tied her hair back into a tight ponytail, and her face was grave.

She watched Angus make his way toward them from the prow, where Lady Ishbel was surveying them.

"It'll be OK," Sunni whispered to Dean. "Just do what I tell you."

He looked up at her, full of questions, but she shook her head.

Angus stood before them, arms crossed. "Now, when I say so, both of you wave and smile for Blaise. I'll be right here, so no messing around."

As their ship grew closer to Blaise's, Angus crouched down so he could not be seen and gestured for them to start.

On the *Venus,* Patchy pointed the waving figures out to Blaise.

"A girl and boy on the ship, Captain."

Blaise cried, "Sunni and Dean! Finally."

On the *Luna,* Angus gave his next command. "Now make a sign that you want to come onto his ship." Nodding, Sunni touched her chest and then pointed at Blaise.

"They want to come over!" Blaise paced up and down. "Right, have your best guys row the boat over and get them."

The *Venus*'s skiff was lowered into the sea.

"They're coming over to fetch me," Sunni said tonelessly.

"Good," said Angus. "Remember, Dean, you stay here with us for now."

"Why can't I go?" Dean whined.

Sunni watched the approaching skiff, her heart in her mouth.

"Because you can't."

"But why not? I thought we were all going to be together."

"We will, but not just yet." Angus's voice was building into a growl.

The skiff slid up to the *Luna,* and its two oarsmen hailed the crew, waving for the children to be helped down.

"Actually, I think Dean *should* come with me." Sunni grabbed her stepbrother's hand and turned herself and Dean to face Angus. They shuffled tentatively toward the ladder and the waiting sailors.

"No, you don't." Angus called out to the crew, "Take hold of the boy."

As men moved toward them, Sunni pulled a blade from her waistband and held it out straight in front of her.

"You let us *both* go!" she shouted.

The sailors shrank back and looked at Lady Ishbel for orders.

Angus burst out laughing at Sunni. "I don't know what's more amusing, you brandishing a dagger or grown men backing down at the sight of it."

"This isn't meant to be funny." Sunni pushed Dean to the ladder. "Get in the boat, Dean."

Lady Ishbel huffed, "Stop her!"

"I have this under control, my lady—"

Ignoring Angus, Lady Ishbel screeched at her crewmen, "Stop the girl!"

Two men lunged at Sunni, and she lashed out with the dagger, slicing one across the arm and the other in the shoulder.

"Don't you come near me!" she shrieked. "Get away, or I'll do worse than that!"

Suddenly one of Blaise's burly oarsmen climbed up over the railing and jumped in front of her, sword in hand, ready to take on anyone who dared to stop Sunni.

"Get in boat now," he grunted. "I kill anyone who stands in our way!"

The dagger shaking in her fist, Sunni hauled herself over the side and almost fell down the ladder in her haste.

Swinging his sword as he descended, the oarsman dropped back into the skiff. He and his mate pushed Sunni and Dean into safe positions and then took up their oars, speeding them back to the *Venus*.

"Mistress, we can stop them with crossbows!" yelled the *Luna*'s first mate to Lady Ishbel. "Give us orders!"

But by the time the crew had seized their weapons, the skiff was out of range. They grumbled among themselves.

"I want my map, and that girl was to get it for me." Lady Ishbel was incensed.

Angus elbowed sailors out of his way as he strode across the deck to join her. "There are *other ways*, my lady, other ways to skin a cat."

Blaise pushed in front of his crewmen to help Sunni and Dean climb the ladder.

"Sunni! Dean! You made it. Man, am I relieved to see you!" He almost hugged Sunni, but his nerve failed and all he could manage was a squeeze of her arm. "But what was going on over there? It looked like a fight was about to kick off. Did your sailors mutiny or something?"

"Get us away from here" was all Sunni managed to say. "Away from them!"

She was still trying to keep her dagger hand from quaking. Twice she'd drawn blood now, and it made her feel sick. She wouldn't let go of Dean's hand.

Blaise called for Patchy, who hurried to his side.

"Go now, full speed," he ordered, his eyes trained on Lady Ishbel's ship. "Stay on the same course to the island. And keep us away from that other ship." He ushered Sunni and Dean along the deck. "Come on, let's go below. And you can tell me the whole story."

In his quarters, Blaise pulled the chair out for his friend and gestured for Dean to take the bunk. Before she sat down, Sunni took the bloody dagger from her belt and laid it on the table.

Blaise whistled. "Where did you get that? Man, it looks like you just used it, too."

"It got us off that ship. I found it during a battle with a pirate ship."

"Pretty gutsy." He sat on the edge of the table. "So what happened back there?"

"It's a long story. That wasn't our ship. We were kidnapped by this guy Marin—"

"If he thinks someone's a spy, he draws their picture and traps them inside it!" Dean broke in. "And he's got one of me half finished!"

"He thinks you're a spy? I heard about him—supposedly he was Corvo's apprentice. So he learned a few magic tricks, huh?" Blaise said. "Talk about capturing a likeness. But he can't finish it if you're not around, Dean."

"Yeah." Dean perked up slightly.

"So he kidnapped you?"

"Yes. And we got dragged through the arch and the maze. Then we got to the sea, and when a ship came, Marin took it over. Then pirates attacked, we went overboard and got rescued by Sir Innes's niece, Lady Ishbel." Sunni scowled. She downed water from a pottery jug and handed it to Dean. "That's her ship we just escaped from."

"Sir Innes's niece is here? That's something—"

"She's a stuck-up cow. She's out for herself, Blaise," Sunni interrupted. "And she's just *part* of our problem."

"What do you mean?"

"You found a map, right?"

Blaise looked surprised. "How do you know that?"

"From Angus Bellini. He's on that boat."

"No way, not again! I thought I'd lost him." He flushed with anger. "He said Mr. Bell sent him to rescue us, but I don't believe that. I've been trying to ditch him for ages. Oh, man, Sunni, he's big trouble."

"We worked that out quickly, too," she said grimly. "You're right: all this stuff about him rescuing us is garbage. He wanted me to steal your map and give it to him behind Lady Ishbel's back—or else he said he would hurt Dean."

"No surprises there. So you fought back!"

"Sunni saved me," Dean murmured from the bunk. "Again."

Blaise looked admiringly at Sunni. "Very cool." Then he moved the dagger aside and unrolled his map on the chart table. "Here's the map I found stuck to the white wall between the maze and the sea. I didn't get all of it, though. Angus was on my tail at the time."

Dean hobbled over to look. "He wants it pretty badly."

"Then he either knows something we don't or he's guessing it's important."

Sunni examined the top corner. "I think he has the missing piece." She found her sketchbook, warped from its previous soaking, and opened it to a page of nine small sketches. "Angus dropped a scrap of paper with drawings on it. I memorized them as best I could and drew these."

"You drew that from memory? Wow." Blaise lined the

map up with Sunni's sketch. "These are definitely connected. That line there finishes the outline of this island on the map, and those little drawings look like they go with the others."

"I haven't a clue what they mean."

"Well, see this rectangle? Doesn't it look like the labyrinth in the Mariner's Chamber?" He hoped Sunni and Dean saw what he did.

"Yeah, it does, actually."

"It could be the symbol for a labyrinth. It might be the way out. That's why I set a course for the island. We're not that far from it now." Blaise rolled up the map.

Sunni brightened. "We came in on a labyrinth, so maybe we have to go out on one."

"Yep, that's my guess."

"Angus and Ishbel will come after the map, though."

"They'll have to catch us first. No way is Angus getting this! I bet he thinks it'll show him where Corvo's lost paintings are. That's all he really wants, and he'll do anything to get them."

"You know about the lost paintings?" Sunni said. "Hugo told us about them."

"Hugo." Blaise lowered his head. "You haven't heard about him and Inko yet. . . ." His voice trailed off.

"What?" asked Sunni and Dean in alarm.

"Hugo probably died in the maze, and Inko got swallowed up by thornbushes near Marin's cave," Blaise said quietly.

"Because of Angus?" Sunni swallowed hard.

Blaise nodded. "He doesn't care who he hurts—or kills."

Dean's face was ashen. He crawled back into the bunk and curled up with his back to them. "It'll be our turn next. We've got no chance."

Blaise crouched down on the floor next to him. "It'll be OK, Dean. We've just got to keep going."

"That's what Sunni keeps saying."

"She's right. You want to know why?" Blaise rattled off a list of advantages they had over Angus and Marin and any other monsters they might come across. He thought Dean was listening until the boy let out a snore.

"Thought I had him mesmerized," said Blaise. "Maybe I can bore our enemies into submission."

"You got Dean to stop whining, at least."

"I'd better shut up, or I'll put you to sleep, too."

"You're good, but not that good." Sunni laughed. "Thanks for coming to get us. I'm glad you're here."

"Really?"

"Yeah."

Blaise beamed at her. "Glad to be of service and everything."

He waited for her to say something. She picked at some lint on her sweater.

"How long did you wait till you came into the painting?" she asked at last.

"Overnight. You wouldn't believe how hard it was to get in. I had to walk the labyrinth in front of two detectives. The only way I could get onto it was to tell them I'd show them how you disappeared—without telling them the password, of course. Plus, I'd already had to sneak into

Blackhope Tower past all the reporters and cameramen."

"Wow." She shook her head. "I suppose that was bound to happen, wasn't it? They've probably gone completely crazy now that you've disappeared, too. Did you hear anything about my family before you left?"

"Not much. They said on the news that your stepmom and dad were too upset to talk to reporters."

"Oh." Sunni hugged herself.

Blaise fished around in his bag and pulled out a bundle of lavender-striped wool.

"Your scarf." He held it out to Sunni. "I—I found it tied around a tree and kept it for you."

She smoothed it out across her lap and smiled at him.

When they climbed to the poop deck later, the children saw the *Mars* anchored in the narrow strait ahead, bearing no sign of damage from the skirmish with Bashir.

"What do we do now?" Blaise threw his hands in the air. "Marin's ship is blocking our way. And we've got Angus and Ishbel tailing us."

"Can't we get around him?" asked Sunni, shielding her eyes from the sun.

"He will attack," said Patchy. "*Mars* is in a good position."

"He wants to finish my picture. I know it," said Dean miserably. "You've got to keep us away from him, Blaise."

"Unless there's another route, we're going to get squeezed between him and Angus," Blaise said, studying the map.

He pointed out a more roundabout northwestern route through a cluster of islands. "Here," he said to Patchy. "What about this way?"

"Very dangerous, Captain."

"How?" Dean asked.

"Domain of crabs. Better not to disturb." Patchy wiped his forehead with the back of his hand.

"Well, what other way is there?"

"No other," admitted the sailor. "Only northeastern route, where Marin waits."

"Then I'll take my chance with the crabs. They don't have a ship, and Marin does." Blaise turned to Sunni and Dean. "Are you with me on this, guys?"

"More crabs." Dean glared at the map.

"Not much choice, is there? We'll just fight whatever comes," said Sunni.

"Change course, then," Blaise commanded. "Now!"

The vessel made a wide arc, heading west into an open waterway.

On the *Luna*, Lady Ishbel screamed at the pilot, "What is that boy doing?"

The pilot's eyes twinkled as he answered, "He goes crab way, mistress. Foolish."

With a stony expression, Marin watched the *Venus* maneuver away, then turned his gaze to the *Luna*. After having trailed Blaise so closely, Lady Ishbel's galley had come to a full stop rather than follow him westward.

Marin spied her on deck and swore as he recognized the stranger from the Janus arch at her side.

"I do not know what their schemes are," the apprentice said to the pilot. "That boy has picked up the other two children and is heading toward the crabs, while Ishbel lets a spy move freely on her ship."

On the *Luna*, Lady Ishbel fiddled with her pendant.

"Oh, let us do something, Master Bellini!" she said. "I cannot sit here any longer."

"Patience, my lady. Marin is deciding his next move. I don't think he will be able to resist following the children and playing spy hunter. Once his ship has moved from the mouth of the strait, you should signal for the oarsmen to take the *Luna* through it at full speed. Then we can bear west to intercept them."

At the same moment, Marin was pacing back and forth. "The idiotic boy attempts escape through crab waters, and Ishbel sits there idly."

"Maybe she waiting for you, Captain," said the pilot.

The apprentice snorted. "I had better not keep the lady guessing, then." He whirled around and pointed at the *Venus*, gliding into the distance. "Follow the boy!"

The *Mars* immediately began to change course, and with a low roar, the oarsmen heaved the galley in pursuit of Blaise's ship. Lady Ishbel gazed doe-eyed at Marin as her ship stormed northeastward past the *Mars* into the now empty strait.

Chapter 20

Dean's stomach flipped, and a queasy chill ran through him. *Someone's walked over your grave,* his grandmother would have said. He clutched the side of the boat and swallowed hard. Something was coming. He could feel it.

A plume of white water shot into the air, and the ocean around it churned as if someone were beating it with a whisk. A misty island loomed on the horizon, then disappeared into the clouds.

Dean could not speak. His heart was banging a thousand beats per minute, and his head felt like it was going to explode. *Get a grip,* he told himself, but his body would not listen.

"I haven't seen any of these crabs you've been freaking out about. And we're coming into open water now," Blaise said, clapping Patchy on the shoulder as he strode up. "Maybe for once we're on the right track."

"Hey, that might be the island on the map!" Sunni was gleeful as she pointed to the land on the horizon.

"Yup." He caught sight of Dean. "Are you OK, man?"

Dean's head hung down.

"Dean?" Sunni held his arm. "What is it?"

"I don't know, Sun. I've got a bad feeling."

Just then, a huge whalelike fish, ivory white, with a deadly skewering tusk jutting from its forehead, leaped out of the sea, making a wide arc in the air before disappearing below.

"Patchy!" Blaise yelled. "More speed! Get us away from that thing!"

There was no sign of the beast for a few moments, but then something white skimmed below the surface like a missile. The ivory monster broke through the water and flew up into midair, its red eye and tusk trained on the *Venus*. In its wake a battalion of dark shapes followed, beating and chopping the water.

The children could make out helmet-like discs of shiny armor with spindly legs underneath. One of the discs breached and flung up a long black spike toward the ship.

"Horseshoe crabs!" shouted Blaise. He had grown up with ordinary ones in New England, but these were gigantic. And they were coming at lightning speed.

Twitching spikes appeared at the port side of the hull, wrenching oars into the sea. Claws gripped the wood and began pulling off great chunks. More and more appeared on the starboard side, making the galley list sharply.

Sunni stood aghast. "They're coming aboard! We're going to have to swim for it, guys."

Sunni and Dean flung themselves over the side into the water, struggling away from the sea of frenzied crabs. Blaise hesitated, dashed across the deck to retrieve his bag and Sunni's sketchbook, then leaped after the others. The crew, too, jumped overboard and vanished into the waves.

The armored crabs crawled onto the ship's hull, their tail spikes moving like lances. Nearby, the tusked creature circled, watching with its crimson eye as the *Venus* was wrenched apart, just as a human would tear a boiled crab's leg to get at the succulent meat.

As the boat disintegrated, the crabs sank along with it, leaving only floating debris.

The children treaded water, trying to catch their breath in the rough sea. Dean's clothes felt like lead, slowing him as he tried to move. He had just convinced himself that he couldn't stay afloat a moment longer when he heard a strained shout.

"Over here!" Blaise spluttered. "There's something to h-hang on to."

Painstakingly Sunni and Dean paddled toward the debris and clung to chunks of the *Venus*, mouths parched and eyes stinging, hoping nothing predatory approached them from below. Before them loomed the monumental, stony island, its top wreathed in mist.

"Land," Sunni said hoarsely. "Swim to it."

"OK," Blaise said, panting.

"Dean?" Sunni turned to locate him.

Before he could open his mouth to answer, a strong current dragged Dean under. Everything around him faded to blue-gray as it quickly swept him sideways. He kicked furiously, but his body was sucked downward, around and around in a dizzying circle.

Marin strained to find Blaise's ship. It had been a constant speck ahead of them but had suddenly disappeared.

The apprentice pounded the hull in frustration.

"Captain!" came a sudden cry from the crow's nest. Marin looked up sharply to see the lookout pointing a quivering hand to the waters off the starboard side. The galley was being drawn toward a gigantic whirlpool. Marin and the crew gazed in horror at the center of the churning maelstrom. The *Mars* was on course to be carried straight in.

As the apprentice bellowed instructions, the helmsman struggled to steer the vessel away. Men chopped at the water with oars, trying to push them out of the current, but to no avail. The ship reared up and was pitched forward into the swirling vortex, the mast and timbers splitting with a fearsome crack.

Marin screamed as he was catapulted into the heart of the dark water below.

"Dean!" cried Sunni when she realized he had disappeared. "Where are you? Blaise, he's g-gone!"

Blaise fought to swim nearer, but he was towed into a cluster of small, spiraling whirlpools in the water. "I can't—something's sucking me under!"

The force of the current caught Sunni, too, and pulled her after him. She saw Blaise's dark head gliding in circles as if he were on a merry-go-round, moving into the center. Then he disappeared.

Sunni was yanked after him, headfirst, nearly deafened by the roar of the water churning around her. As she fell, she tried to straighten her body into a dive position, but the force of the water tumbled her over and over. Eventually, she found herself gliding upward into a remarkably still, electric-blue pool. She floated there, dazed, and stared up at an arched cave ceiling as lofty and magnificent as a cathedral, shimmering with reflected light. Carved out of the wall of the grotto were six giant stone goddesses, holding up canopies of stalactites that grew from the ceiling.

"Sunni," said a voice.

She rolled over and looked around. Pieces of shredded sail and shattered hull littered the pool. The high arch of the ceiling curved down into a horizontal stone platform. Blaise was huddled at its edge, his hand extended.

He helped her out of the water. "You made it!"

"You too," she whispered.

"Only just."

"Dean. Have you seen Dean?" Sunni staggered along the edge of the rock platform, her eyes streaming with seawater and tears.

Blaise walked with her, his arm hovering around her back. "No."

"He was right there with us. I should have held on to him! I am so stupid—"

"No, you are not—"

"Listen. What's that?" She wiped her eyes and cocked her head at a distant rushing sound. The rush grew into a roar. Bubbles rose to the pool's surface as if it were coming to a boil.

A ball of seaweed, silver fish, and bubbles blasted

upward and splashed over them. The smell of kelp filled the cavern, like a beach at low tide.

As the water settled again, placid and glowing blue, Sunni and Blaise swept startled fish back into the pool and picked seaweed fragments off themselves. A giant clump of kelp had surfaced, and something was stuck underneath it. A hand emerged from the seaweed.

Dean's streaming face peered out, and Sunni dived frantically into the pool to help him.

"Sun." Dean grabbed her arm, his eyes half-shut as she fished him out and hugged him close.

"You're alive! I thought you'd gone for good." Sunni sniffled and laughed at the same time. "I think crabs have it in for you, Deano."

"I thought I'd drowned." Dean buried his head in her shoulder.

"One minute you were there, and then you weren't. Stop doing that to me!"

"The water just took me," murmured Dean, "and I came out here."

"I know. It got me and Blaise, too."

"Is he OK?"

Blaise crouched down and ruffled Dean's wet hair. "Yup. Hey, man, nice swim."

"I couldn't have swum if I'd tried!" Dean spat and worked his finger around in his mouth. "I've got seaweed stuck in my teeth."

A gigantic bubble burped up in the pool and pushed a billowing dark shape to the surface.

"What the—?" Dean exclaimed.

"Come on, Blaise, help me," Sunni said urgently. They swam out to the floating shape and turned the figure over to reveal Marin's unconscious face. With all the strength they had left, they towed him back to the platform and laid him out. Corvo's apprentice was clammy and still, his olive skin drained of color.

Dean crawled over to see. "Is he dead?" he asked hopefully.

Sunni touched the side of Marin's neck for a pulse. "No, just alive." She knew what she had to do because she had practiced many times in junior life-saving class. She shook his shoulder gently and said loudly, "Marin? Marin, wake up."

There was no response, so she tilted his head up and carefully lifted his neck. She put her ear to his mouth, but no breath came. Sunni opened Marin's mouth, took a deep breath, and put her mouth tightly over his. After four breaths, she drew back and listened. Within a few seconds, he spluttered and came to, coughing water.

"Marin!" Relief washed over her. "You're all right. Just rest for a minute."

His eyes fixed on Sunni, then Blaise and Dean, before he rolled onto his side, spewing.

"Gross!" Dean wrinkled his nose.

Sunni's stomach was a cage of butterflies. *I kissed him,* she thought, *sort of,* and wondered what it might have been like if he had been awake at the time.

"So this is Corvo's apprentice." Blaise's face knotted up with resentment as Sunni pulled off her jacket and pushed it under Marin's head. "You don't have to make him too comfortable, Sunni."

"Yeah. Why don't we throw him back in?" Dean jeered.

"Give it a rest, will you?" murmured Sunni.

"He left us in the water after we went overboard!"

After a few moments, the apprentice said in a choked voice, "I gave you a rowboat, boy! Bashir would have caught us all if I had stopped to pull you from the sea." He had a coughing fit and went on, "You should not have been on deck. I told you both to stay inside, but you disobeyed."

Dean was sullen.

"And you survived, did you not? No simple feat in this place," Marin went on.

"We did manage to get in the rowboat," said Sunni. "And then Lady Ishbel's ship picked us up."

A look of annoyance crossed Marin's face. "Ishbel."

"Everybody rescues us and then wants something for it!" complained Dean. "Secrets, maps—"

"What is he saying?" Marin interrupted, pulling himself up to sitting. "What maps?"

"Blaise found a map," said Sunni. "Lady Ishbel decided it was her property. Then Angus tried to double-cross her and get it for himself."

"Angus—the stranger on her ship, who was also at the arch?"

She nodded. "He was going to hurt Dean unless I stole the map for him, but we escaped to Blaise's ship. Then the crabs attacked us."

"If you hadn't been blocking my way, I never would have had to go near the crabs!" Blaise glared at the apprentice.

"Did your crew not warn you?"

"They did, but it was the only way."

"To where?"

Blaise's mouth was set in a stubborn line.

"We are shipwrecked here!" shouted Marin, struggling to his feet. "What difference does it make if you tell me now?"

Blaise stayed silent.

"It was a location on your map, was it not? Come, boy, do you think I am a simpleton?"

"All right!" Blaise burst out. "It's an island."

"That tells me nothing. This sea is full of islands." Marin held out his hand. "Let me see this map that everyone thinks is his."

"I don't know," said Blaise, his chin jutting out. "Hugo Fox-Farratt told us you were working for Soranzo."

"That is untrue! He is spreading lies about me."

"Hugo's not the only one. You don't have a great reputation."

"Yeah," said Dean. "Lady Ishbel said she heard bad things about you from Zorzi. He rescued her from this ocean while he was keeping away from you."

Marin reeled as though he had been punched in the stomach. "Zorzi is here—and avoiding me?"

"Who's Zorzi?" Sunni asked, puzzled.

"My fellow apprentice. The youngest of us three, only thirteen and like a brother to me."

Blaise noticed Sunni's face softening at this and said, "Hugo said Sir Innes didn't want you here, either. But you sneaked in anyway, like a rat."

"You would have done the same if you had been me."

"Betray Corvo? No way."

"I did not betray my master!"

"Then why does everyone think you did?"

Marin let out a rueful laugh. "Because they are like sheep, believing without thinking."

"So you did nothing wrong," said Sunni. "Capturing us and treating us like criminals was the right thing to do?"

"I have protected you and kept you alive!" Marin stopped and gave Sunni a grateful look. "As you have me."

Sunni's shy smile and the way she looked back at the apprentice made Blaise interrupt. "Yeah, OK, we're all alive. The question is, how do we stay alive? We've got to find water and food."

"Where do we think we are, exactly?" asked Sunni.

"Well, we were close to the island when we went down."

"Yeah, really close," said Dean. "It was the last thing I saw before I went under."

"Maybe we're underneath it somehow," Sunni ventured.

"Come, come, enough of this," Marin said tartly to Blaise. "I know this archipelago far better than you, but you still will not show me the map."

"Let him see it," Sunni said with a sigh.

"I don't know." Blaise kept his hand firmly on his messenger bag.

"Blaise," said Sunni, "I think it'll be OK."

Reluctantly he took out the map and unrolled it. Marin spent a few moments feeling the paper and studying the drawings.

When he looked up at them, his face was unusually soft. "My master did not make this."

Blaise slumped. "Does that mean it's worthless? We wasted our time coming here?"

"No, I meant that someone else drew this map. Zorzi. Where did you find it?"

"Stuck to the white wall between the maze and the sea." Blaise regarded Marin coolly. "It wasn't attached very well and peeled off pretty easily, but I was running from Angus and had to leave a piece behind. He snagged it, but luckily Sunni saw it and copied what was on it."

He produced Sunni's sodden sketchbook from his bag.

"You saved my sketchbook!" Sunni hugged it to her chest. "Thanks, Blaise." She opened it carefully and pointed out the nine little drawings to Marin. "We don't know what these mean."

The apprentice studied the images of a fish-tailed man holding a trident, a winged woman, a man with a sickle, a woman cradling two young children, a woman on horseback, two men holding cornstalks, a man with a lyre, and another woman on horseback.

Marin's face lit up. "I know them. They are part of a code we used in the workshop. It came from the time when our master taught us to read."

"Is that when you learned English?" asked Sunni.

"I learned some from my master and more from Lady Ishbel. But that was long ago, when she first arrived here and things were different between us," he said brusquely. "Someone hand me something to draw with."

Using one of Sunni's pencils, Marin drew a grid of squares on a damp blank page. In the first box he sketched a man holding a lyre and wrote *A* above him. In the next he drew a man holding a cup and grapes and put a *B* over him.

"*A* is for *Apollo*, and *B* is for *Bacchus*," said Marin. He drew a few more Roman gods and the first letter of each name. "This is a picture alphabet. We used it for remembering letters. If we saw *A* written down, we thought of Apollo, the god of music, and his lyre."

"Zorzi spelled out a word in pictures," said Sunni excitedly.

"A message for me or Dolphin, the other apprentice." Marin was actually smiling. "Perhaps he is not avoiding me after all."

"What does it say?"

"First is a labyrinth symbol, but the word starts with Fortuna, goddess of fortune. After her is Iris, goddess of the rainbow. Then the sea god, Neptune, with his trident, Iris once more, and Saturn, holding his sickle."

"F-I-N-I-S?" Dean spelled out.

"Exactly," said Marin. "The next picture is Tellus, the goddess of earth, with Epona, the goddess of horses. Then twice we see Robigus, protector of corn crops, with Apollo and Epona again."

"FINIS TERRAE."

"*Land's End* in Latin," said Marin.

"Does that mean it's the way out of Arcadia?" asked Sunni.

"It may be. I do not know."

Blaise arched an eyebrow. "In all the time you've been here, you've never come across a way out?"

"I was not looking for one," said Marin. "Though I have found paths that transport you back to the upper layers unexpectedly. The night before I captured you, I had been fighting with Bashir but was pushed up through a weak place in the painting and into the naiads' lake."

"So part of the game for Sir Innes was taking the right path to avoid going back to the palace and starting again?" Sunni broke in.

"Yes, I suppose so."

"We'd better not be heading into one of those," said Dean. Sunni hugged him and said, "I hope not."

"So, now what do we do?" asked Blaise.

Marin walked to the edge of the shimmering water. "Pray that this treacherous pool is not the only way out."

Chapter 21

Angus gazed at the towering island before them, its surface dotted with boulders and marked with veinlike paths that disappeared into the clouds obscuring its top. The *Luna* had crept along the entire shore searching for signs of the other ships and a place to moor.

"Your clever plan did not work," said Lady Ishbel. "Neither of the two ships is here."

"That's because we were faster, I suppose," Angus replied. "We must be ahead of them."

"I thought Marin would follow my ship, not that boy's."

"So that's what's bothering you, my lady," Angus said with a smirk. "Marin."

"What do you mean?"

"A problem of the heart."

"How dare you! My business with Marin has nothing to do with you." Her face was crimson.

"Let's see, what was it? He didn't return your affection? Or he preferred someone else?"

Lady Ishbel's anger robbed her face of all its beauty. "You are impudent! Pray be silent!"

He rolled his eyes and changed the subject. "Have you been to this island before, my lady?"

She struggled to contain herself. "Some time ago, I

can't remember when. It's a forbidding place, with hardly anywhere to land."

"That bay we passed earlier will do nicely."

The vessel glided along the south coast of the island, passing sea stacks and rocky islets, and anchored in a solitary bay.

"Presumably the kids were heading here." Angus frowned. "It's a shame we haven't got the map yet. We need it to know what's so interesting about this place."

"*My* map."

"*Your* map," he said. "I suggest we explore this hunk of rock. Would you care to accompany me, my lady?"

Lady Ishbel shivered as she studied the island's rocky terrain. "I do not care for this place. But, yes, I must see it again for myself."

Two oarsmen rowed them toward the shore on the *Luna*'s skiff and Angus helped Lady Ishbel onto a level piece of land.

As they slowly progressed along the shore, she struggled to walk. Angus hauled her over ledges and across rocks as they approached the western side of the island, fuming all the way.

"I am fatigued," Lady Ishbel declared, and sat down on a rock, her vast skirt flipping up like a ringing bell.

"Fine." Angus continued along the path.

"You must wait," she called.

"No, I mustn't. If I find anything, I'll bring it back."

"Turn round and face me when you speak. I must see your face."

Angus whirled around and fixed her with his stony eyes.

"I do not believe you will come back!" shouted Lady Ishbel. "What do you want with this place?"

He turned and began walking again. Lady Ishbel leaped up and dashed after him. Her voluminous gown made it impossible for her to see where she was putting her feet, and it was not long before she stumbled and rolled, shrieking, down the rough slope.

Angus merely looked back at her over his shoulder and, saying nothing, walked on.

Blaise squinted at the cave's cathedral-like ceiling. "Look at those statues in the wall. Behind them there's some sort of path up, but it gets dark toward the top and I can't tell whether it goes anywhere."

"We have two choices," Marin declared. "If we do not take the path, we must dive back into the pool and find an underground waterway to the sea."

"Too risky. We'll end up back here again if we're lucky, and drown if we're not."

"Let's try the path," said Sunni.

Marin rolled up the map and went to tuck it into his satchel.

"Hey," said Blaise, "I found that. Give it back."

"It was meant for me."

"I don't see your name on it." Blaise thrust out his hand. "Hand it over."

The apprentice snorted. "As you wish. I am not a thief."

"Yeah, yeah. So you say." Blaise made a great show of stashing the map away.

"There. You are happy now?"

"Can we get a move on?" Sunni took a few impatient steps toward the row of stone goddesses. Blaise caught up with her, and she gave him a pointed look.

"What?" he whispered.

"Why are you giving him a hard time?"

"Huh? The guy kidnaps you and threatens to put you in a prison drawing, and you're worried about *him* being given a hard time?"

"We're all right," she hissed. "He ended up helping us."

Blaise let out a frustrated breath. "I still don't trust him."

Sunni shook her head and bustled to the last statue in the row. Carved into the side of its body, a narrow staircase of shallow steps led straight up.

"Dean, you follow me." Sunni edged her way up the steps and along a catwalk behind the row of goddesses, the others inching along behind her. She reached a sharp turn, and the way ahead was dark.

"Something's in there," she whispered. "I can hear sounds."

"What?" Dean's voice quivered as Sunni felt her way along in the blackness. Suddenly an explosion of wings slapped her around the face and shoulders.

"Bats!" she screeched. The cloud of creatures veered away into the higher reaches of the cave.

There was scuffling behind her. Marin shouted in Italian, and Blaise barked something back at him.

"What is it?" Sunni asked.

"Nothin', keep going." Dean's voice pierced the dark. "One of them kicked the other or something."

Sunni moved forward. The path twisted again, and a dim glow shone from above.

"Light," she called. "Come on, there's light up here."

They crawled hand over hand through the slimy passage toward a chink of blue sky and emerged aboveground on a scrubby hillside studded with boulders and cacti. The sun scalded the earth and forced them to shield their eyes.

"Three paths," said Blaise, considering the junction of rough walkways before them.

"We should follow the one going up," said Marin.

"How do you know?" asked Blaise, rubbing his filthy hands on his pants. "Have you been here before?"

The apprentice put his hands on his hips. "No. Those other two paths would lead us down, and I do not see the point of going back to the sea."

"How do you know that?" Blaise repeated.

"I have eyes to see," said Marin. "Look, the paths lead down."

"No, I mean how do you know there's no point in going toward the sea?"

"I do not know for certain. I just have a feeling that we should walk upward." Marin's eyes narrowed. "You do not trust my judgment?"

"Oh, I'll take a chance on your path," said Blaise. "But no, I don't really trust you. Too many people think you're a traitor."

With that, he set off briskly, swinging his arms. Sunni and Dean followed, bent over in the burning sun.

Marin pushed past them, his tattered cloak blowing wraithlike in the scouring breeze, and dogged Blaise's footsteps. "I did not betray my master!"

"Heard that before," grunted Blaise as he wound up the rugged hillside.

Sunni's head was spinning with the heat. She licked her dry lips and tried not to stumble. Dean panted at her heels and shouted for Marin and Blaise to slow down. A chorus of hidden cicadas grew louder the higher they climbed among the clusters of brushy trees and weirdly shaped stones.

"You know nothing!" Marin gasped.

"Then tell me." Blaise stopped between two man-size slabs of rock and blocked the path with outstretched arms, his face blazing red. "Get it over with."

Marin came to a halt just below him, glowering.

"Come on, I want to know the truth before we go any farther," said Blaise as Sunni and Dean staggered up and collapsed into the shade of some boulders.

"The truth." Marin gave a crooked smile.

"You owe it to us," Blaise taunted.

"I owe nothing to anyone except my master." Marin leaned against a tall, jagged rock.

"Yeah, your master. So why does everyone think you betrayed Corvo?"

The apprentice turned and pressed his face briefly against the searing hot surface of the stone. "Because of a man named Bellini."

Chapter 22

Sunni, Blaise, and Dean exchanged surprised glances, but before any of them could speak, Marin continued, almost spitting with disgust.

"Maffeo Bellini. He called himself a painter, but he was usually in the taverns drinking wine instead of working. Maffeo copied other painters' ideas and said they were his own. Because of this, my master refused to allow him in our workshop." Marin squeezed his eyes shut as if he were in pain. "But Maffeo kept appearing when I was on my own in town, in alleyways, by food stalls, telling me I should leave il Corvo and work for him."

"But you didn't," said Sunni.

"No, but I allowed him to talk. I was flattered. Every time he appeared, his offers grew better and better."

"What made you so special?" Blaise let his arms drop from the boulders to his sides.

Marin looked miserable. "My master had taught me a small amount about making enchanted drawings. But I began to read his books in secret and practice on my own. I boasted to my friends — and, to my shame, even to Maffeo — that before long I would be able to make even more powerful paintings than my master's."

"So that's why Maffeo wanted you to work for him?"

"Yes," said the apprentice. "Yet I did not understand how this lazy painter suddenly had so much to offer me. Where did his new wealth come from? By the time I found out, it was too late."

"Where was it from?" Sunni asked.

"Soranzo," Marin said through gritted teeth. "Maffeo told Soranzo all about my master's enchanted paintings. If it had not been for my vain boasts, the existence of the paintings would have remained a secret. But once Soranzo knew, he would rest at nothing until they were his. My master sent us three apprentices away with parcels and directions to different locations. I was sent to Alexandria, in Egypt. But the address was false, and the paintings I carried were blank."

Blaise jumped in. "Corvo didn't trust you anymore."

"I cannot deny it. My master taught me a harsh lesson when he sent me to Alexandria. I worked hard to earn my passage back across Europe so that I could ask for Sir Innes's help in finding my master."

"And he didn't want anything to do with you either, so you went into Arcadia behind his back."

"Soranzo's spies were everywhere. I merely protected myself. You must see that!" Marin pushed himself away from the rock. "I had to steal into the painting and keep out of everyone's sight. With enough magical knowledge to create my hidden cave and charm the dryads, I dedicated myself to fending off the spies who began arriving to hunt for my master and his paintings, while searching for him myself."

Blaise crossed his arms over his chest. "So you don't want Corvo's lost paintings yourself?"

"No, I want only il Corvo's forgiveness. And even if I cannot have that, I will continue to defend Arcadia and the paintings if they are here." Marin shrugged. "Believe me if you choose to. It makes no difference."

"I'm still not sure what I think of you," Blaise said, wondering fleetingly what Sunni thought of Marin, deep down. "But maybe this is your chance to prove yourself. There's a new enemy here now. *Angus* Bellini. Yeah, that's right—Bellini. He claims our teacher sent him to rescue us, but he's really after the lost paintings. And he'll trample over anyone to get them."

"Bellini," repeated Marin, his eyes wide. "That man is named Bellini? Yes, yes, I knew there was something familiar about him." He began pacing about like a penned-up animal until something came to him and he stopped short, a look of disbelief on his face. "This Angus Bellini is from your century?"

"He must be," said Blaise. "If he wasn't, how would he know about me and Sunni, our names and everything?"

Marin seemed satisfied with this. "And you do not work for him?"

"I'd rather eat crab shells," Blaise snorted.

Marin pulled his leather satchel from under the cloak. Dean cringed at the sight of it and skittered behind the boulder.

"What now, boy?" asked Marin impatiently as he rifled through the bag.

"My portrait. You're going to finish it, aren't you?"

"You are the least of my problems. I see now that you are no spy, after all." He drew out Mr. Bell's book and carefully peeled the pages apart.

"No joke?" Dean's mouth hung open.

"I do not joke about such things."

"Yes!" Dean's relief was so great, he punched the air.

Holding the book out in front of him, Marin tapped his finger on a painting of fauns and nymphs dancing in a forest glade. Blaise, Sunni, and Dean gathered around.

"That's Maffeo," said the apprentice, pointing at a laughing faun. "He once modeled for my master. Before il Corvo knew what he was really like."

"Maffeo looks just like Angus," said Sunni, aghast. "But he can't actually be him." She looked at the date of the painting. "1580."

"Angus told me that some of his ancestors came from Italy and settled down near Braeside, so maybe they're related." Blaise shook his head. "And Angus is an artist, too, but I wouldn't want to see any of his drawings brought to life! Really creepy stuff."

"Perhaps your Bellini is a devilish incarnation of his ancestor," said Marin, shutting the book. "If only I had found the paintings myself and knew they were safe. I have searched many islands, as well as the maze and the palace, but there is no sign of them."

"Maybe they're not even here," said Sunni.

"It would be a relief if no one could ever find them. Those paintings have cost many lives."

Blaise let out a long breath and said, "Like Hugo's and Inko's."

"What?"

"Angus pushed Hugo into the maze and something attacked him. And he made Inko go into the brambles below your cave. Th-they swallowed him up."

"Unfortunate for Fox-Farratt . . . But Inko is stronger than you think. Do not worry about him." Marin's hands curled into fists. "So another Bellini dares to hunt my master's paintings and will kill to own them! I shall make this devil pay."

He looked at them each in turn. "I may need your help to stop him."

"In return for two things," said Sunni cautiously. "First, give me Dean's portrait to prove you won't finish it."

Marin slid the damp sketch out of the Corvo book. "I will gladly give it to you and tell you a secret. I can bring people back out of their portraits. The imprisonment does not have to be permanent. But do not ask me to release the other spies — they would only make trouble." He handed it to her. "Keep this drawing safe in your satchel."

"Why can't I just tear it up or dump it in the sea?" Dean burst out.

"Let her keep it safe. It is unwise to throw enchanted paper away."

Sunni sandwiched Dean's half-finished portrait between the pages of her sketchbook.

"What is your second request?"

"That you'll help us find the way home to our world."

"Of course," he replied. "I can see now that you stumbled upon Arcadia in error."

"We stumbled in and brought trouble with us. So have you, Marin." Sunni's voice cracked. "You might not be a traitor, but you're a bully. Inko was so scared of you, he did anything you ordered him to."

Marin lowered his gaze to the ground. "Even though Inko could not speak, he could lead enemies to me. I had to tell him I would erase him from Arcadia if he disobeyed."

"Erase him!"

Marin hastily opened the book of Corvo's paintings and held it up when he had found what he was looking for. A drawing of Inko smiled out from the page.

"Sir Innes asked il Corvo to put Inko in Arcadia. My master copied this portrait into one of the underpaintings, and when he conjured everything into life, Inko lived, too. Sir Innes wanted this because the real Inko, Sir Innes's cabin boy, had died of disease years before."

Sunni's eyes stung at this.

"But I could not have erased him," Marin continued in a hollow voice. "The Inko who lives in Arcadia cannot die. My master drew him, along with every stone and tree in this place. As long as this painting exists, Inko will be alive in it."

The four figures weaved along the straggly path, pushing through spiky undergrowth and scrambling over rocks.

Blaise walked at the front, muttering warnings about

stones or thorns over his shoulder from time to time. Dean clambered behind him while Sunni and Marin brought up the rear. Blaise could hear the hum of her voice—she kept on finding new questions for the apprentice, which didn't seem to bother Marin now that he'd already spilled his guts to them. He answered every question and had Sunni completely absorbed.

Blaise had heard more than enough from Marin. With a heavy sigh, he plodded on. Suddenly, after rounding a hard bend in the trail, he came to a halt at the edge of a steep cliff. The path continued as a high, narrow ridge across a bay, which led to a towering, sheer-sided needle of rock jutting up from the water. It rose from the surf far below, edged by majestic cliffs that vanished into mist. A dark indentation in the cliffs suggested that the path ran on around it.

Blaise held one arm out to shield Dean from the edge. "We've got to follow the path to that big stack."

"Just like that?" Dean gulped. "Look how narrow it is. One wrong step and you're gone."

"We can do it."

"I don't know."

Sunni and Marin bounded up behind them.

"Oh, great." She peered down at the deep drop on both sides of the path and shuddered.

"It's doable," said Blaise.

"But what if—what if something bad happens to one of us trying to get across, and it turns out it wasn't even the right path?"

They were all silent.

"There is no room for doubts—they steal our courage and concentration," said Marin after a time.

"I'm not scared," Sunni said, her chin jutting out. "I just wish we knew we were on the right road."

"We're going to have to take a chance," said Blaise.

"I know, I know."

"Being scared didn't keep us from going through the maze or into the boats. And it didn't stop you from coming into the painting in the first place, to find Dean. You didn't think twice about that!"

Sunni nodded sheepishly.

"I'll help you. It'll be fine." Blaise flexed his arms. "I'll go first, then Dean. I can figure out the best places to step and guide you, OK?"

"OK," Dean murmured, trying not to look down.

Holding his arms out fully for balance, Blaise gingerly walked the ridge until he reached the stack and hugged it, his fingers scraping the rock to get a grip. He edged along to a safer perch and waved back at the others.

"It's not too bad. You can do it, no problem. Come on, Dean."

Dean braced himself at the edge. Blaise, with his long legs and quiet determination, had made it look so easy.

"Are you OK?" Blaise called. "You don't look like you're breathing. Stop holding your breath, man!"

Dean let out a long sigh and began to breathe again.

"All right!" Blaise called. "That's more like it. Look, why don't you crawl on your hands and knees? That might be easier."

He kept chattering encouragements as Dean made his

way across on all fours. At last, Blaise pulled him in away from the edge.

"No problem at all!" Dean turned and grinned at Sunni triumphantly. "Your go, Sun."

Sunni focused all her concentration on the ridge and moved slowly but steadily across, jumping onto the ledge without Blaise's or Dean's help.

"See? You did great." Blaise grinned at her as he guided her away from the edge.

Marin was a lonely sight, staring at the crashing surf below.

"Don't look down," said Blaise. "Not a good idea."

"You can do it, Marin, but you're going to have to use your arms for balance," Sunni called, giving him a tight smile of encouragement. "Or just do what Dean did."

"Come on, you've lived through worse than this in Arcadia," Blaise said, secretly pleased to be telling the apprentice what to do.

Marin pushed his cape over his shoulders. "Quiet!"

He shifted his satchel around onto his back and stepped onto the ridge, his teeth bared slightly. Jerkily, like a marionette, Marin tottered across and came to a standstill near the end of it.

"Keep going, don't stop there!" Blaise said. Marin flung himself toward the ledge, stumbling and starting to topple backward.

Dean grabbed Marin's tunic and was pulled, howling, toward the apprentice, before the others hauled them both in. All four collapsed in safety on the ledge, sending alarmed birds screeching from their roosts in the cliffs.

To their surprise, Marin began to laugh.

He sat up and playfully shoved Dean, who had only just let go of his tunic. "You surprise me, boy. I thought you would be the least likely to help me."

Dean shoved him back. "My name's Dean, not Boy."

"Come on," groaned Blaise, getting to his feet.

He began to feel his way around the stack, along the rough path. One by one, the others followed, their faces pale and strained with concentration.

"Almost there," Blaise said. "Just coming to—"

Suddenly he was pulled forward and yanked off the path into a dark recess. For a moment they heard him shouting, but then another snarling voice drowned him out.

"Blaise!" Sunni plastered her back to the stack's wall.

Dean froze, his eyes shut.

"Keep going!" Marin hissed. "Go! Blaise is in danger!"

Sunni felt for Dean's hand, and with halting steps she edged herself around to the opening in the stone. She pulled Dean close as Marin pressed in behind them, propelling them deeper into the recess.

What they found was far more than a crude hollow in solid rock. It was a perfectly round room, its smooth walls lit from above by an opening in the stack.

In its center loomed Angus, one hand twisting Blaise's arm behind his back, the other pressing the blade of a dagger to his throat.

Chapter 23

"Welcome." Angus's smooth voice cut Sunni and Dean to the quick. "What a pleasure it is to see you again."

Blaise's free arm strained to tear the dagger away from his throat. "Get off me, you crazy—"

"Shut up, kid, or the blade will do it for you," snapped Angus, wrenching Blaise's arm sharply. He looked up at Sunni, Dean, and Marin. "A fascinating place, is it not? The walls are alive."

Sunni flicked her eyes away from Blaise long enough to take in what was on the wall behind him. It was a huge drawing—and it was moving. The color drained from Marin's face as he noticed the mural.

It showed two boys, who went about their business apparently unaware of what was happening in the chamber. They inhabited an airy workshop with tall shuttered windows, full of pots, benches, artists' materials, and drawings. At one table, a boy with short curly hair, dressed in clothes similar to Marin's, stirred something in a cauldron. The other, older boy stood at a slab, grinding nuggets of something into powder with a pestle.

Angus's face was lit up with a diabolical energy. "A living mural," he announced, turning Blaise around to survey the drawing. Angus was so enraptured that he didn't notice Sunni edging her way closer.

But before she could reach him, he glimpsed her out of the corner of his eye. He brandished the dagger and muttered, "Stay back."

"You've got no right!" shrieked Sunni.

"Oh, no, have I upset you?" Angus puffed. "Again?"

"You're supposed to be rescuing us!" Dean exploded.

"What a shame that Marin hasn't finished your portrait and I still have to listen to you!" He nodded a greeting at the seething apprentice.

"He's not going to finish it!" shouted Dean.

"Congratulations."

"Bellini." Marin's face was a rigid mask of anger. "The boy Blaise has done nothing wrong. Release him immediately."

"I disagree," said Angus. "He's got stolen property in this bag."

Blaise choked out, "Wha—?"

"The map, *mon ami*, the map."

"It's not stolen. I found it!" Blaise shouted.

"It belongs to Lady Ishbel," said Angus.

"Where is she, then? Did you dump her overboard?"

"She's around. Somewhere."

Marin took one half step forward. "It is *my* map. It was meant for me. But you may have it in exchange for the boy."

He moved quickly toward Blaise and retrieved the map from the messenger bag. Angus snatched it and crushed it into his trouser pocket.

"Well, there goes your bargaining chip. I look forward to seeing what's so special about this map." The painter peered over his shoulder at the mural. "Now, let's take a closer look at this drawing."

Never taking his eyes off Angus, the apprentice said nothing.

Angus dragged Blaise toward the mural. "If I'm not mistaken, this is il Corvo's workshop in Venice. And the two boys are very busy. What's the younger one doing? Ah, of course, boiling linseed oil to mix with the pigments and thicken them to perfection."

Marin glanced at Sunni and Dean, dabbing one finger to his temple.

"He's mental all right," agreed Dean in a whisper.

"Pay attention! You'll learn more here than in all the lessons my cousin Lorimer could ever give you," Angus said. "Look, the other boy is grinding nuggets into powder to make paints. Lapis lazuli, verdigris, malachite, umber, ivory . . ."

As Angus peered at the boy with the pestle and mortar, a man with a short dark beard and hooked nose appeared in the mural, taking his place in front of a huge easel. He contemplated a picture of a ship being attacked by a giant whale.

Marin gasped.

"The Raven himself," whispered Angus. "The master who can turn paintings into miracles."

As if on cue, Corvo briefly looked in their direction, but by the way he looked through them, it seemed he could not see them.

"I regret that the Raven is oblivious to us. Is there no way to communicate with him?"

"No," Marin said. "He is beyond us while in the mural."

Angus's smile twitched. "That's a terrible shame. Is this mural your doing? Did you put Corvo and the others into it? I imagine your drawing style is much like the Raven's, since you learned from him."

Marin said icily, "This is not my work. It is the work of my master himself."

"And what's this I see?" said Angus, squinting at the mural. "So many paintings in the workshop. So many new masterpieces."

He walked slowly along the wall, dragging Blaise with him, his eyes trained on the mural. Then suddenly, he stopped. A grin spread over his face. "That painting there, hanging behind Corvo's easel, the one with the dead stag at the bottom of the cliff and the men on horseback. What's that painting called?"

"I do not know," said Marin.

"Really?" Angus raised an eyebrow. "It matches the description of a lost painting I read about called *The Chalice Seekers*. See? It even has the chalice floating in the sky."

Sunni sucked in her breath. *The magical paintings Hugo talked about.*

"I'll wager that the two paintings next to it are *The City of the Sun* and *The Jewel of Adocentyn*," said Angus, breathless. "The three missing canvases, found at last! It's the perfect hiding place—paintings within paintings within paintings. Genius. Now all we need to do is get them out of there so I can see them."

Marin folded his arms over his chest.

"You seem to be a clever lad, Marin. You know how to

trap people in your drawings. It stands to reason that you can remove them, too. Objects should be even easier to transport in and out," said Angus. "So, there's a good chap. Bring those three paintings out of the mural."

Marin did not move.

"I'm not asking you. I'm telling you." Angus smiled but his eyes were steely. "And if you do not do as I say, what happens next will be your fault." The knife glinted in his hand as he pushed it against Blaise's throat.

"I cannot remove what my master has drawn there. It is impossible."

Angus considered this. "But you could transport a person *into* this mural. Yes?"

The apprentice's face fell for a split second, and Angus pounced.

"Aha, it can be done. A simple proposal, then. I want you to draw *me* in."

"It is too dangerous. I do not know how you would ever get out again."

Angus hesitated. "All right. Send the girl in. Let's find out how dangerous it really is." He leered at Sunni. "You can fetch them for me, can't you, Sunshine? You're a strong lass—I reckon you can carry all three in one go."

"No, I c-cannot be responsible . . ." stammered Marin. "What if something were to happen to her?"

"Matey, you'll be responsible for what's going to happen to *him* in a minute." Angus tightened his grip on Blaise. "And don't tell me you've suddenly developed a conscience after trapping people in your little sketches. Now, get on with it."

Blaise struggled as he tried to wrench himself from Angus's grasp, but the dagger nicked his skin and a scarlet pearl of blood appeared on his neck.

Sunni screamed and took a step toward him. Marin put a hand on her arm.

"What guarantee do we have that you will hand back the boy once you have the paintings?" he asked Angus through gritted teeth.

"None!" Sunni said. "His guarantee isn't worth anything!"

"Well," said Angus, "if you feel that way, we can't do business." He grunted into Blaise's ear, "Your fair damsel won't help you. I'm afraid it's all over, my friend."

Blaise spat out a defiant, "Good!" but his eyes were terrified. Angus traced the dagger across Blaise's throat, lightly, his eyes fixed on Sunni.

Sunni's heart beat so hard it ached. "Draw me! Marin, just draw me!" she cried. "I'll do it!"

Angus relaxed his grip slightly and smiled. "Ah, she's all heart, that girl. It would bring a tear to a glass eye."

Marin brought his face close to Sunni's ear. "Are you certain? You are willing to risk this?" He squeezed her shoulder and said in a low whisper, "Do you trust me?"

Trembling, she breathed out, "Yes."

With an almost imperceptible nod of his head, Marin let her go.

"I will draw the girl there." The apprentice pointed at a blank area of the wall, away from the Raven and the other apprentices. He opened his satchel and rummaged about for a stick of charcoal.

"Very good," purred Angus.

Marin stood Sunni in the position he wanted. Dean scampered close to them and said, "I'm right here, Sun."

Angus heaved Blaise nearer so they could watch Marin draw. "We're about to watch a miracle happen."

Sunni saw the fear in her friend's eyes once more and said, "It's all right, Blaise."

Marin stared at her, his charcoal stick poised to begin. He was studying every detail, from the width of her nose to the length of her foot, and it made her shake.

His hand began flying across the wall, furiously sketching and rubbing out, cursing in Italian. From the corners of her eyes, Sunni watched herself take shape, scarcely breathing.

When the drawing was finished, Marin began murmuring something in a monotone voice. He drew strange swirly symbols above Sunni's head, then dropped his hand to his side.

Sunni's fingertips dissolved first and then her hands. It was as if she were being dunked into a vat of invisible ink.

Angus exploded with gleeful laughter.

The sound was odd, muffled, as if she were under the sea. She tried to scream, but nothing came out.

Her feet prickled with pins and needles. The burning spread up her legs, and she could not move. When her eyes finally focused, Sunni was in a strange room, warm with golden light and reeking of pungent oils. Corvo and the two boys were hastening toward her, their startled faces full of suspicion, their hands reaching out to seize her.

She opened her mouth and wailed, "Help us!"

Suddenly all Sunni could see was streaks of color and light as the room dissolved again before her eyes. The three figures faded, and everything went gray.

Sunni was only in the mural for a matter of seconds. Her feet reappeared on the floor of the round room, quickly followed by the rest of her body. Complete once again, she staggered back against the mural.

"It didn't work!" Angus shoved Blaise aside and lunged at Marin. "You filthy—"

The apprentice kicked out and sneered, "Bellini, you and all your ancestors are dogs!"

"My ancestors? What are you babbling about? You snide little toe-rag!" bellowed Angus, circling Marin, the dagger brandished before him.

"That devil Maffeo!" Marin roared. "He ruined my life!"

He leaped at Angus, fists flying, sending the dagger clattering across the room. The startled painter grappled with Marin, attempting to wrestle him to the floor. "You're crazy!"

The others hurled themselves at the pair, trying to haul the painter off Marin.

"Villain!" shouted Marin.

All at once, Angus released the apprentice and lunged at Sunni, crooking a thick arm around her neck.

"Stay away!" he cried. "Or Sunshine here gets it." He backed toward the mural, dragging Sunni with him.

Suddenly, a hand clamped onto Angus's shoulder. He

froze, then turned his head slowly to see who had appeared behind him. It was one of the apprentices from the mural.

"What the—?" gasped Angus as the other apprentice materialized, seizing his other arm. He released his grip on Sunni, then flailed wildly, trying to throw the boys off. Blaise and Dean rushed forward, and together the four of them pinned Angus to the ground in a messy scuffle.

Panting and sore, Sunni looked over toward Marin. His face was white, streaming with tears, and his shoulders trembled. His eyes were fixed on something behind them.

"What is it, Marin?" Sunni panted.

"*Signore*," he croaked. Gesticulating wildly, he began chattering in Italian.

A dark figure moved softly across the room and regarded Marin with crow-black eyes.

"We will speak English, Marin," said Fausto Corvo, gesturing toward the heap of bodies on the floor. "For our guests. Now, what in heaven's name is happening, my son?"

"Master," said Marin. "Can this be? I cannot believe I have finally found you. . . ."

"One thing at a time," replied Corvo. He examined his apprentice's portrait of Sunni. Then he smudged his forefinger across the symbols above it.

"This is how you attempted to transport the girl, Marin?" He knit his brows together. "Small wonder it did not work in my mural! This is the wrong formula. Like pouring oil into water—they will not mesh."

"I know, master. But I thought she might appear for long enough to attract your attention."

"And she did," said Corvo. "For how long have you been able to transport beings in this way?"

Marin lowered his eyes. "A—a long time. I have been capturing your enemies. They are all here in my satchel. I will show you—"

"Not now." Corvo rubbed the magical symbols out with the palm of his hand, then turned to the captive on the ground. Angus looked up at him in wonder.

"Maffeo Bellini," Corvo said with weary distaste. "After so many years."

"I am *Angus* Bellini, sir," the painter said. "It is an honor to meet you. Please—release me, I've done nothing wrong."

"This descendant of Maffeo has hurt and killed in pursuit of your magical paintings," Marin said with feeling. "I present him for your judgment." He hung his head. "And myself also."

"I will hear your story later, Marin," said Corvo. "And who are these children?"

"Innocents who wandered into Arcadia and are trying to return home to their world. They are Bellini's victims, too."

"I don't have any victims!" Angus protested. "Is it a crime to be interested in your work, Signor Corvo? I only sought the paintings because I wanted to share your genius with the world!"

"Indeed?" asked Corvo. "And why do you think it is that I have given up Venice—my friends, my family, everything I love—and hidden myself away for so many years? The world must not learn the secrets of my work—it has been my greatest challenge to keep them hidden for this long."

"I beg you. Let me go."

"There is but one remedy," said the Raven.

He pulled a piece of parchment from under his short black cloak and cradled it in the crook of one arm. He gave Angus a pitying look and, while muttering something, began scribbling on the parchment with a piece of charcoal.

A flash of realization crossed Angus's face. "Get off me!" he howled, but the apprentices held him rigid.

Sunni and Dean huddled together nearby. Blaise stood by their side, his mouth slightly ajar as he watched the magician's hand.

"He—he's going to trap Angus," stammered Dean. "That's just what Marin nearly did to me."

As he drew, Corvo crooned in a low voice as if he were soothing Angus with a lullaby. He sketched and corrected, hardly taking his eyes from his subject. At last he held the drawing out and turned it to show his three apprentices. "Have I captured Bellini's likeness?"

Marin, Dolphin, and Zorzi smiled at their master.

Angus panted, "No, no!"

Then Corvo showed the drawing to Sunni, Dean, and Blaise. He had caught Angus's hard eyes and sneering mouth, the gouges in his cheek and the tangle of his hair.

"That's amazing, sir," Blaise managed to whisper.

Sunni gulped. "It is."

Dean said nothing, daunted by the fierce look in the magician's eyes.

Corvo nodded and scrawled something across the top of the drawing to finish. "So you want my secrets, Bellini? Impossible!"

He flung the drawing across the room.

Angus started to blur around the edges, his face fading and his body as indistinct as a wisp of fog. Last to vanish were his outraged eyes, as the parchment floated to the ground.

The three apprentices got to their feet and hugged one another.

The Raven retrieved the drawing and held it up for them to see. Angus was squirming and shouting to be released, his stringy hair flying around.

Dean retched, his face drained and damp with sweat.

Sunni's bottom lip trembled. "Are you going to draw us?"

"No, I am not." Corvo wondered at these three staring, white-faced children. "But I do not understand. Are you sorry I trapped this man? My apprentice says he is your enemy, yet you are upset at his fate."

"He was our enemy," said Blaise quietly. "But I don't think he deserves a living death inside a drawing."

"He—he can't even move in there," Sunni murmured.

The Raven gestured to Dean. "Do you agree?"

"Yeah." Dean wiped his face. "That could have been me. I don't wish it on anybody else."

Corvo stroked his beard. "Then what would you have me do with Signor Bellini?"

"Put him on a really faraway island," ventured Dean, "where he can't do anything bad."

The magician's eyes lit up. He turned Angus's drawing over to the blank side, drew an island, and held it up. "A new home for Bellini. What will he do there?"

"Be a farmer," Dean said.

"Ah!" Corvo chuckled. "Very good. I will give him two pigs and some chickens." He drew these onto the island. "Shall I give him a wife?"

"Please don't," said Sunni. "I'd feel really sorry for her!"

"Wait until you see the wife I will give him." The magician's eyes twinkled. "Then you may feel sorry for *him*."

The apprentices burst into laughter, and the children grinned.

"No, you are right. The pigs and chickens are company enough for Bellini at the moment." Corvo finished the sketch and bowed to the children. "I thank you."

He whistled a lilting tune, and in a few moments a raven swooped into the room and perched itself on his shoulder. "My friend will take Bellini and his new home far out into the sea, beyond the knowledge of my sailors. There he will be released to make a life on his island."

"We could take the drawing home with us, sir, and release him in our world," said Sunni. "Wouldn't that be better?"

"You do not possess such powers." Corvo shook his head in a kindly way. "Bellini is a violent thief. It is best for him to stay with us. He will not have a bad life on his island."

"It won't exactly be Paris," Blaise said to Sunni, "but at least Angus will be alive." He looked hopefully at the magician. "And maybe someday you'll let him come back to our world."

Corvo shook his head and patted the raven's feathers.

"I have decided that you must close the labyrinth in Blackhope Tower when you return. It is time to bring peace to Arcadia. Will you do this for me?"

"Yes, sir. But how?" asked Blaise.

"When you leave us, continue along the path. It will take you to the top of the island—*finis terrae,* the land's end. Find an amphitheater with a labyrinth within it. This labyrinth will take you back if you say 'chiaroscuro' as you walk." Corvo smiled. "As you entered, so you will leave. And, most important, the last of you to arrive in the Mariner's Chamber must walk that labyrinth backward from the center, repeating the password. This will close the entrance forever."

He murmured something, and the raven took hold of Angus's portrait in its beak. It circled their heads and then flew from the room.

"Bellini is on his way." Corvo bowed again. "It is also time for us to take our leave and for you to return to your home." He went to the mural where the portraits of Zorzi and Dolphin had stood like empty shells since their subjects had left them. Mumbling to himself, he drew a line of curling symbols above their heads. One by one, the two younger apprentices faded into the air and reinhabited their portraits.

"Where did you send Dolphin and Zorzi when we left Venice, master?" Marin asked in a small voice.

"Here," said the magician. "I sent them to Sir Innes, where they would be safe until I could join them."

"You sent me to Egypt with blank canvases."

"You know why I had to do that, Marin."

Marin knelt before his master. "I repent of everything, Signore. Forgive me."

Corvo pulled his apprentice to his feet and grasped his hands. "I think you have spent long enough suffering for your sins. It is time you came home with us."

His face twisted with emotion, Marin placed himself in front of Corvo, who found a large empty space in the mural to draw his eldest apprentice.

The magician murmured several unfamiliar words as he had before starting Angus's portrait. Sunni, Dean, and Blaise hovered as close as they dared, to watch Corvo draw.

First he made a sweeping oval for Marin's head, then he moved the charcoal down the wall and blocked out his body. Humming, Corvo sketched Marin's tunic and torn sleeves, the leather satchel slung over his chest, then his breeches and flat shoes. He returned to the oval and sketched in Marin's nose, chin, mouth, and black hair.

When he came to draw Marin's eyes, he paused. It was all there: four hundred years of anger, regret, and loneliness. The magician saw his apprentice's longing for peace and forgiveness. As Corvo traced the arc of the young man's eyelids, he prayed that the angels, planets, and stars would guide his hand.

Finally, Corvo and Marin stood back from the mural and the children surrounded them.

For what seemed like an age, Marin considered the portrait his master had conjured on the wall. Then he turned to the others. "It is time for me to say good-bye. My brothers are waiting."

"Bye, then," said Dean. "Thanks for not killing me,

trapping me, or taking me into another stupid under-painting."

"Farewell, Dean, worst spy I have ever met." Marin smiled, then nodded at Blaise. "Farewell, Blaise. You are a foolhardy ship's captain, but you would make a worthy apprentice in our workshop."

Blaise shook his head. "I'm not so sure about that. I wouldn't want to make drawings that have the power yours do. I don't know that I'll even be able to look at my own drawings in the same way again."

Marin's eyes blazed. "I hope you will look at your drawings with joy and not distress. Do not turn away from your passion because of Angus Bellini's fate—it was my master's decision, not yours. If you stop drawing, you will die inside."

He turned to Sunni. "You are the most baffling female I know. Handling weapons, swimming, and drawing as well as a boy—and saving my life. I did not treat you with the respect I should have."

"No, you didn't. But everything turned out OK, so it's all right. There are lots of girls like me now," she said.

Marin smiled. "I cannot quite believe that." He opened his satchel and took out Mr. Bell's book. "This is yours. But may I show it to my master before I give it back?"

After an explanation in Italian, Marin handed the book to Corvo, who was dumbfounded as he leafed through it.

"I am famous in your time," the Raven said at last, his eyes shining. "And this book—a miracle! Many people can see my work." He was momentarily at a loss for words.

"And they care about *these* paintings? The ones that are not enchanted?"

"More than you can imagine," Sunni said. She, Dean, and Blaise clustered at Corvo's side as he thumbed through the pages of the book.

"I've loved that one since I was little. I saw it in a museum in London!" Sunni pointed at a Venice street scene.

Corvo slapped Marin on the back. "Who would have believed it? That little painting lives in London now."

Blaise leafed forward to another page. "And this picture is in America. I saw it there."

"Another miracle. My work has crossed a vast sea to the New World."

When he had seen every page in the book, he closed it carefully and handed it back to Sunni.

"You can keep it," she said. "I'm sure Mr. Bell won't mind."

"Thank you, but no." Corvo put his hand over his heart. "The memory of it will always be here now."

He nodded to Marin, who bowed low and stepped over to the mural.

"Farewell, Sunni."

Sunni's cheeks went hot as the apprentice said her name. His eyes caught hers and held them for a moment.

Corvo moved his chalk in spirals, making shapes above his drawing. A line of symbols appeared across the top of the portrait. At the completion of the last one, Marin breathed out and smiled. His body grew dim and vanished from the fingertips and toes upward. His face faded, the amber eyes the last to go, gazing out with a look of utter peacefulness.

The drawing shook on the wall. The lines faded, then sharpened, quivering and filling out as Marin took possession of the portrait.

They watched him roll his head from side to side. After a moment, he stretched his arms and legs out and walked tentatively around the workshop. Dolphin and Zorzi flew to him, jumping on him and patting his head.

"My friends," said Corvo, turning around. "You have witnessed the magic of the heavens, a miracle few have ever seen. That I have allowed you to see it means that we have a bond of trust. You are privy to my work and must help protect it. Remember, the labyrinth must be closed down. I put my faith in you to do this."

The children nodded, their faces bright, moved at being part of Fausto Corvo's great work.

Then, after a last bow, the Raven traced the same symbols over his self-portrait and, his black eyes glowing, receded into a dim shadow before vanishing altogether. They watched him take possession of his portrait and welcome his long-lost apprentice home with a fatherly hug.

Chapter 24

"Come on, let's go," said Dean. "We don't need to hang around here anymore."

Sunni could not take her eyes from the mural, where Marin stood, presumably telling the others his story. The two younger apprentices hung on his every word, while Corvo stroked his beard and nodded occasionally.

"A few more minutes. I just want to see . . ."

"See what?" Dean huffed. "Marin's gone."

"Dean's right, Sunni." Blaise scowled to himself as Sunni watched Marin, a melancholy look on her face. "They're all set now. We don't need to keep watching them. It feels kind of like spying. And we've got our own homes to go to."

"OK." She followed the others out but looked back at the mural once more, just long enough to see Marin smiling toward her but not seeing her.

"How are we going to tell Mr. Bell about Angus?" Blaise asked. "I feel kind of sick at the idea."

"I do, too," Sunni murmured. "We'll tell him together, OK?"

"Yeah, strength in numbers, I guess," he said more brightly. "Hey, Sunni, what was it like in Corvo's workshop?"

"I was barely there," she answered. "But it smelled wonderful, like oil paints, and the light was all golden. It was magical."

Blaise smiled ruefully. "I wish I'd gotten to see it."

"Will you come on?" said Dean. "All this talking is slowing us down!"

One by one, they edged across the ridge on the other side of the stack to the continuation of the path and climbed up, weary and thoughtful. The air grew dank as they entered the mist, and the craggy rocks made weird shapes in the gloom.

Then came the faint sound of a man's voice, low and tired, echoing somewhere ahead of them.

"One is one and all alone, and evermore shall be so."

The voice dropped to a murmur, but after a few moments, it erupted as if the singer had had a burst of energy. "Five for the symbols at your door, six for the six proud walkers."

Seconds later they saw a shadowy figure fading in and out of the smoky mist.

"Seven for the seven stars in the sky, eight for the April rainers . . ."

The figure stretched and tried to walk more upright as he sang, "Nine for the nine bright shiners—"

"It's Hugo!" Dean shouted.

At this the figure stopped dead and crouched down to survey the murk below him.

"It can't be." Blaise was incredulous. "I left him dying in the maze."

"It is, too. It's Foxy Farratt. That's the song he was singing when we met him. Hugo! It's me, Dean—and Sunni!"

There was a strangled sound from the figure, now hobbling quickly. Blaise scrambled up the path and hurried toward the voice, which called out, "I see your path. You're not far now. Keep on, now. You are nearly here."

The waiting silhouette was the color of mud against the dim light. It was almost birdlike, its legs bent, with a long tail drooping behind.

Blaise slowed his pace. What if this was not Hugo but another predator? "I thought you'd died."

"I very nearly did," answered the silhouette.

"You were in bad shape."

"True. But hearing your voice was a tonic, dear boy. That was you, was it not, behind the hedge in the maze?"

Blaise smiled broadly. "Yes, Mr. Fox-Farratt, it was."

"It was a voice in the wilderness to me. I gathered all my strength and carried on, evading my feathered enemy and finally escaping the maze."

Blaise pressed on and as he grew closer, he recognized the shape of Hugo's frock coat, its tails shredded and flapping behind him.

Hugo burst from the murky cloud, his arms spread out. "Thank heavens you are safe and sound."

He was practically unrecognizable in the washed-out light, his face a constellation of sores and rivulets of dirt. The cherry-red coat was caked with dried blood and slime.

"Shocking, I know." Hugo's grin was dazzling against his worn face. "Soap and water are rather lacking around here, I'm afraid."

"What happened to you?" asked Blaise.

"Almost more than I can comprehend, dear boy, and none of it enjoyable. After being bundled onto a rattletrap ship, I was attacked by pirates, snakes, and a giant hound with fangs." He paused suddenly. "See here. That ruffian you were with—he's not around, is he?"

"No, sir. Angus won't be bothering anyone again."

Hugo nodded gravely, but his smile grew as Sunni and Dean caught up to them. "I say! I despaired of ever finding you, my friends."

"You've been looking for us?" asked Dean.

"Yes, ever since you disappeared from the palace. I would never have forgiven myself if something had happened to you."

"I'm sorry we ran away," Dean murmured.

Sunni glanced at her stepbrother in wonder. "Me too."

"You had good reason," said Hugo. "You wanted to return home." Sadness crossed his face. "I cannot go back to my time, but you can go back to yours, with any luck. I see now how selfish it would be to make you stay. I do not wish you to spend your lives here, knowing your families will grow old and die without you." He bowed. "I put myself at your disposal, my friends. I will help you return home in any way I can."

"Thank you," said Sunni. She could barely contain her growing excitement. "We're actually near a place we think can take us home."

"Good heavens," said Hugo, perking up. "Then let us go, by all means."

They wandered across a stretch of dead grass and scrub, retelling their adventures.

"My word—il Corvo—alive and working with the apprentices in his Venice workshop!" Hugo said breathily. "And Angus Bellini, banished to a far-off island." He shook his head. "But no sign of Lady Ishbel."

"Knowing Angus, he dumped her along the way," Blaise said.

"Probably," agreed Hugo grimly.

A rhythmic *caw-caw-caw* sound came through the mist ahead.

The fog dissolved to reveal three stone columns and a shallow amphitheater beyond, bordered by more columns and filled with black birds, all cawing like rows of spectators. The words LUX IN TENEBRIS were carved above the entrance.

"*Light in the darkness,* if my Latin serves me well," exclaimed Hugo. "Let us hope this path does indeed take us into the light, past this unkindness of ravens."

"Huh?" Dean said.

"The collective noun for a group of ravens. An unkindness."

"Good description," Blaise muttered, eyeing the noisy crowd of birds.

"Look," Sunni said. "The labyrinth."

The rectangular maze was overgrown with weeds and was hard to make out in the odd light, but Sunni ignored the din of the ravens and ran to the opening of the snaking path. It led to four interconnected quadrants, just like the labyrinth in the Mariner's Chamber.

Sunni positioned herself at the first stone. "This is it. Let's go home."

Hugo raked his hand across his filthy hair. "I am sad to

see you go, my friends. I will miss you. But it is the right thing, of course."

"I'm sorry, Hugo."

"I could come with you. Perhaps there is a place for me in your century."

Before he could stop himself, Dean blurted out, "Yeah, a cemetery!"

Hugo looked hurt, even under his layer of dirt.

"Dean didn't mean it like that," said Sunni. "It's just that you have been in here so long, you might not survive in our time. We don't want you to end up as a skeleton in the Mariner's Chamber."

"I see," said Hugo in a small voice. "Yes, I am aware of the difficulty. And I cannot in good conscience keep you here any longer."

"There's something else," said Sunni. "Corvo asked us to close the labyrinth from the other side, so no one can ever come into Arcadia again."

Hugo bowed his head. "Then remaining here is my fate."

"Inko is out there somewhere, waiting for you to come back." She twisted her hands together.

"Perhaps. But I do not know whether our friendship can be repaired. Not after what you have told me about his betrayal of you to Marin."

Sunni bit her lip. "Marin bullied him into it. He had no choice."

Hugo nodded. "I cannot forgive what Marin did, but I understand."

"What will you do once we're gone?" asked Blaise.

"Perhaps I will be lucky enough to find a way back to the palace."

"I hope you do," said Sunni wistfully. The boys murmured in agreement. "I wish you could let us know you were safely home."

"I will find a way to send you a sign," said Hugo.

"All right." Sunni took a deep breath and turned to Blaise and Dean. "Who goes first?"

"I'm game," said Blaise.

"Then me!" Dean grinned.

The ravens cawed loudly as Blaise entered the labyrinth. Once he had, the squawking faded and he felt the peaceful sensation of following the path once again. As he walked, murmuring, "Chiaroscuro," he remembered sketching *The Mariner's Return to Arcadia*. He would soon be back there, an ordinary boy again.

This thought faded, too, as he felt himself grow weightless. The center of the labyrinth was in front of him, sharp in focus and then evaporating as he came to a stop there. Everything drifted away as his body did.

Dean waited to follow Blaise and gave a whoop after he vanished. "I'm right behind you!"

Sunni squeezed his arm, and Hugo saluted.

As Dean walked stoutly along the labyrinth's path, a low rumble began in the bowels of the island. The ravens flew into the air as one, hovering above the amphitheater like a black cloud.

"Whoa!" Dean shouted as the ground heaved up great clods of earth. The stone tiles of the labyrinth juddered and leaped into the air, falling back in a new formation.

"No! It—it's changed shape."

The labyrinth was no longer rectangular, but round, its paths winding into a spiral. The ravens sat back on their seats and cackled.

"Try again, Dean," called Sunni.

Dean set off carefully. The stones stayed as solid as if they had never moved, and he soon arrived in the center. He put both arms up and closed his eyes as he was transformed from a boy into a wisp of air.

With a grave bow, Hugo escorted Sunni to the mouth of the labyrinth. Before she set off, she rifled through her backpack and handed him something that made him smile—Mr. Bell's book.

"It's had a bit too much seawater, but I hope you'll enjoy it anyway." She shook Hugo's hand and stepped onto the path. "Good luck."

"And to you, Miss Forrest."

Please be stable. No more earthquakes, she prayed. As she began mumbling, "Chiaroscuro," she wondered how she would explain everything that had happened.

"Chiaroscuro, chiaroscuro," she muttered more loudly as the chorus of ravens shrieked.

Suddenly Sunni heard noises nearby.

Hugo shouted, "You must not!" But someone or something made a hoarse sound and he cried out in pain.

Don't look! Don't listen! Sunni urged herself.

Hands grasped at Sunni's arms and backpack.

"Where is my map?" hissed a voice.

"Chiaroscuro," whimpered Sunni.

"Lady Ishbel, come away!" Hugo was pulling at the girl, but she dogged Sunni's steps.

"You were with him! Where is the boy who has my map?"

"Ishbel!" screamed Hugo. "Come away from her!"

Sunni stumbled along the path as the other girl clasped her by the elbows. *Chiaroscuro.* She could barely make out the center of the spiral, but she moved forward instinctively, dragging Lady Ishbel along. From the ground a low rumbling began. The stones of the spiral began to shift once more.

Hugo tried to peel Lady Ishbel away from Sunni, but she lashed out at him. With every ounce of her strength, Sunni staggered toward the center as Lady Ishbel clung to her like an outraged cat. As the familiar weightlessness took over and Sunni felt the stones' positions changing under her feet, the shrieking of the ravens was almost as loud as Ishbel. The digging fingers fell away, the ravens' noise faded, and Sunni felt herself swirling like a snowflake in a breeze.

When she came to, it was in a chilly place and a hard one at that. Her cheek was against something cold. She opened her eyes and, to her horror, came face-to-face with a skull. The ivory bone was delicate, even around the black hollows where the furious green eyes had been only a few moments before.

Sunni scrambled to her feet. Lady Ishbel's skeleton, still dressed in her ridiculous golden gown and pendant, was sprawled across the center of the labyrinth in the Mariner's Chamber.

An alarm wailed, and Sunni clamped her hands over her ears as she staggered away.

"Sunni!"

Sunni backed straight into Blaise, her whole body shaking. He caught her and calmed her as best he could, though he was shaking himself. "We're here. It's OK!"

Dean crouched over the bones and touched the dress. "Is this, is this—?"

"Lady Ishbel. Sh-she tackled me as I was coming through." Sunni couldn't take her eyes from the remains. "She wanted the map."

They stood quietly for a moment, and then Blaise asked her, "Are you OK to do what Corvo asked?"

Sunni ran her hands over her tired face and nodded. She closed her eyes as she stepped over Lady Ishbel into the fourth quarter of the labyrinth. "Chiaroscuro, chiaroscuro."

Winding backward along the path, she spoke it out loud, against the shrill sound of the alarm. When she had passed though all four corners, she leaped away from the labyrinth and turned back to watch it.

"Look!" Dean pointed. The black tiles faded in front of their eyes and blended with the surrounding flagstones. They could barely make out the labyrinth anymore.

"You shut it down, Sunni," said Blaise. "It's finished." His voice was weary. "We'd better get our stories straight. What do we tell people?"

"The truth," said Sunni. "What else? If they think we're making it up, that's their problem."

"So we tell everyone about Angus?"

"I want to forget about him," grumbled Dean.

"We've got to let people know he's still in there. Especially Mr. Bell."

Police sirens were shrieking in the distance, adding to the din of the alarm. Suddenly the chamber door swung open and a guard cautiously put his head around it.

"You!" He gasped when he saw the three disheveled figures on the bench. "How did you—? This room was locked!"

The only response he got was tired shrugs.

The sounds of engines and voices filled the air outside Blackhope Tower. Before the children knew it, blankets were placed around their shoulders and they were sipping cups of sweet tea as they waited for their parents to arrive.

Chapter 25

*L*orimer Bell was pinned against a wall in a darkened room.

Blaise's father looked closely into his face and repeated, "It's not good enough." Behind him stood Mr. Forrest, nodding incessantly.

"But, but—"

"It's just not good enough, never was, never will be." Mr. Doran's eyes were flat and blank as he bore down on the art teacher.

Lorimer protested, "I've done everything I can, honestly."

"You have not, you have not," intoned Sunni's father, and Mr. Doran repeated, "Just not good enough."

The two fathers pushed Lorimer farther into the wall. He felt something against his back. The painting—he was leaning against The Mariner's Return to Arcadia.

"No, give me some air!" Lorimer gasped.

"You should be in that painting, not our children," said Mr. Forrest, not moving an inch.

"Go into the painting and get them," Blaise's father commanded, and he pulled something metallic out of his pocket. It glinted as he raised it over his head and, in one swift move, *slashed it across the surface of the painting. "I have made you an opening. Go and find our children."*

Lorimer leaped away from where the knife had split the canvas open. "Nooo! Why did you do that? They can never get out now!"

The art teacher awoke with a violent jerk. Another nightmare. He had had so many since the children and Angus vanished.

The telephone's ring sliced through the silence. It had barely rung a second time before Lorimer had fumbled it to his ear and glanced at the bedside clock. Six thirty in the morning.

"Lorimer, great news," boomed the headmaster. "All three children have been found at Blackhope Tower, worn out but unharmed, barring a few scratches. They won't be coming to school for a day or two, of course, but we shall see them very soon."

Lorimer nearly cried with relief. "I am delighted, George, absolutely delighted." He could hardly focus on what the headmaster said next and hung up as soon as he could.

But as he got up and sat on the edge of his bed, his smile faded. The children were back, but what about Angus?

Later that day, Sunni rolled over and hugged her comforter in close around her face. Her bed was the softest place she could imagine being, and the quietest. She could have stayed there the rest of the afternoon, sleeping more deeply than she ever had before, but sun was filtering through her curtains and the fragrance of roast chicken was wafting up from downstairs. She looked around her room. She remembered choosing the colors, but now it felt like someone else had, in some other life.

On the desk lay her warped sketchbook. She had shown it to the police and told some of her story, but the officers had left scratching their heads and promising to return when Sunni felt "more herself again."

She swung out of bed and went to peer at something on her bulletin board that caught her eye. Digging a postcard out from under layers of other pictures, she recognized with a jolt the painting of three young men in high-collared white shirts and tunics. They stood against a familiar landscape: a lake and a marble palace with woods and hills beyond. On the left was Zorzi, dressed in green. In the middle, dressed in blue, stood Dolphin. And on the right, proud and confident, was Marin, dressed in rusty red. Sunni turned the card over and read the caption: "*The Apprentices*, by Fausto Corvo, circa 1581."

"So you've been inside the painting all this time and you got there by walking around the maze." D.C. McNeill read over her notes as she spoke.

"Labyrinth, not maze." Blaise sat next to his father on the sofa. He had slept for fifteen hours straight and then devoured the juiciest burger and biggest mountain of fries in his life.

"Don't get used to this, buddy," his father had said with a chuckle. "Tomorrow we're back to healthy eating."

Blaise rubbed his full stomach, ready for any questions the police could throw at him.

"You were saying something under your breath when you walked the labyrinth, Blaise," McNeill said. "We were watching. Remember?"

"You were watching, all right," said Blaise's father. "That's about all you were doing, seems to me. One minute I get a call saying Blaise is with you in the Mariner's Chamber, and the next minute you're telling me I just missed him and he's vanished into the ether."

"I can only apologize again, Mr. Doran," said McNeill, gritting her teeth.

"It's not their fault, Dad," Blaise said. "I wanted to go into the painting, and I kind of tricked them into letting me because it was my only chance."

Mr. Doran let out a long sigh. "Guess we did a good job raising you to be curious and explore the world. But you outdid yourself this time, son."

Blaise smiled sheepishly at his father and then answered McNeill's question. "The word I said was *chiaroscuro*. It means "light and dark" in Italian."

McNeill made a note of it and continued in a flat tone, "And once you got in, you had to make your way through a series of worlds and fight off predators before you found the way out."

"Yes," said Blaise. "And we met some people who had been in there for four hundred years."

The three adults exchanged incredulous glances at this.

"Did you meet a man from, er, our world who vanished after you did?" D.C. Nash asked from the armchair.

Blaise sucked in his breath. "Yes."

"What was his name?" asked McNeill.

"Angus Bellini."

A small but triumphant smile crossed the detective's face as she made a note. "Do you think he's still inside the painting?"

"Y-yes." Blaise felt a rush of unease.

Nash leaned forward. "Please, Blaise, if you have information about him, tell us. He put a security guard from Blackhope Tower into the hospital, and we'd like to get him if we can."

"He's still in the painting," said Blaise. "And he's not coming back."

"How do you know that, son?" asked Mr. Doran.

"He's trapped there." A shiver ran up Blaise's back. "The labyrinth is closed now. No one else can get in or out."

McNeill took all this in and pinched the bridge of her nose as if she had a headache coming on. "You're sure about that?"

Blaise nodded, and his father reached over to squeeze his shoulder.

"Any idea about the skeleton?" Nash asked.

"Lady Ishbel Blackhope," answered Blaise. "She was alive in the painting, but she was too old to survive once she came out into our time."

"How did she get through if the labyrinth had gone?"

"She came out with Sunni before we closed it down."
Blaise was grateful for the warmth of his dad's hand.

McNeill shook her head as she wrote more on her pad.
"This is some story, Blaise."

"You don't believe me? Then how did we show up in
that locked room?"

"I didn't say I don't believe you. But it's a lot to get my
head around."

"Sunni and Dean told us the same story," said Nash.
"Not that it makes it any easier to take in."

Blaise relaxed a bit at this.

"We'll give you a bit of time to rest and see if you
remember anything else." The detectives stood up.

When Mr. Doran let them out of the front door, a
chorus of voices outside began calling out.

"Mr. Doran, how is Blaise? How about a photo?"

"Mr. Doran, can Blaise speak to us?"

"No, thanks, folks. Please give us a bit of space. If Blaise
was your son, you'd want the same," said Mr. Doran,
firmly closing the door on the reporters.

Blaise took the phone to his room and looked up Sunni's
number.

"Hi," she said cheerfully when she came to the phone.
"How are you doing?"

"Eating loads, sleeping even more." He laughed. "What
about you and Dean?"

"Fine, but Rhona, my stepmom, wants Dean and me to speak to a counselor. She thinks we need professional help with our trauma."

"Are you feeling traumatized?"

"Only about being stuck indoors. All these reporters are hanging around trying to talk to us and take photos."

"Same here," said Blaise. "But I'm going to school tomorrow and I don't care who follows me."

"Me too — totally. I can't believe we've been away for three weeks. It seemed like we were only there three *days*."

"I know. Bizarre. Just think — it could have been longer," said Blaise. "We've got to see Mr. Bell and tell him about Angus. He phoned and talked to my dad while I was asleep."

"Yeah, he phoned here, too, and when he asked Rhona how we were, she gave him an earful about our *terrible ordeal* and how it wouldn't have happened if we hadn't been doing his project," Sunni said, fuming. "When actually, it was all because she dumped Dean on me that afternoon!"

"Do you wish it had never happened?"

Sunni paused. "While we were there, I just wanted to get home, but now that I am — I don't know. I'm glad, but I can't stop thinking about Arcadia."

"Me too. And nobody but us will understand what it was like — if they even believe us."

Sunni sighed. "I know."

"Is Dean feeling the same as you?"

"To be honest, I don't know what Dean thinks — he doesn't want to talk about Arcadia at all. He's right back into his creature comforts, eating constantly and stuck on his computer, playing games. Rhona is spoiling him rotten."

"Can I talk to him for a minute?"

"Yeah, if I can tear him away from the screen." She shouted her stepbrother's name. "OK, see you at school tomorrow."

"Bye, Sunni."

Dean was crunching something as he said hello, sounding distant.

"Deano," Blaise greeted him. "All right, man?"

"Yeah. I just ate three pieces of pizza. And chocolate cake." He gave a little *heh-heh*.

"Better than dried fish."

There was a long pause. "Yeah."

"So," said Blaise, "you're OK, huh? Your legs all right?"

"Got Band-Aids on." Dean slurped a drink on the other end. There was another pause.

"Cool." Blaise wasn't sure what else to ask.

"Gotta go. My mom's taking me to buy a new game."

"Sweet. OK, man. Take care."

"Are you sure you don't want me to go in with you?" asked Mr. Forrest as he pulled the car up to Braeside High School's main entrance. Groups of students hung around outside, waiting until the last possible second to saunter in.

"I'm sure, Dad. I'll be fine." Sunni stepped out of the car into the mild March air and waved back at him.

Before the car had pulled away, several girls ran up and enveloped Sunni in a group hug. She was pelted with questions and ushered into school like a queen bee at the center of her hive. At first it was amazing to feel all this welcoming warmth. But as the day went on, a ball of apprehension began to grow inside her.

Every head swiveled to look at her in the hall. Her name floated in and out of conversations to an alarming degree. Kids even cornered her in the bathroom to ask more questions and tell her what they thought. It began to dawn on Sunni that coming home wasn't going to be easy, not by a long shot.

That afternoon Sunni dodged more curious kids and escaped to her art class.

She bumped into Blaise at the door and let out a deep breath. "There you are. I've been looking for you all day. You missed Spanish."

"Yeah, overslept." He scratched his head. "I've been keeping a low profile since I got in. You wouldn't believe some of the stuff people have said to me. That we're liars and we made Arcadia up. People I don't even know."

"I'm getting it, too," she said. "Some people are nice, you know, really glad to see me. But others are just mean."

"I don't get why it even matters to them so much."

Sunni shrugged ruefully. "Are you ready to talk to Mr. Bell after school?"

"Yeah. I guess we'd better," he said, and flashed a hopeful smile.

Applause greeted them as they walked into the classroom.

Lorimer Bell stood by his desk, looking like he might burst with emotion. Blaise and Sunni slid into their seats, their faces pink and bashful, until Lorimer called out for quiet.

"We're all very, very pleased to have you both back. It has not been the same in here without you."

"Yeah, I had to think up my own ideas to draw," said one boy, and the class tittered.

"Tell us what happened," said a girl.

Lorimer put his hands up. "Let's give Sunni and Blaise a chance to catch up first. There will be plenty of time for stories later." He took a box of charcoal sticks from a cupboard. "Besides, we have work to do. Charcoal portraits. Everyone else is already paired up, so why don't you two draw each other? Taking turns, of course."

Blaise and Sunni raised their eyebrows at each other. Lorimer looked puzzled, so Sunni shook her head and said, "Sorry, Mr. Bell, it's nothing. Portraits sound fab."

Their charcoal sticks flew across the paper. The other students glanced over at the pair, who seemed to be in their own bubble, far away from the classroom.

When everyone else had left for the day, Sunni and Blaise stood by Lorimer's desk.

"Do you have to leave straight away, Mr. Bell?" asked Sunni.

"No, no," said Lorimer. "I hoped we could catch up." He pulled up chairs for them. "We were all so worried about you."

"Why didn't you come get us, then, Mr. B?" Blaise's voice was flat. "You knew how."

A stunned look passed over Lorimer's face.

"But you sent your cousin instead."

"I did not send Angus—believe me." Lorimer put his hand to his throat, remembering their last encounter. "He forced me to help him work out the password, and then he assaulted a guard to get access to the labyrinth."

"The police told me about the guard." Blaise nodded.

"The Mariner's Chamber was closed off after Angus got in. I couldn't have followed then, even though I wanted to help you."

Blaise leaned forward. "But you knew more about Corvo and the painting than you told me."

"How could I risk putting you in danger? Besides, I didn't know the password, Blaise. Angus realized you had to have used a word you'd seen that day in the Mariner's Chamber. He knew the only likely clues would be on the information card next to the painting and made the right guess."

"Did you tell anyone else?" Sunni asked.

"I was sure the police wouldn't believe me—it sounds like such a far-fetched story. And I hoped that Angus would bring you back." Lorimer smiled, but his hands trembled. "How *did* you manage to find the way out?"

"Thanks to Angus, we almost didn't get out. He nearly killed Blaise and didn't blink an eye."

"Angus is no angel, but he wouldn't go that far—"

"I'm sorry, Mr. Bell, but he did." Blaise opened his sketchbook and pointed at a drawing. "That's Hugo Fox-Farratt and a servant boy, Inko. Within an hour of meeting them, Angus had gotten rid of Hugo, luckily not for good, and left Inko for dead. We never saw him again."

"That is not the Angus I grew up with."

Blaise could only shake his head. "Something must have twisted him up pretty good since then."

"When did you draw these?" Sunni turned the sketchbook around so she could get a better look.

"On the *Venus*, when I was alone," Blaise said. "Lucky I had a plastic bag to keep my sketchbook mostly dry."

"My sketchbook is totally warped, and a lot of the drawings look like they were done on wet paper towels. But at least Marin's sketch of the Roman gods is still in there," she said. "These drawings are fantastic, Blaise."

"They most certainly are." Lorimer thumbed through the drawings and stopped on one page. "That's a beautiful one of you, Sunni."

"You drew me on the labyrinth? How?"

Blaise was beet red. "It's from memory."

She smiled at him. *You're really, really nice,* she thought. *How did I miss that before?*

"So these other people found their way into the painting before you," said Lorimer.

"Yes, into paintings underneath the top one, that have living things and water and food just like here," said Sunni. "Corvo made them as a sort of adventure park for Sir Innes Blackhope, with monsters and mazes and sailing ships."

Lorimer flipped the sketchbook to a drawing of Angus in his fedora and overcoat.

"But what's happened to my cousin? You haven't said." Lorimer's voice was hollow. "The *Braeside Sentinel* says he's still in the painting. Is that true?"

"He is, but . . ." Sunni said. "Oh, Mr. B, it's really hard to tell you this. Angus is alive, but . . ."

Blaise broke in. "But he's trapped. Fausto Corvo is in there, too. We found him and his apprentices in one of the underpaintings. And they have his three lost enchanted paintings with them for protection."

"The lost paintings," said Lorimer. "So they do exist."

"Yes. Angus made out to everyone that he was searching for us, but he was really after those lost paintings. So Corvo drew a magical prison portrait of Angus and captured him inside it."

Lorimer's face drained. "Angus—captured by Corvo's sorcery?"

"W-we're really sorry, Mr. Bell. We tried to see if there was a way to bring him back, but there wasn't."

"But—" The art teacher slumped back in his chair. "This is horrible. Caught in a piece of paper. Horrible."

"No, no, Corvo is going to free him from the portrait, but only after Angus is banished to an island."

"I can't take this in."

"Angus can't ever come back," said Blaise in a soft voice. "Corvo told us to close the labyrinth, so Sunni shut it down after she came through."

Lorimer put his hand to his forehead. "He's trapped in the painting we were obsessed by. If I had known twenty years ago that this was how things would end up—"

"Twenty years ago?" Sunni interrupted.

"Angus and I were fascinated with Corvo's work when we were teenagers. We learned everything we could about him and his supposed sorcery." He gave a hard laugh. "We even tried to do our own magic—but it never worked.

Over the years, I lost interest, and I thought Angus had, too. But as soon as the news reported you'd vanished, he guessed you must have learned how to get into the painting—and that's when he turned up. I told him to leave it alone, but he never listened to me. Now Corvo's magic controls him."

"I'm really sorry this happened," said Blaise miserably.

"It's certainly not your fault! Angus knew what he was doing, and he is paying a very high price for it." Lorimer sat up. "I didn't think my cousin could ever be a killer, but he was a criminal. He was in prison until last summer."

"Prison!"

"For forging old masters. It started after we finished art school. He was so good, he could copy almost any painting. Angus liked to show off his copying skills and make a bit of cash on the side. But he got greedy. He wanted really big money, so he made up false documents to go with his forgeries to make them look authentic. He started making paintings to order for some very sketchy people who sold them to museums. I'm glad Angus didn't get hold of Corvo's paintings. He didn't deserve to be the custodian of such treasures—they would have ended up in the wrong hands."

"No one can reach Corvo now," said Sunni. "Or his paintings."

A knock on the classroom door startled them. When he saw Blaise and Sunni, the visitor nodded and waited outside.

"Well," said Lorimer briskly, "I am delighted you stayed

to talk to me. Don't worry anymore. Just go back to your normal lives. Speaking of which, the deadline for your projects is the week after next!" He tried to smile.

"Your book!" Sunni exclaimed. "I—I left it in the painting. It got really waterlogged. I'll replace it, I promise."

"Don't worry, Sunni. I can get another," said Lorimer as they walked to the door. "I hope that in time you'll tell me more of your experiences in the painting."

"We will. You're probably the only person who'll believe us," said Blaise.

That night Lorimer sat in his studio, bewildered. No more Angus. His cousin had gone, and he was free. He knew he shouldn't feel relieved, but he did.

One thing still bothered him though: Angus's mysterious associate and his packet of information about Lorimer's forged paintings.

Oh, hang it, he thought. *I'm not going to live the rest of my life in fear. If he comes forward, I'll be ready for him. Anyway, knowing Angus, he probably made the whole thing up, just to keep me in line.* He jumped to his feet and said aloud, "Well, no more. It's over."

He stacked all his photocopies, notes, and scribbles about Corvo back into their box and carried it into the sitting room, where he stuffed each sheet into the fireplace before setting them ablaze.

Sunni tapped at Dean's bedroom door.

"What?" Dean was swaddled in his comforter with a bag of chips wedged next to him, intent on a video game. "I said, what?"

He turned and saw the warped sketchbook in her hand.

Sunni slid Marin's parchment from between its pages and held it out. "I forgot I had this. You should keep it."

Dean glared at his half-finished portrait. "What—to give to my mom for Christmas or something?"

"I don't know. Just keep it as a souvenir." Sunni studied the sketch. "It's a really nice drawing, even though Marin didn't finish it—"

"Yeah, good thing, too!"

"But just think if he'd been able to stay in Venice and become a painter—he might have become as famous as Corvo."

Dean scowled at his game and wrestled with the controls. "Instead he dropped off the face of the earth and no one's ever heard of him."

"We knew him."

"I want to forget about him." He nodded at the portrait. "You keep it. You know you want to, anyway."

Chapter 26

The next afternoon, Sunni and Blaise strolled past the lions at the gates and up the driveway to Blackhope Tower. The castle had become a major attraction now, and the parking lot was full.

"Did you tell your parents we were coming here?" asked Blaise.

"Yeah, no choice. They've been tracking my every move since we got back. It's a miracle they let me out at all. Did you tell your dad?"

"Uh-huh. I'm not sure he gets why I want to come back, but he's OK with it, as long as I don't disappear again."

"Rhona doesn't understand, but that's nothing new. I had to beg my dad to let me come without her shadowing me," Sunni scowled.

"What about Dean? Where's he?"

"He told me to get lost when I asked if he wanted to come. He gets angry if I bring up the smallest thing about Arcadia."

"Boy," said Blaise, "I'm just the opposite. I want to talk about Arcadia because I can't stop thinking about it. Angus jumps into my head during math, and while I'm playing soccer, I wonder whether Hugo made it back to the palace."

"I'm the same. The painting is always at the back of my mind, even in my dreams."

"I wonder if we'll ever get back to normal."

"Whatever that is," she said with a sigh. "Everyone seems to set us apart now, whether we like it or not."

"Like staring at us and stuff like that?"

"Yeah. Will we always be the weirdos who claim they went into a painting?"

"Well, we are, aren't we? And even if people think I'm a weirdo, I don't regret meeting Corvo. Do you?"

"No way."

"The only thing I regret is having to finish my project. Work is the last thing I feel like doing."

"Maybe it'll help chase away the ghosts. That's why it's good we're working together," she said. "I can kick your butt."

"Not so long ago, you hated the idea of me doing your artist," Blaise scoffed.

"That was then. After what we've been through, the art project isn't all that important anymore."

A guard hurried over to them as they entered the hall. "It's Sunni and Blaise, isn't it? Do your parents know you're here?"

"Yes, it's fine," said Sunni. "We're not staying long. Just having a quick look at the Mariner's Chamber again."

"You'll find things are a bit different up there now. But my colleague on that floor will show you around."

"Thanks." She caught up with Blaise, who was already climbing the spiral staircase, and scurried with him toward the buzz of voices on the second floor. They were astonished to find a line of people outside the Mariner's Chamber.

"Four at a time," said a bored guard, counting them off as they shuffled in.

Sunni and Blaise joined the line, and before they knew it, people were taking photos and asking for autographs.

"No photography!" barked the guard.

"It's Sunni and Blaise!" someone exclaimed. "Come on, let them in ahead of us."

Everyone stood aside to allow Sunni and Blaise into the chamber. *The Mariner's Return to Arcadia,* bursting with color and detail, beckoned them in as before.

Sunni sucked in her breath as she walked over what had once been the labyrinth, feeling again the chill of Lady Ishbel's skull against her cheek.

"What happened to Ishbel?" she asked Blaise in a whisper.

"I heard they buried her in the family graveyard out back. You OK?"

"Yeah." Sunni headed for the painting, her spirits lifting as she neared it.

But when she got close, she saw a rope barricade in front of the masterpiece.

"Keep back, please!" commanded the guard, and Sunni jumped away from the painting, startled.

Blaise turned to him, incensed. "You can't go right up to it anymore?"

"No, son. Those days are over."

"How else can you look at it properly?" asked Sunni, but the guard just smiled.

"I think you'll find most museums protect their valuable paintings similarly," he replied.

"They must have done that because of us," Blaise said to Sunni under his breath.

They stood as close to the painting as they dared, drinking in the familiar scenes. Sunni could almost feel herself back in the winding lanes, searching for Dean. Her eyes roved through the fields toward the cave leading into Arcadia, and she wondered for the hundredth time whether Hugo was safe.

Blaise sensed visitors waiting for him to move out of their view. Then someone pushed in front of him and he drifted away, fed up.

Sunni found him sprawled on the bench, staring at the decorated ceiling.

"What's up?"

"There are too many people here now. And they all recognize us."

"Yeah, and—?"

"I want to take my time and really look at the painting. Just in case we can see Hugo."

"You think he'd come into the top painting?"

Blaise shrugged. "He'll have to if he wants to give us a sign he's all right. Unless he's forgotten about us—or he didn't make it."

"Don't say that."

"Let's come back first thing Saturday morning, before anyone even thinks about visiting here. We can be the first ones in and take as long as we like."

She nodded and followed him out of the Mariner's

Chamber, past the line of curious visitors.

"I feel anxious all of a sudden," Sunni said, making her way down the staircase at Blaise's side.

"Why?"

She paused on one step and he looked back at her. "Because I'm worried about Hugo. And because the Mariner's Chamber is ruined and we helped ruin it."

"All right, I hate that barrier and the crowds and Sir Innes is probably spinning in his grave right now, but we can't do anything about it." He wanted to touch her hair but kept his hand in his pocket. "Listen. Eventually people will get bored and find something else to stare at. And then the Mariner's Chamber will be ours again."

Blaise began descending the staircase, but Sunni's hand caught his elbow and lingered there for a moment.

"Thanks," she said softly.

Blaise's heart galloped as he and Sunni made their way into the hall. Casting a happy smile toward the staff, he made for the exit.

"Hang on a minute, Blaise." Sunni stopped at the display of information leaflets. A stack of photocopies with the title, *The Blackhope Enigma Continues* stood out.

"Those are brand-new," said the lady behind the desk. "We're just waiting for the rest of the leaflets to arrive."

Sunni took one and followed Blaise outside.

"Listen to this," she said, reading aloud from the leaflet.

"With the return of the three missing children, another chilling discovery was made in the

Mariner's Chamber. A female skeleton dressed in late sixteenth-century clothing was found on the labyrinth. This echoes the last discovery of a skeleton in 1862. While that skeleton's identity remains a mystery, experts believe this one is Sir Innes Blackhope's niece, Lady Ishbel, because it wore a distinctive pendant engraved with her name. Castle accounts say she disappeared in 1600, just before her marriage to the Laird of Muckton, who had arranged with her father for Lady Ishbel to become his third wife."

"Poor Ishbel." Sunni shook her head and tried to push the image of the girl's skeleton out of her mind.

"Yes and no."

"What do you mean?"

Blaise's eyes were bright. "Well, she got to do things no girl from her time would ever have been allowed to do — be a sea captain, fight pirates, and hunt for treasure."

"You're right. But the way she died . . ." Sunni shuddered.

"She's peaceful now," said Blaise. "And she's with her family."

Sunni bit her lip and nodded.

"Come on," he said. "Let's go home."

Sunni gazed back at Blackhope Tower. The sky had darkened behind the turrets and the rain had started.

"What do you think Marin is doing right now?" she mused.

"Forget about him, will you?" Blaise grabbed her hand.

Sunni arched one eyebrow.

"That guy's too old for you." He gave her a sidelong glance and grinned as they ran to the bus shelter. "By about four hundred years!"

BLACKHOPE TOWER

Epilogue

I'll sing you twelve, oh, green grow the rushes, oh!" Hugo sang as he turned down another crooked lane and passed the fountain in the square. "I say, Inko, it has been a long time since I was last here. Can't say I've missed it. Silent as a tomb. Not nearly as nice as Arcadia!"

He chatted away as they got closer to the harbor and the ships moored there. "Ah, yes, that's the *Speranza Nera*. And there stands Sir Innes, master of all he surveys."

Hugo strode up the gangway, splendid in burgundy trousers and a peacock-blue coat. When he reached Sir Innes, he stopped and looked around.

"Where to put it?" He tapped his chin. "Can't be too obvious. But the children must be able to see it. What do you suggest, Inko?"

The servant boy tugged on the hem of Sir Innes's cape.

"You could be right. It would be framed nicely and just visible from all viewpoints," Hugo declared.

He peered under the cape, where Sir Innes's hand rested on his hip, almost hidden by the heavy fabric. With a nod to Inko, he maneuvered the object under the captain's hand and wedged it against his crimson tunic. After a few adjustments to make sure it was secure, Hugo stood back.

Peeping out from behind the captain's arm was Lorimer Bell's battered book, *The Mysterious World of Fausto Corvo.*

"A sign for you, my friends."

*Turn the page for an excerpt from
Sunni and Blaise's next adventure:*

The Crimson SHARD

Prologue

*T*aking care not to wake anyone, the traveler crept back into the house, shielding his candle.

In the scullery, he rinsed the last traces of blood from his hands and dried them on a cloth. He felt for the leather sheath sewn into his tunic and slid out a flat shard of bone, smoothed and sharpened to a point at one end and carved into an animal's head at the other.

Every time the shard cut into flesh, the mark was harder to remove afterward. He found a piece of lye soap and a rough cloth and scrubbed the bone. As he worked, the face of the dead alchemist, Peregrin, edged into his mind. He scrubbed harder and cursed his associate for being so reckless with the lethal substances in his laboratory. If only Peregrin had taken more care, he would still be alive and producing the miraculous elixir.

The traveler seethed, knowing he could no longer make unlimited use of the elixir's astonishing powers; with so little left, there would not be many more crossings into other centuries. And there would be even fewer opportunities to obtain the information he needed to track down Fausto Corvo.

When he was satisfied that the crimson stain had faded, he returned the bone shard to its hiding place and, stealthy as a cat, climbed upstairs to his study. He ran his eyes over the

AN EXCERPT FROM *The Crimson Shard*

bookshelves, then glanced at the door in the far wall, its frame crowned with two carved faces.

Content that nothing had been disturbed in his sanctuary, he settled himself at his desk, dipped a pen in black ink, and on the first page of a notebook bound in red Moroccan leather, he scrawled two names:

SUNNIVA FORREST
BLAISE DORAN

They were only children, and twenty-first century ones at that, but they had the knowledge he needed. And destiny had just brought them to London.

Whatever it takes, *he thought, patting the bone shard in its secret place.* Whatever it takes.

Chapter 1

Sunni raised her face to catch the sun and wished she were lying on the grass in Hyde Park instead of hanging around in Phoenix Square while her friend Blaise tried to decipher a map scrawled on a paper napkin.

A distant siren wailed, and something clicked in Sunni's head.

"It's so quiet here," she said. "Like someone closed a window on the rest of the world."

"Mmm," Blaise mumbled, turning the napkin upside down. "OK, I've got it now. It's that house over there with the blue plaque on it."

"So, you still want to see this place?" Sunni said with a sigh as Blaise stuffed the napkin in his pocket.

"No, I've made us come all this way for nothing." Blaise had that look of bright intent he always got when his mind was set on something. "What's the matter—don't you want to see it?"

"I don't know. Just because some weird beardy guy in a café says it's a cool place doesn't mean it is."

"It sounds cool to me," Blaise said. "I thought you'd want to check it out, too."

AN EXCERPT FROM *The Crimson Shard*

"It's just that it's bound to be full of sheep-like tourists, same as all the other museums in London," she said.

"That's what *we* are—tourists. And by the way, I am not sheep-like."

"No, you're more dog-like, with a bone he won't give up," Sunni said. "I'm sick of museums, Blaise. We've seen tons ever since we arrived. If I have to look at another china shepherdess or Roman mosaic, I will curl up and die." She stopped walking. "Let's hang out in a park for a change. We've only got a few hours till we meet your dad—and it's our last day in London!"

"If you don't want to come in, go sit in that garden over there," Blaise said, nodding at the fenced-in scrap of grass and elm trees in the middle of the square. "I'll meet you after."

A jolt of irritation coursed through Sunni. "No, I'll come along," she said. "Unless you *want* to go on your own."

"Of course I want you to come! Why are you making such a big deal about this?"

"I'm not making a big deal."

"Yes, you are." Blaise gave a gentle tug on her ponytail. "Hey. You look like a celebrity with those sunglasses on. Trying to hide from all your fans?"

"Yeah, right. Can we get this over with? Which house is it?"

"This one." Blaise stopped in front of number 36. "And look, no lines of sheep trying to get in."

"Except us. Baa!" Sunni bleated like a sheep, and Blaise laughed.

AN EXCERPT FROM *The Crimson Shard*

"Look," he said. "We'll go wherever you want after this. I just want to check it out."

He stepped up to the red door with columns on each side and an arch above it. In the middle of the door was a bronze head with a ring-shaped knocker in its mouth.

"Now we'll see if the guy in the café sent us on a wild goose chase or not." Blaise rapped the knocker.

"Yeah," said Sunni. "I wouldn't put it past—"

She stopped in mid-sentence as an outlandish figure pulled the heavy door partway open. The man wore breeches and a red silk waistcoat topped with a long dark overcoat. His extravagant cravat was as white as his powdered wig.

"Good afternoon," said the man in a light but resonant voice with a slight accent. He had languid, heavy-lidded eyes and a nose that had been broken at least once. But the uneven angles of his face did not diminish his handsomeness—they made him all the more striking.

"Is this Starling House?" asked Blaise.

"Yes. Have you an appointment?"

Blaise's shoulders slumped. "Appointment? No, we didn't know we needed one."

"One usually makes an appointment to see the house." The man consulted a leather-bound book on a side table. "But today it is not a problem. We will find the time for you."

"OK . . . thanks."

The man swept the door fully open and ushered them into the hall.

AN EXCERPT FROM *The Crimson Shard*

They both stopped short, gawping. It was as if someone had peeled away the walls and ceilings to reveal an unspoiled landscape that had existed there before houses were ever built—a 360-degree panorama of rolling hills, trees and pastures below a canopy of light blue sky.

"This is all painted, Blaise," Sunni said, inspecting the wall. "You can hardly tell it's not real."

The man looked at them with polite amusement, as if he had heard comments like this a hundred times before. "Yes. It takes a few moments to remember you are in a house, not in the countryside."

Even the staircase continued the illusion, decorated with painted sky, clouds and flocks of birds all the way up the stairwell.

"Whoa!" said Blaise, teetering backward. He crouched down and touched a brightly colored spot on the floor. "I almost stepped on that, whatever it is. Wait, it's a ladybug. Not a real one, a painted one."

Sunni knelt down beside him. "Look, there's another one over here."

"Who painted all this?" Blaise found a painted spiderweb almost hidden in a corner.

"I will explain in a moment," said the man.

"Are you an actor?"

"An actor? No. This house was built in 1753, so we wear period costume to enrich the visitor's experience."

"Cool," said Blaise.

"My name is Throgmorton. I conduct tours here." The man slid an enameled watch from his waistcoat and studied it. "We shall begin in a moment. Please wait here."

AN EXCERPT FROM *The Crimson Shard*

Throgmorton closed his watchcase and disappeared down a staircase. He returned with two pairs of oversized felt slippers and handed them each a set.

"Put these on please," he said. "Over your footwear."

Sunni and Blaise pulled the slippers over their sandals. The felt tickled the tops of their feet. Sunni was about to do a quick moonwalk when she caught Blaise staring at something behind her. The blissful look in his eyes alarmed her somehow, and she whirled around to see what he was looking at.

A girl stood motionless near the top of the stairs. It was as if she was floating in the blue expanse, held up by a few clouds.

She was dressed in a billowing silver gown, and her pale blonde hair was pulled up into an elaborate arrangement of knots and twists. Without a word, she gathered up her skirts and glided down the stairs, like a goddess descending from the heavens to join the mere mortals on Earth.

AN EXCERPT FROM *The Crimson Shard*

Acknowledgments

Writing *The Blackhope Enigma* was an extraordinary experience that transformed my creative life. Along the way, I received invaluable support from many sources.

I thank my husband for his good-humored and unwavering faith in me; my parents, who raised me to love art and to find the magic in everyday life; my agent and mentor, Kathryn Ross, whose wise counsel and caring attention to my work helped make this book possible; Amanda Wood, managing director of Templar Publishing, for giving this book the perfect home; my wonderful editors, Anne Finnis and Emily Hawkins; and the Scottish Book Trust, which provided me with the opportunity and support to develop my writing. I also acknowledge support from the Scottish Arts Council toward the writing of *The Blackhope Enigma*.

I am deeply grateful to all of them and to the network of friends and colleagues who spurred me on to bring this book to life.